MR. PARK LANE

LOUISE BAY

Published by Louise Bay 2021

ISBN – 978-1-910747-711

BOOKS BY LOUISE BAY

The Mister Series
Mr. Mayfair

Mr.Knightsbridge

Mr. Smithfield

Mr. Park Lane

Mr. Bloomsbury

Player Series
Private Player

International Player

Standalones

Hollywood Scandal

Love Unexpected

Hopeful

The Empire State Series

Gentleman Series
The Wrong Gentleman

The Ruthless Gentleman

The Royals Series
The Earl of London

The British Knight

Duke of Manhattan

Park Avenue Prince

King of Wall Street

<u>**The Nights Series**</u>

Indigo Nights

Promised Nights

Parisian Nights

Faithful

Sign up to the Louise Bay mailing list at
www.louisebay/mailinglist

Read more at www.louisebay.com

ONE

Hartford

At twenty-nine, I was a doctor who'd travelled and worked in some of the most deprived places in the world, but just the *thought* of Joshua Luca had me sliding my sweaty palms down my jeans and wishing I could steady my racing heartbeat.

I hadn't seen him in over a decade, but Joshua could still get to me, and I hated it.

It wasn't like we'd ever dated.

It wasn't like I'd been pining for him all these years.

It wasn't like he'd even ever noticed me. Certainly not in the way I'd noticed him.

Joshua had been an almost obsession until, at seventeen, I broke my leg and swore off teenage infatuations for good. In one night, I grew up and let go of my silly crush.

I'd forgotten all those old feelings before my mum announced she'd arranged for me to stay with Joshua for a couple of months until I "found my feet"—unintentional irony, given the cast on my left leg. I didn't argue. It wasn't worth telling her that if I'd figured out living in a war zone, I was pretty sure getting settled in London would be a piece of cake.

Cake. My much-missed friend. Not something there was a lot—or any—of at the Medicines Sans Frontiers outpost in Yemen where I'd been stationed. As soon as I'd dumped my bag and showered, I'd go on the hunt for something lemony. With sprinkles.

I should try to keep my focus on cake. Anything but the memories of Joshua's summer sun-streaked hair. His long, lean, tan legs. The way the dimple in his left cheek would appear whenever my sister was around. His permanent half-smile hinted that he was always in on the joke. And his cool confidence meant that if he ever ended up in trouble, he managed to talk his way into forgiveness. He'd seemed like a god to my teenage self.

I wasn't sure he would remember anything about me. Maybe the unibrow? The braces?

Our parents had been friends since I could remember. Joshua was the same age as my brother. My sister was a year younger, and to my eternal frustration, I was the baby. The baby with a crush on her older brother's best friend.

I was nothing more than a lurking spectator during games of tennis, dares, and talks about girls. Almost like I'd been a part of the scenery—the background in Joshua and my brother's summers. Unlike my older sister, Thea, who'd embraced the denim mini-skirt trend like she was a twenty-five-year old supermodel. Thea was always at the center of everything. I'd watched as she twirled and giggled in front of Joshua, who responded with cocky grins and pouty lips. He'd definitely remember Thea. Unlike forgettable, invisible me.

I'd never told a soul my fantasies about Joshua. And at

seventeen I'd swallowed them down, determined to keep them tucked away in a deep, dark place forever.

Now, as I stood in the airport, about to come face-to-face with him, an unwelcome, familiar shiver breezed across my skin and tripped my pulse.

My phone buzzed. I dipped out of the queue so I didn't breach the mobile ban. It was my mum. I released my right crutch and slid open the phone.

"Have you landed, darling?"

The thing about working in war zones was that your parents always worried. War zones didn't worry me. Reunions did.

"Yep. Will be heading to get my bag in a minute. Can I call you when I get back to Joshua's place?"

"Of course. Marian said it's a wonderful flat. He's such a good boy. Has his own company, a marketing agency. Just bought them a new car, you know."

I must have heard about the new car at least three times. "Yes. The Lexus. I remember." I was never going to be the daughter who bought her parents a brand-new car. I didn't earn that kind of money. And even if I did—they didn't need one.

"He's done very well for himself. Very reliable. I'm sure he'll be waiting for you."

"I could have made it into town on the Heathrow Express." I hated the thought of Joshua going out of his way for me. I was sure he had better things to be doing on a Tuesday than playing chauffeur to me.

"You have a broken leg, Hartford," she said in her you-don't-get-a-say tone. As soon as I'd told my parents I was coming back to London, my mother had pushed her perpetual interfering into a higher gear. I knew it was an expression of her relief. After three years abroad, I'd be a couple of hours away instead of a couple of time zones. Now I was back, I'd have to get better at dodging her well-intentioned help bombs.

I glanced over my shoulder at the wave of people herding down the corridor, heading for the queue. A flight must have just landed, and I didn't want to be stuck behind them all. "I shouldn't keep him waiting. I'll call you later."

"Send my love to Joshua and call me when you've settled in."

There was my icebreaker with Joshua. I could tell him I'd spoken to my mother and she sent her love.

I re-joined the queue and told myself if I could handle treating sick kids on folding beds in searing heat, I could handle Joshua Luca.

No. Big. Deal.

THE DOORS out onto the landside concourse slid open. I scanned the audience of cab drivers with signs and people waiting for loved ones to appear. Set back from the crowd, as if a spotlight was positioned over him, Joshua stood, leaning against a post, head down, focused on his phone.

A fizzle of desire bloomed in my chest. I had to remind myself to breathe. He was still gorgeous. And I was furious about it. I'd set down my torch for Joshua a long time ago and wasn't about to pick it back up. It could only lead to trouble. Again.

His shoulders had broadened, but the dirty blond hair still had a way of looking perfectly tousled. And that magnetic confidence? It was still palpable from ten meters away.

He glanced up and right at me, as if he could hear me thinking. I felt his lopsided smile between my legs.

Vagina, you're a traitor.

I grinned and started toward him as if I'd just been searching him out in the crowd, rather than drawn to him like lightning to a metal rod.

"Hey." I tipped my head back to meet his gaze.

He took his time and made a slow, unapologetic sweep of my body from head to toe and back again, lingering on my lips and my cheeks on the way back. "Hartford?"

Should we kiss? One cheek or two? Hug? Why did I feel so awkward?

Twenty-nine, I reminded myself.

A doctor.

A crush on Joshua Luca leads to nothing but trouble.

I pulled him into a one-handed hug, pushing myself up awkwardly onto a one-legged tiptoe so I could reach around his neck. He stiffened almost unnoticeably before hugging me back.

"Good to see you," I said into his hairline.

I could feel his large hand through my jacket span almost the entire width of my back. And that smell? I'd forgotten that. What was it, and how had it not changed in all these years?

Without asking, he pulled my backpack from me like it weighed nothing and slung it over his shoulder. "That's it? No more luggage?"

I shrugged. "Nope. Just me."

He nodded toward the exit and I followed him. "What happened to your leg?"

I glanced down at my cast as if I needed to clarify which leg he was talking about. "Oh nothing. Just an accident." I didn't want to get into it. I just wanted it to heal.

Quickly. So I could get back to work. "Tell me about you, Joshua Luca. What have you been doing since I last saw you?"

He shot me another trademark smile. "When was the last time I saw you?"

"I can't remember . . ." I knew exactly. I refused to think about what had come after my accident. For years afterward, I ruminated about the night I broke my leg. Joshua had come to collect my brother before heading out to celebrate the New Year. He was in his second year at university and had just turned twenty. As I'd watched him from the top of the stairs, I'd never been so aware of our age difference thanks to the new stubble on his jaw and the flat, toned stomach he unintentionally revealed when he'd reached for my brother's jacket. He'd turned into a man and I still felt like a child. My glimpse of him had lasted thirty seconds max, but it was etched in my memory like a tattoo. Those few seconds had been the last good memories I had of Joshua.

"You lost your braces."

Of course he would remember those.

"Shocking, isn't it? I thought I was going to have to wear them forever. I also tweezed my monobrow. And I got a couple of degrees along the way." People could change. I wasn't who I'd been back then. "It's been a while."

"Right." He glanced over at me and furrowed his brow before looking away. "This is us."

He pressed a button on his key fob and the boot opened on an expensive-looking car. He slung my backpack in before heading the wrong direction to the passenger seat.

And then he opened the door. The passenger door. For me.

I shook my head. Had he grown up in the fifties? It was

all part and parcel of that Joshua Luca charm he'd had since he came out of the womb. I wanted nothing to do with it.

"What?" He looked genuinely confused.

"I can open my own door," I said as I hobbled into the vehicle, pulled my crutches with me, and settled into a buttery leather seat. I wasn't going to be reduced to a melting mess by a small act of chivalry. Not that he was *trying* to make me melt. He didn't see me like that. Joshua didn't have to *try* to make women melt.

Joshua shrugged and shut the door before moving around to the driver's side.

"Sorry if I smell like Yemen. You might need an air freshener in here after our journey."

He pulled out of the parking space and we started twirling through the narrow passages of the multi-story car park. "Yemen? I thought you flew in from Saudi Arabia."

"No direct flights from Yemen."

"Should you be going to places that don't have direct flights?"

I laughed. "You sound like Patrick. I was working with Medicines Sans Frontiers. I wasn't on holiday. But I appreciate the big-brother vibe."

"Right," he said, that frown appearing again. "You want a water?" He pulled open the lid to what looked like a built-in cool box under the arm rest between us and took out a bottle.

"Thanks. You got any cake in there?"

"This isn't Tesco, but you might find an apple."

"I haven't had an apple for thirteen months." I scrambled about and found an apple as green as I'd ever seen. "You want a bite?" I held up the fruit then abruptly pulled it away as my imagination offered up an image of him sinking his teeth into . . . me.

Was he a biter? For a split second, filthy images reeled through my brain: Joshua in bed, naked. Joshua over me, arms flexed and gaze trained on my lips. His hips pushing—

Stop.

I needed to get a grip, buy some brain bleach and dose the butterflies in my stomach with propofol. I was going to be living with this guy for a couple of months. I couldn't be following him around, drooling like some teenager with a crush. Besides, I knew that an obsession over Joshua was dangerous. Literally. I needed to construct an impenetrable Joshua Luca forcefield around myself.

This was strictly a friend zone.

I DIDN'T KNOW where to look first: the amazing one-hundred-and-eighty-degree view toward the Millennium Wheel, the ginormous living room with sofas that looked like gooey marshmallow, or that pesky dimple in Joshua's left cheek that had had me hypnotized since I was twelve.

"This is where you live?" I asked, trying to pretend I hadn't noticed the dimple. "You have exceptionally good taste for someone whose greatest childhood pleasure was giving my brother wedgies when he least expected it. It looks like a huge hotel room."

He shoved his hands into his pockets and his gaze hit the floor in exactly the same way as when he used to flirt with Thea. He managed to combine confidence with bash-fulness in a way I'd always found completely adorable. Joshua didn't have a shy bone in his body, and I wondered when exactly he realized how sexy a little humility can be. "I can't take credit for the decoration. It's residences of the Park Lane International."

"Residences? As in, you live in a flat that's part of a hotel? You can order room service whenever you like? And use the gym and stuff?"

"And stuff," he confirmed, nodding.

"Wow." I'd spent the previous year sleeping under canvas on a fold-up bed. Five-star luxury was going to take some getting used to. Except I wasn't about to get used to it. I glanced around, trying to see where I might put my things. There only seemed to be one door. Maybe I was on the sofa. "Where am I sleeping?"

"The oven? The bath?" Joshua grinned. "Or maybe the bed in the bedroom? It's a conventional choice but definitely the most comfortable."

Joshua towered above me, his chest wider and broader than it had been when I'd last seen him. He still had the sense of humor of a seventeen-year-old boy. "I'm laughing on the inside. Seriously, Joshua. Which way?"

He shrugged. "I've not been in here before. I'm next door in apartment P1. I guess it's over here." He strode across the living room and pushed open a door. "Yep. This is the bedroom."

"Wait, you don't live in this flat? I thought I was coming to stay in your spare bedroom."

"You hoping to see me in my boxers in the morning?" He grinned and widened his eyes suggestively.

I couldn't deny I'd wondered what Joshua looked like in his boxers in the sixty minutes since we'd left the airport, but I certainly wasn't about to admit to it. "Mum told me you had a spare bedroom."

"This is like the guest bedroom for the penthouse. It's a separate flat that's only available for residents of my place. It's like having a pool house or something."

Decoding the guy-speak, he wanted his own space.

"Joshua, if you didn't want me to stay with you, you just needed to say. I have other friends." I wasn't sure I had that many in London, actually. Most of them were scattered about the country. And the world. But I didn't need Joshua taking pity on me—I could have figured it out. My mother had begged me to stay with him—told me that he was lonely in London and needed the company. Clearly she just wanted to get her own way. Past experience should have been a warning, but I'd been too tired to argue with her and agreed to stay with him until I found a place of my own.

"You're acting like I've asked you to stay in the boot of my car." He was completely unfazed by my reaction. "I got this place for three months. It's no big deal."

"Wait, you rented it for three months?" I couldn't bear to think how much that might be costing. "Return the key. There's no way I can afford—"

Joshua stepped toward me and stroked my arm as if he were trying to tame a wild horse. I tried to ignore the heat, the way his fingers seemed to press into me with authority, the way he smelled so incredible when he was so close.

"It's no big deal. I'm not expecting you to pay for any of it."

I shook off his arm. Physical contact threatened to ignite my old crush like a match to tinder. "Joshua!" He didn't get it at all. "That's even worse. I'm not expecting you to cover my rent. The entire reason you stay in someone's spare room is to avoid incurring the expense at all."

"But *you* don't have the expense. If it makes you feel better, you can pretend it's my spare room."

"I need a shower." I collapsed on the sofa, jetlag, travel, and the last thirteen months catching up with me all at once. I sank into the marshmallow cushions and wondered if I'd ever move again. "Have you paid? Can you get your money back?"

"No. I signed something. And anyway, where else are you going to go? Someone's spare room or worse, a *sofa*, when you can be here?" He nodded toward the view. "You've been off curing the sick in faraway places. You can see this as your reward."

I didn't want praise or thank-yous. "You're ridiculous."

He smirked. "You're welcome. I presume you're hungry." He messed about on his phone. "You haven't turned into one of those do-gooding vegans, have you?"

"Yes, I'm hungry, and no." I'd been dreaming about eating a burger as big as my plaster-covered leg for the last year. Nothing about my fantasy involved vegetables.

"Thank God. Burgers then?"

Despite my irritation with Joshua, a small smile crept across my lips. He might be my exact opposite when it came to lifestyle, but when it came to taste in food, apparently we'd been separated at birth. *And maybe some cake*, I didn't say. I was picky when it came to sponge, and I wanted to be able to take some time deciding on my first post-Yemen piece. "There isn't much I wouldn't do for a burger right now."

"Interesting," he said, sliding a glance at me as he tapped away on his phone. Then he sat down on the sofa opposite. "Maybe I can think of a few things." I wasn't sure how a dimple could be suggestive, but Joshua's managed it.

His bold flirtations had never been directed at me before. It was sort of flattering, but I had to remind myself it was simply how he operated. He didn't know how *not* to flirt. To Joshua, flirting was some kind of unconscious habit, as automated as breathing.

"It's nice to see you haven't changed a bit."

"It's nice to see you have." He paused and for a split second, looked at me like we were long-time lovers rather than virtual strangers. He blinked twice, cleared his throat. "Except the disapproving scowl is still the same."

"Hey," I said, tossing an expensive cushion at him. He batted it away like candy floss. "I don't scowl."

He chuckled. "Don't worry. It's cute."

Cute?

I was going to have to supercharge my forcefield.

TWO

Joshua

I glanced up at the bleak, gray London sky and mentally checked what month we were in. Summers were never guaranteed in England but today felt like November, not June. Hartford certainly hadn't brought Middle East heat back with her when she'd landed earlier today. I turned onto Piccadilly and tried to search my brain for memories of Hartford. I remembered her braces, long gangly limbs, and hair pulled back into a bun. Her whole family used to complain she had her head in the clouds. Other than that, there were an awful lot of blanks. She'd always been around; I just couldn't recall many specifics.

A detail floated to the surface—a nickname. Something to do with fairies or ballet . . . That's right, she'd been a ballet dancer. A far cry from the intense but undeniably beautiful doctor I'd picked up from the airport today. I shook my head—I couldn't think about her now. I had other things to focus on.

I pulled up the collar on my jacket to stop the cold air

burrowing down my back. I should have brought a coat for the short walk to the restaurant where I was meeting my biggest client. As marketing director of GCVB, Eric was one of the most powerful people in luxury goods, which meant he got to pick the restaurant. The one he'd chosen was popular and had all the right number of stars for Eric. I thought it was a little pretentious, even for my tastes. At least the steak was fantastic. I ducked down a side alley and the red-cloaked doorman greeted me. I headed in.

I was five minutes early and Eric wouldn't be here yet. He liked to be fashionably late.

"Good afternoon, Mr. Luca." The blonde hostess tilted her head as she greeted me. "Your guest is already seated. Can I show you to your table?"

Hairs at the back of my neck stood up despite now being in the warm. I stared at her, processing what she'd said. Why was Eric early? That never happened.

The hostess showed me to a table in the corner, where Eric was seated in his crisp white shirt, his sleeves rolled up and his suit jacket draped casually on the back of his chair. Not only was he early—he'd been here long enough already to settle in.

"Good to see you," I said, shaking Eric's manicured hand and then taking a seat.

"Joshua. I'm having the sweetbreads and then the steak. What about you?" Eric's English was almost perfect, but his French accent was always evident in a restaurant. Perhaps because he was *usually* a relaxed diner, chatting with the wait staff about menu options. He liked to discuss wine with the sommelier. Not today. Today, Eric had already ordered, and his French accent was nowhere to be heard.

"Excellent choices, Eric. I'll have the same." I wasn't going to waste time looking at the menu when I could be focusing on what Eric was here to tell me. Because he definitely had something to say.

"We haven't had lunch for a while," he said. "Things have been busy back at Head Office."

"If you're going to be busy, no better place that Paris."

Luca Brands specialized in helping luxury brands, and the biggest luxury brand business was GCVB. We were responsible for the branding and marketing for all thirty brands the GCVB group owned, which ranged from skincare and perfume, to champagne and eleven of the top design houses. GCVB wasn't just Luca Brands' biggest client—they contributed around forty percent of our revenue.

"How long have we worked together now?" He took a sip of the wine the sommelier had placed in front of him. "Six or seven years?"

"Seven years next month." I leaned back, stretching out my legs, trying to give off the impression that this was just an ordinary lunch between us. But we both knew it wasn't.

"And I like your work. You know I do." He didn't have to add the "but" for me to hear it.

"I'm pleased. Your business is our business."

He wasn't listening. He was acting like he was too interested in the bread basket between us. More likely he was focused on what he was going to say next. "Yes, yes. And in all that time, Luca Brands has never wanted to expand outside the luxury space?"

I took a breath in, considering whether to answer the question. "What makes you ask?"

His gaze lifted to mine and revealed one of his mischievous grins—the kind that said, *I know something you don't know.*

"Well," he said, drawing out the word. "You know how GCVB like to buy new companies?"

Since Luca Brands started working with GCVB, they had done acquisition after acquisition. After each new company had been brought into the group, Eric would force a pitch process for all brand and marketing agencies in the new group along with Luca Brands. Whoever won the pitch was appointed exclusively across the newly enlarged group. We'd comfortably won each pitch. So far.

"As you know, GCVB dominate in luxury brands. Recently we've felt that we've acquired every business we were interested in the space. So . . ."

He was enjoying this. I couldn't tell whether or not he was just excited about the new acquisition or he enjoyed trying to make me squirm.

"So we're dipping our toe into pharmaceuticals."

It was like he'd dropped a turd on the table. His revelation was both unexpected and unwelcome. "Really?" It seemed like a stretch of strategy, not to mention an industry Luca Brands had absolutely no experience in.

"Yes. High margins. Growth sector. At first glance, it looks like it wouldn't be a natural industry for us to expand into, but our shareholders want growth and the CEO has a background in pharma. It makes sense." Eric popped a hunk of bread into his mouth and chewed. When he swallowed, he asked, "So what is Luca Brands experience in the pharma industry?"

Eric could be a dick. He knew we didn't have pharma experience. Luca Brands was a specialist agency and we kept our edge by not having too many competing priorities. "You want one brand and marketing agency to cover the newly enlarged group? Or will you keep specialists in each division?" I wanted to cut to the chase.

"So many agencies cover all industries these days."

"That's true," I replied. "But we're not a one-size-fits-no-one kind of agency. We're specialized. Focused. And we're the best at what we do."

Eric nodded vigorously as he cut into his sweetbreads. "I've always appreciated your work. Which is why I'm inviting you to pitch for the enlarged group, despite Luca Brands' lack of experience."

That sounded like he didn't think we had a hope of success. I tried to keep my voice even and my face neutral. "You're not concerned you're going to have to compromise on the quality of the work no matter who you appoint?" I asked.

"No." His tone was decisive, like he knew this was going to be an accusation he'd have to contend with. "I'm confident that whoever wins the work will be as good at luxury as they are at pharma and vice versa."

I nodded.

"You look worried." Eric delivered another lupine grin before taking a sip of the expensive wine I was paying for. Meanwhile, he held the future of my business in his hands.

"Do I?" My poker face was on point. I didn't look worried. Eric just *hoped* I was worried. "If you're not concerned, I'm not concerned. After all, you've worked as marketing director in luxury brands for twenty years. If you can handle pharma, so can we."

Truth was, I knew that when I walked away from lunch today, I'd have thousands of concerns I didn't have before I'd arrived at this restaurant. If Luca Brands lost GCVB as a client, we'd lose nearly half our business—not to mention our dominance in the luxury brands space. Everything I'd built could be lost, and hundreds of jobs and livelihoods would be ruined.

Eric raised his glass. "It's a growth opportunity. Isn't that what they say?"

I raised my glass in return. "No doubt, we'll both rise to the challenge."

Fuck. I wanted to ditch lunch, get back to the office and start strategizing. The first thing I was going to have to do was recruit some pharma talent. I needed people who knew the industry. *Great* people. I started mentally flicking through my contacts. Who did I know?

"I shouldn't be telling you, but the pitch won't be a normal presentation of credentials. I'm going to ask you to create a specific campaign for a very exciting new drug Merdon is going to be releasing."

My heart was pounding like I was sprinting between bits of bad news. "GCVB already purchased the company?"

"Yes. It will be announced today. Merdon. They have lots of great ideas to democratize the distribution of drugs."

What the hell did that mean? "Democratize?"

He shrugged like what he was saying was obvious. "Particularly in the US market, where pharma companies charge astronomical fees until patents run out."

I nodded ambiguously. I had little clue what he was talking about. The US pharmaceuticals market was as far outside my expertise as a market could be.

"Merdon's strategy is to target hugely overpriced drugs, still under patent, and re-engineer them so they can be produced at an affordable price. Then they distribute them over the counter where possible. They cut out the middleman—the greedy doctors who take a huge slice of the profits. They get medicines to the people who need them for a much lower price. Isn't that wonderful?"

The way he explained it sounded impressive. Although I don't think I'd ever heard the word *affordable* from Eric's lips before. It just seemed like such an odd decision by GCVB to enter an industry that was so very different to luxury goods. But I wasn't GCVB's CEO and shareholders. My job was to deal with the reality I was faced with rather than question it.

"A lot of the work will be aimed toward the US, but Luca Brands have a great track record on that front. Whoever wins this pitch will be helping people, Joshua. So instead of just focusing on making the world stylish and beautiful, this is Luca Brands' opportunity to do something with real meaning." It was the first time he'd tried to sell the idea to me, and it gave me a glimmer of hope that he wanted us to succeed.

"Sounds interesting," I said, the sentiment genuine. I enjoyed my work. I loved the luxury industry and the creativity that surrounded it, but I liked to stretch myself and set bigger goals. "I like the idea of being able to do good —bring medicines to those who need them most."

"Exactly," Eric said. "It's good to see you're not totally turned off by the idea of doing something outside your wheelhouse."

"Our wheelhouse is unique, quality brands and marketing services. And we'd be delighted to help you with Merdon along with the entire GCVB portfolio. Who else is pitching?" I'd be a fool not to ask about my competition.

Eric grinned. "There's you, two incumbent agencies at Merdon, and I'm going to invite two fresh agencies to pitch as well. You know, just to keep you sharp, Joshua."

I smiled as good-naturedly as I could manage. I was going to have to be more than sharp to land an account in an industry where I had exactly no experience. But there wasn't an alternative. I had to win this pitch or watch my business and employees suffer. Losing wasn't an option.

THREE

Joshua

While Dexter was at the bar, I took a deep breath as I mentally flipped through my day so far. First Hartford had arrived, which had been . . . unsettling. Then Eric's news at lunch had the potential to devastate my business and the hundreds of employees who depended on me. It was only Tuesday. What else did this week from hell have in store?

I wasn't sure a pint and a chat with my mates was going to make me feel any better. But it couldn't make me feel worse.

"You seem deep in thought." Dexter, one of my best friends, set a drink down in front of me and took a seat. "Did you suggest a drink because you want to talk about your feelings?"

"How did you guess?" I grinned, trying to act as if I didn't feel the pressure from Eric's announcement. I might not want to talk about it, but I didn't want to go home and mope either. It was unusual of me to suggest an impromptu drink to our group of friends on a Tuesday. Normally, Tuesdays meant working until I met Kelly for a drink before going back to hers. Or to a hotel. I didn't like people in my space, so my flat was kind of off-limits to women. Which was one of the reasons I'd taken the flat next door for Hartford. I had an extra bedroom in my place, but Hartford was pretty much a stranger to me.

Hartford.

"You pick up that girl from the airport today?" he asked, almost reading my thoughts.

"Yup." I'd complained to the guys at our drinks last week that I was getting a new neighbor. But that news had paled in comparison to what I'd heard at lunch.

"Is she the reason for this . . . mood you're in?"

I wasn't in a *bad* mood. I was just tense, which wasn't my normal M.O. Not only was I facing my business being upended, I couldn't shake the feeling of disquiet that had settled with Hartford's arrival. Normally I'd go home and have a soak in the bath. But with Hartford next door, what I'd normally do didn't seem so appealing. I'd expected to give some vaguely familiar kid a lift back into town, give her a key to the residence next door and then get on with my day. But when she appeared . . . there she was. Unexpected.

Despite the haziness of my memories, Hartford was instantly recognizable. She gave off a feeling of warmth and familiarity that *should* have been comforting. And it was. And it wasn't.

"I'm not in any kind of mood."

"Has Miss Tuesday Night dumped you?"

I wasn't sure what irritated me the most about Dexter and the rest of my circle calling Kelly "Miss Tuesday Night." Maybe it was the way it made her sound like a chore, or the way it made me sound like a slave to routine. Sex was never a chore and I wasn't anyone or anything's slave. "Don't be ridiculous."

"Oh that's right, she can't have dumped you. Because first you would have had to be in an actual relationship." Since Dexter had gotten together with Hollie, he'd become one of those men who thought everyone was better off with a serious girlfriend. I'd been down that route and didn't plan to travel it again.

"In case you've forgotten, I got down on one knee way before you did."

He didn't even try to hide his wince. "I know, mate."

Tristan interrupted the two of us and took his waiting pint without even saying hello. After a long sip, he sat on the small stool between us.

"Thirsty?" Dexter asked.

"Only for attention." I smirked at my own joke and Tristan rolled his eyes.

"Joshua was just telling us about Hartford," Dexter said.

"No, actually, I wasn't. I didn't suggest a drink so we could discuss women. You should know me better than that." I wanted to be surrounded by people in my corner. People I could count on to be cheering for me.

"I thought Miss Tuesday Night was named Kelly," Tristan said. "Did she break up with you?"

"You're correct that I usually see Kelly on Tuesdays. And no, we didn't break up. We're not in a relationship that can be broken up from." Kelly and I were strictly no strings. There wasn't any expectation of anything more from either side. That was how we both liked it.

"Okay then, Mr. Pouty. Did *Kelly* tell you she didn't want to have sex with you on Tuesday nights?"

"No. She's just busy tonight." It was a lie. I'd been the one to cancel our plans. I just wasn't in the right frame of mind for shagging.

"So, who's Hartford?" Tristan asked.

How were we still on this topic?

"Joshua, who's Hartford?" Tristan was relentless.

"The daughter of a friend of my mother's." That under-played our connection. My mum and Marion—Hartford's mother—spoke to each other at least five times a day. I could guarantee my mother's best friend knew how often my dad took a shit. And I'd grown up with the Kent kids. Or more specifically, I'd been best friends with Patrick and developed my flirting skills on Thea. And then there was Hartford.

Hartford, the gangly kid with her head in the clouds, now a woman who walked up to me and wrapped me in a hug like she was my best friend. Her shapeless scrubs hid what felt like quite the grown-up body beneath. I'd tried to think of something else as her breasts pressed against my chest, but I found myself swapping my thoughts of her breasts to the feel of her lips ever-so-close to my neck.

"Right, and why are we talking about her?" Tristan asked.

"Joshua picked her up from the airport and he's not been himself since," Dexter said. It was meant to be a joke but it cut a little too close to the truth for my liking.

"Is she hot?" Tristan was nothing if not on-brand.

"Not my type." That was true. Nothing about Hartford reminded me of the women I usually spent time with. I was accustomed to women who looked like they just stepped out of the pages of *Vogue*, and sometimes they had. Glamorous, beautiful women.

Hartford, on the other hand, clearly didn't give a crap about her appearance. Her hair looked like it had gone five rounds with a cat before being piled on top of her head, and there was no trace of makeup or carefully chosen wardrobe.

But there was no doubt she was beautiful.

I didn't like surprises. But everything about Hartford's high cheekbones, full pink lips, and very grown-up body had knocked me off my feet. I wasn't sure whether it was the way she was so open and unfiltered, or the way she clearly wasn't impressed with me, but something about her had thrown me sideways.

As we drove home from the airport, she'd chattered away. I'd been trying to figure out what exactly it was about her that was so unsettling. Then she bit into her apple and groaned at the taste, the noise shooting sparks right to my groin. Images swooped into my brain of her naked, riding me, her head thrown back, her nails digging into my chest.

That's what was disconcerting. I was imagining having Hartford naked in my bed.

Hartford, the gangling kid sister of a girl I practiced my flirting on.

Hartford, the daughter of my mother's closest friend.

Hartford, my new neighbor.

I needed to give her some space. Or more accurately, I needed to give myself some space from her.

There was no way I was going to cross the line with Hartford. There were too many reasons why it was a bad idea. First, she was so far from my type it was actually comical. Second, I wasn't about to have casual sex with someone who might end up hurt, especially when that someone was so inextricably linked to my family, and most importantly, I didn't do relationships. Ever.

Hartford was only next door for three months and then

she'd be gone. Between now and then, my time would be taken up trying to stop my business from going under.

I glanced up as Andrew took a seat at the table. I hadn't expected him to make it.

"So, why are we here?" Andrew asked, peeling off his suit jacket and carefully placing it on a free seat behind him.

"I'm trying to figure out a way of stopping my business from collapsing."

"Collapsing?" Dexter asked. "What's happened?"

"My biggest client just bought a pharmaceuticals business."

"Who? GCVB?" Tristan picked up his pint. "Why would a luxury goods company buy a pharma company?"

"Maybe they want to repackage the muscle relaxants?" It wasn't the right time for Dexter to crack jokes. "Apart from that not making business sense—why is that a problem for you?"

"It's more than a problem." I told them how Eric wanted to appoint one agency for the entire enlarged group.

"Right," Andrew said. "But you've won the pitch every time. You'll end up doing Merdon's branding and advertising as well as the rest of the companies in the group."

"We brand and market *luxury goods*," I said. "Not pharmaceuticals. We have zero experience. There's no way Eric is going to have us do the branding and marketing for Merdon."

"Looks like you might have to go full time and figure this out," Dexter said.

I couldn't suppress an eye-roll. "I *do* work full time. I'm in a creative industry; number of hours at my desk doesn't correlate with productive output." I wasn't in the mood for Dexter giving me a hard time about not working long-enough hours. I needed to try to devise a plan, a way out of what was sure to be wreckage.

"First step, hire some people who know pharma," Andrew said. "GCVB obviously knows and likes you. It's not a foregone conclusion that they're going to drop you. I know a few people. I'll put you in touch."

Luca Brands was the best there was in the luxury goods market. Eric knew that. But he also knew that I didn't know anything about pharma. Then again, I hadn't gotten to where I was by giving up. If Luca Brands was going to go down, we'd go down fighting.

"Every pitch you go into, you end up winning," Dexter said. "Yes, this is a different industry, but the underlying business of what you do is the same. You've got this. I have no doubt."

I exhaled. This was why I'd cancelled on Kelly. I needed someone to tell me this was doable. Who better than the men who knew me better than I knew myself—and all of them titans in their own industries?

"And in the meantime, you have a hot new neighbor you can distract yourself with," Tristan said.

"I can tell you now that I'm never going to touch Hartford. Not like that. Not at all."

There were lots of logical reasons to stay away from Hartford that mainly involved her connection to my family. More than that, the overriding reason I planned to avoid Hartford was because today, riding home with her in the car, I'd felt like a teenager again. Like I'd done before I'd launched Luca Brands. Before I'd made my first million. Before I'd been dumped by my fiancée. It was unsettling—like traveling backward through time in my own body—which was exactly what I didn't need at the moment. Saving my business and my employees meant I had to be laser focused. Nothing about the next few months was going to involve unsettling women who'd moved in next door. I was going to be fighting for my professional life. Hartford might be a doctor, but she didn't have a cure for my condition.

FOUR

Joshua

As I headed out of the lift after my Saturday morning session in the downstairs gym, I couldn't keep my gaze from Hartford's door. Despite the concerns about my business that should have been occupying all my waking hours, over the last few days, my thoughts kept sliding to Hartford. What was she doing? How was she getting on with that broken leg? Maybe I had imagined those feelings she'd stirred in me. Most importantly, why couldn't I get this woman out of my head?

Just as I turned the key, her door swung open and Hartford appeared, a knotted bag hanging from her right crutch.

"Joshua!" she said, her smile so wide my heart tripped in my chest. "How are you?"

"You want a hand with that?" I nodded toward the bag. I'd been a selfish dick, not checking on her. She had a broken leg and probably could have done with some help unpacking and getting settled.

She laughed. "It's just rubbish. I'm going to the chute. I'm a bit obsessed with it to be honest. Any excuse to use it."

"You're obsessed with throwing things out?"

She wrinkled her nose. "No, just the chute bit. Pull it open, drop it in, and voilà, it's gone."

I couldn't help but laugh. "Okay."

She gave me a one-shouldered shrug as if she couldn't care less what I thought. "It's so convenient."

She'd switched out her scrubs today but replaced them with what looked like pajamas. I was getting the distinct impression that Hartford didn't really own normal clothes.

"Are you unpacked?"

"I am. It didn't take long. I was just about to go to the supermarket. Want to come?"

I should go inside, run a bath, put on some music and relax—ready myself for the next week of chaos—but I hadn't seen Hartford for a few days and . . . Well, I had promised my mother I'd make sure she was okay. "Is there one around here?"

She narrowed her eyes at me. "Joshua Luca, tell me you shop for your own groceries."

There was just something about this woman that made me smile, even when she was semi-scolding me. "I can't do that because I'd be lying."

"Then I insist you come with me." She hobbled past me and I caught the scent of cinnamon. "I'll just use the chute and then we'll go."

It didn't seem to occur to her that I might have plans. Or that if I didn't shop for groceries, it was because I didn't have time or didn't want to or had someone to do that sort of thing. Something about her assumptions drew me in. That, and the fabulous arse I couldn't stop staring at as she limped down the corridor.

She turned back after using the chute. "There." Her eyes were wide and bright and completely focused on me. "I just need to wash my hands, grab my bag, and we'll go. Yes?"

I got the feeling she wasn't looking for an answer as she disappeared back in to ready herself. I let myself into my flat and shrugged off my jacket, then pulled it back on. This was ridiculous. I didn't want to go shopping. I was looking forward to some thinking time or "Genius Time" as Tristan liked to call it. I hadn't told Tristan that I liked to have my Genius Time in the bath. There was such a thing as over-sharing, even among best friends. The bath was where I figured out solutions to problems. I'd had a bath every day since I'd learned about the Merdon acquisition. I was still waiting for inspiration to strike.

I guess I could get my Genius Time after a trip to the supermarket. It would mean I could carry back what Hartford bought and then leave her to it and shut the door. I'd probably discover that the frisson of . . . whatever I'd felt, and the deep stir of my gut when I'd picked her up at the airport, had dissipated. A shopping trip with Hartford would clear my head, allow me to focus my thoughts on my business.

"You ready?" Hartford poked her head around my door.

"You know where you're headed?"

"Of course. But tell me *you* know where your local supermarket is."

I couldn't help but chuckle. She liked to prod, but in a way that was . . . charming almost. "There's a Waitrose just around the corner."

"Then we'll head there." She grinned at me as if I were her student and I'd unexpectedly given her the correct answer to a question.

As we stepped into the London drizzle, she took a deep breath in. I forced myself to glance away from her rising chest. Had she always had a chest like that? "I'd forgotten what rain felt like."

"London's different to Yemen, I imagine." I led us to the crossing.

"Couldn't be much more different." She turned her head to look back on the hotel residences. "We slept under canvass in a compound, obviously."

"A compound?"

Hartford expertly navigated the crossings and pavements like she'd always had her leg in plaster. My mother might have thought she needed help to settle in, but she was wrong. She didn't need anyone's help to do anything by the looks of things. "Like a little village ringfenced by security where we could move freely without . . . worrying. It's where we were safe."

"And you didn't leave that compound, apart to go to the hospital?" It must have been like living in a prison. I couldn't imagine living like that for a week, let alone a year.

"Sometimes to collect supplies or help a child who'd been injured and couldn't be brought to the hospital. But not on our own."

She'd basically been putting aside her safety and comfort to look after people. That was so . . . admirable. "So why are you back?"

She nodded at her leg.

"Was that, like, a bullet or something?"

She snorted, almost as if she was disappointed. "No. I tripped, but my leg must have been weak from the first time I broke it. This time wasn't so bad."

I would have thought tripping was better than being

shot, but maybe I didn't understand the nuances. "Mum said you have a job starting here. So, you're back to stay?"

"Yes. Starts next week. I'll be a little hampered from a practical perspective, because . . . you know, the leg. But I'll figure it out. I always do."

"You looking forward to it?"

She nodded and glanced away, as if not entirely sure. "It will be a change."

Hardly an enthusiastic response. At my raised eyebrows, she continued.

"It will help my specialty, I think. I just . . . you know, I just enjoyed Medicines Sans Frontiers for the last few years. You're so all-in, you know? In a place like London, I'm not sure how . . . busy I'm going to be." Her voice flattened like it had been sat on.

"People need medical attention in London."

"We'll see. Anyway, I didn't have any choice. I had to come back and it's a good hospital. I have a lot to be thankful for. My boss is like *The Guy* in pediatric medicine, so I'm bound to learn a lot, if nothing else."

I couldn't believe that anyone would be so unhappy to be back in London, the best city in the world—and in a penthouse overlooking Hyde Park no less. But her obvious disappointment tugged at something inside me and I wanted to make it right.

"Give yourself a chance. You might love it here, sleeping under Egyptian cotton and cashmere."

She laughed and her nose wrinkled in a way I'd never noticed when she was younger. I had the urge to circle her waist and pull her closer so I could examine the freckles that sprinkled her cheeks. I wanted to make her feel that everything was going to be okay.

Why had I agreed to this shopping trip?

———

"THIS IS THE BEST BIT," she said as I set the bags on the side. "Unpacking it all. Seeing what you've bought."

"I'd find that an easier concept to grasp if we'd come back from Hermès, not Waitrose."

She grinned at me and I tried to tell myself it didn't feel good to make her smile.

"Grab a potato peeler and get started," she said. "And don't give me that *I don't know how to use a potato peeler.* I've eaten your mother's apple pie; I know you can peel."

She was right, I'd been roped in to peeling duties as a kid more often than I cared to remember. "It's been a while. Remind me again why we can't just order something in? That way, I don't have to peel anything. And we would have had the entire morning to do something more exciting than shop."

"More exciting?" She made a puffing sound through her completely bitable lips. "Like you could have a more exciting time than battling your way up and down supermarket aisles. Especially when you had me for company."

I couldn't help but smile at her comfort around me. The feeling was mutual. There was something too easy about being in her presence. "Yes, so exciting." I had to fake the sarcasm.

She laughed, a warm, sunny laugh that threatened to clear the rainclouds. "Aha! This will be perfect." She presented an empty, oversized jam jar that she'd found lurking in one of the cupboards. "How much do you think you would have spent ordering in dinner tonight?"

I couldn't help but wonder if whatever I said would result in a scornful reprimand. "I'm not sure. Why?"

"I want your money."

"I thought you *didn't* want my money, or at least the apartment I rented. What do you need?"

"What would you have spent on dinner tonight?"

I gave up trying to understand what she was trying to say. "I don't know. Fifty or sixty quid."

She gave an almost imperceptible shake of her head and held out her hand. "Okay, hand it over. Give me fifty pounds."

She was asking me for money to peel her potatoes? I didn't have the energy to argue with her. I just pulled out my wallet and handed over three twenty-pound notes.

"Perfect." She unscrewed the gold metal lid of the jar and dropped the money inside. "Medicines Sans Frontiers is always in need of additional funds. This will help. Thank you."

I wasn't sure if it was the cause or her, but something in my gut shifted. Her passion for doing good was admirable. "You going to volunteer with them again?"

She pulled out a baking sheet then shrugged. "I've done it three times. My mum doesn't want me to." She fell silent. "But I like to be busy."

"You really don't think you're going to be busy in a London hospital, Hartford?"

She nodded enthusiastically, like she was trying to convince herself. "I hope so. My job at the hospital starts on Monday. Plus, I'll try to get as much experience as possible by volunteering for extra shifts."

This focused, driven woman didn't seem to share any resemblance to the flighty dancer I'd known when we were kids. Had this side of her always been there, and I simply hadn't noticed? I tried to think back but couldn't remember.

"Somewhere in there, you should find some time to have a social life."

"What do you call this?" She shot me a smile as she sprinkled rosemary on the chicken.

It was strange how shared experiences and people in common could create a history with someone. I wasn't sure I'd said two full sentences to Hartford before she turned up at the airport, but it was as if I'd known her intimately for the last thirty years.

"*This* is manual labor," I replied, smirking. A part of me liked the idea I was her social life. "You want me to arrange a massage for you at the spa or something? My treat." I mentally batted away images of her laying face-down on a massage table, curves sloping gently under a thin sheet, waiting for—

"You're so funny."

I wasn't trying to be.

"Tell me about your job," she said. "What does 'PR and marketing' really mean? It's easy to think that medicine is the only thing in the world when you're surrounded by it all day."

"My company devises and implements marketing and PR strategies for luxury brands."

"Yeah, I'm going to need more detail."

What was this? An interview? Usually I loved to talk about my business, but not today. Not with her. "It means that a luxury goods company—"

"Give me an example of what a luxury goods company is."

I couldn't help but chuckle. I was surrounded by people who didn't need to be told. Even outside of work, my best friends were wealthy and knew how to indulge. Hartford came from a different world. A simpler one. One I hadn't known for a very long time. "You know—Moet et Chandon or Tiffany or Dior. You might not like to indulge, but tell me you understand the *concept* of luxury?"

She narrowed her eyes as if she were trying to work it out, and I got the feeling she was only half-joking. I couldn't help but laugh.

"These companies give us money to devise a brand strategy. Sometimes we just put together an ad campaign. Sometimes we get involved in everything from packaging and price points to which shelves the products are going to sit on."

"I think I get it. And this hotel," she said, gesturing around vaguely, "is it a client?"

"No, but I'd like it to be." This small group of international luxury hotels was in our wheelhouse, but at the moment I was too focused on keeping my current clients —and one client in particular—to think about anything new.

"Is that why you live here?"

"No, I'm here because I've got to live somewhere convenient, and the views are great. It's right in the center of things. The hotel facilities are useful. And I like it. Who wouldn't want to live here—except you? I can arrange for a bed of nails to be delivered and you could only use the cold tap when you shower. Would that make you feel more comfortable?"

She shrugged. "As long as I have somewhere to sleep and food in my stomach, that's enough for me. I'm focused on other things."

It was such a different way of looking at the world than I was used to. Did she judge me for having different aspirations? And why the hell did I care if she did judge me. I wanted to ask what her priorities were if they didn't involve comfort. I wanted to dig deeper and find out more. But I stopped myself. That wasn't who we were. We didn't need to go deeper. I was helping her out because it made my mum happy. I needed to focus on my business.

My hands stilled as an idea struck me.

Merdon. Pharmaceuticals. Experts.

I should be picking Hartford's brain to help strategize the GCVB presentation I knew we'd have to make in the very near future. Hartford was a medic, far closer to the pharmaceutical industry than I was. At the same time, she worked with these company's end-users—her patients. I needed to get inside her head, understand her mindset. Apparently, the bath wasn't the only place for inspiration to strike.

Before I got a chance to ask her the first of a hundred questions I had, her phone buzzed on the side with a message. She picked it up in one hand, dropping the spoon she was holding in the other when she saw who the message was from. "My boss," she said, swiping up. Then she groaned. And swore. And groaned some more before tossing the phone.

"What happened?"

"Gerry invited me for dinner next Friday with his wife and some other people at the hospital. And I can't even say I'm working because he has access to my shifts and he knows I'm not."

Had I missed something? Was a dinner invitation the worst thing in the world? "So, go to dinner with your boss."

She groaned again, but picked up the spoon and resumed stirring. "Like it's that easy. First, I don't know the man. Second, he's one of the greatest minds in pediatric medicine."

"Right, and pediatric medicine is what you do. So what's the problem?"

"That's my specialty, yes. Getting to work for him is intimidating enough. Now I have to go to his house and . . . you know, talk to him and his wife and . . ." More groaning. "Third, I have nothing to wear. And to top it all off, he's told me to bring someone." She snapped her head around to look at me. "Oh my God, would you come with me?"

Friday nights were normally reserved for Candice. "I think I have something this Friday."

"Right," she said. "Of course you do. And what do I even wear for dinner with my boss? I mean, for the last year, I've not worn anything but scrubs and this—" She swept her hands down her body, indicating the shapeless khaki tracksuit-slash-pajama ensemble she was wearing. "And even before I went to Yemen . . . I mean, I worked a lot. I've never been much for socializing."

Nothing she was saying was a surprise. "You need clothes," I said, pulling my phone from my pocket. "I know a few women who might be able to help."

"I don't want your girlfriends dressing me, Joshua."

"That's good because I don't have a girlfriend. I'm calling the cavalry."

"This isn't going to be a *Pretty Woman* moment where you call the concierge who knows someone at a department store and—you know?"

I chuckled at her analogy. I didn't believe in fairytales. "Don't worry. No *Pretty Woman* moments for me. I'm no Richard Gere."

"And I make it a rule not to have sex for money, or to floss. Life is *far too short* to floss."

I looked at her again, wondering if she meant to be as

funny as she was. I shook my head and turned back to my phone.

"Okay, Friday, early evening, before dinner with your boss, you have a date."

Her face flushed a delightful shade of pink and I had to stop myself from sweeping my thumb across her cheekbone. *Focus, Joshua.*

"I don't want a date. I want a dress to wear to my boss's house. Are you even listening to me?"

"I'm going to take you to some friends of mine. Beck and Stella's place. Stella will have something you can borrow. And if I know Stella, she'll have roped in Hollie and Autumn and—"

"Oh my God, Joshua. What have you done?" She looked genuinely worried.

"I've sorted you out with something to wear. You'll love these women. They'll figure it all out and—"

She groaned again, the sound taking on a slightly hysterical edge.

I didn't understand why she wasn't delighted. "If it makes you feel better, I'll be your plus one." *Shit.* I was supposed to be focusing on work, which meant less time with Hartford, not more.

She locked her gaze on mine, eyes going wide. "You will? I thought you had plans." Just one look at her and I knew I couldn't take it back. Her expression was all vulnerability and gratitude. She reached out and grabbed my shoulder and I froze, not because I was turned to stone by her touch, but because all I could think about was how I wished I could strip off my shirt to feel the tips of her fingers press into my skin.

Shit. Shit. Shit.

I cleared my throat, trying to get a handle on myself.

"Nothing I can't cancel." She gave my shoulder a quick squeeze before pulling her hand away.

Dinner with Hartford's boss could be an opportunity. That's all. I'd do it for any friend of the family. Hopefully, spending the evening among a room full of medics would help me gain some insight into their world, which would help me prepare for the pitch with GCVB.

This wasn't about Hartford. This was about business.

FIVE

Joshua

I let the smooth heat of Beck's whiskey drizzle down my throat. We'd been at his place for hours. I wasn't quite sure what Stella and Autumn were doing to Hartford, but going by the time they were taking, I was bracing myself for Frankenstein's monster to appear at some point.

"How's the pitch for GCVB coming along?" Beck asked.

I nodded. "Okay actually. I'm in the process of recruiting some external expertise and feeling energized by the idea of doing something new." Seeing Hartford so completely dedicated to helping others through her work had given me a lift when I needed it. At first I'd been focused on wanting to win the Merdon pitch because I didn't want to lose GCVB's business. Now, I was actually excited about the idea of doing something in a different sector for a business that wanted to change people's lives for the better.

"My, my, how the tables have turned. What brought this about?"

I shrugged, glancing at the stairs where I expected Hartford to appear sometime soon. "The client sent over a bunch of documents setting out the positive impact of what they're trying to do in the US to help make important drugs available to the people who need them. They're really trying to make a difference. Maybe it's time for a new chapter in Luca Brand's story."

"You sound excited. Is it time for a new chapter in Joshua Luca's story, too?" He nodded toward the stairs. "She's pretty."

"She's a family friend. I'm doing her a favor and anyway, I like the chapter I'm in right now. I don't believe in going backward."

"Backward?" Beck asked.

Before I could remind him I'd gone down the serious relationship route already, Stella came into the living room, a grin the size of China on her face. "She's so completely perfect." Her hands were clasped together like she might burst if she let go. "She's so down to earth and beautiful, but has that 'gorgeous but doesn't know it' vibe."

It sounded like Stella was trying to convince me of something. But there was nothing I needed to be convinced about. I just wanted to get to the party and meet Hartford's colleagues.

"She's a nice kid. Are you nearly done with her? We have to get going." They just needed to put her in a dress and maybe do something with her hair. How long could it possibly take?

"She's a *woman*, Joshua. A beautiful, clever, funny *woman*." She shot a glance at Beck, who nodded dutifully.

"I only met her briefly," Beck said. "But she seemed very nice."

Stella rolled her eyes. "Wait until you see her, Joshua. Her skin is amazing. Her face is so pretty she's like a little doll. And if you're a boob man, Joshua, her boobs—"

"Stop it, Stella." I grimaced. I didn't want to think about Hartford's breasts. Again. Or her flawless skin. Or her fingertips on my arm, or the way her smile warmed my insides. I wanted to ignore it all.

"Well, you'll see for yourself."

Just then, Hartford appeared from behind Stella at the bottom of the stairs. My cock lengthened and I had to fight a groan. She looked like Vivian Leigh had a baby with Adriana Lima.

Stella had been right—Hartford looked spectacular. Her long hair, which I'd only seen a glimpse of at the weekend, was down and styled into glossy waves; her iceberg-blue eyes seemed to sparkle; and had her lips always been that full or was it the flash of red lipstick? And Jesus, I hadn't been imagining those curves hiding under her shapeless scrubs.

"We only have one issue," Autumn said, entering the room behind Hartford.

There didn't seem to be any issues as far as I was concerned.

"She won't wear the shoes. Or one of them, at least." Autumn raised a pair of black strappy heels in the air. "And they're Jimmy Choo."

"They're a client of mine," I said. "Apparently they're very comfortable."

Hartford spluttered. "Well, you can wear them then."

I never was one to back down from a challenge. "Toss them over," I said, unlacing my shoe.

"You're not wearing women's shoes, Joshua," Hartford said, scowling at me.

I retied my lace and stood so I could see her entire outfit. "What do you think you're going to wear with that dress? Your normal trainers?" Two strappy sandals would be better, but given her cast, one would have to do. Her dress was a perfect choice for dinner with the boss. It had sleeves, didn't show too much cleavage, and hit below the knee. "Is that Roland Meurier?" I asked.

"You think it's too clingy?" Hartford asked.

"I think it looks great," I said.

"You don't need to look so shocked." Hartford sighed.

I rolled my eyes. "I've known you a long time, Hartford. I'm not shocked." Fragments of memories began to piece themselves back together: Hartford with her hair pulled back into a severe bun, slim legs sheathed in yoga pants, torso outlined in a cardigan that wound around her waist. I couldn't remember if she'd been beautiful back then, but there was no doubt she was now.

"These aren't going to fit me," I said, holding up Stella's shoes. "So you'll have to wear them. Or one of them."

"No way," Hartford replied. "That's a step too far. I'm not going to twist my good ankle when one leg is already in plaster. I'm meant to be making a good impression."

"You won't twist your ankle," I said. "I'll be there to support you."

"Just try them," Stella said. "Please?"

Hartford looked at me from under her lashes and for a split second, our eyes locked. The air shifted. Autumn's cooing and Stella's cajoling fell away until it was just the two of us.

"For me," I said.

She paused mid-breath, as if she was going to say something else. "I'll try."

She blinked and we were back in the room.

"It looks great," Autumn said as she watched Stella slip the shoe onto Hartford's foot.

I stalked over to her. We had to get a move on.

"I'm going to fall," Hartford said.

"You're going to be fine," I whispered into her ear.

I tried to ignore my friends muttering to one another behind me. They were probably creating a story about how I would be married by the end of the year and this was going to be the woman I fell in love with. They didn't get that I wasn't going on a date. I was attending this dinner to get the scoop on healthcare. And I was helping out the daughter of an old family friend. One who just happened to be gorgeous.

SIX

Hartford

It had been a long time since I'd worn a dress. The ten-year-old scar on my leg had faded so it was almost invisible now, but every time I glanced at the silvery river on my calf, panic started to stir. Memories threatened to push through, and I remembered why my teen crush on Joshua Luca had ended so abruptly. Tonight, at least, the scar was hidden by the plaster.

I lifted my chin and forced a smile at nothing and no one in particular.

"You okay?" Joshua whispered. Gerry, my soon-to-be boss, had gone to collect drinks while Margo, his wife, was checking on dinner. The other four diners—all members of the pediatric department—chatted and laughed at in-jokes I just knew I wouldn't get even if I'd been working with Gerry for five years. Luckily, my broken leg gave me an excuse to perch on a bar stool off to the side, away from the center of the action. Joshua stood dutifully by my side, looking as comfortable in his skin as he always did.

Margo was impossibly glamorous, so my dress and ruffles weren't out of place at the dinner. Just out of place on me. I wasn't built for styled hair. Or ruffles. Or glamor. By the time I might have cared about those things, I had already trained myself to focus on work to the exclusion of nearly everything else. Slowing down long enough to wander through shops or experiment with hairstyles would have invited my mind to wander—and that was the last thing I needed.

"I'm going to stain this dress," I whispered back, deliberately looking over Joshua's shoulder so I wasn't taking in the crisp, white, open-collared shirt that made him look even more tanned than usual. He looked like he belonged on a yacht.

"Impossible. It's black."

He didn't know me very well. I was pretty sure I could ruin anything in my way. Especially when I was nervous. I pulled the skirt of the dress down.

"Below the knee isn't short," Joshua said through smiling teeth. He'd spent the car ride trying to convince me that anything below the knee was acceptable in a business setting. Except we weren't in a business setting. Medicine wasn't business. Not to me, at least.

"Do you even know who we're eating with? Gerry is the pediatrician that all other pediatricians want to be. Rumor has it, the Prime Minister has him on speed dial and he's turned down the job as Chief Medical Officer for the UK more than once. How on earth am I going to impress him?" I replied.

"Just be yourself." He glanced between my eyes and my lips, down to my chest and then back up again. Unintentionally flirting. He really couldn't help himself. "You're funny, sort of charming, and you look beautiful."

I rolled my eyes. Joshua had all the charm over on his side of the room. This was why he had women flitting around him constantly. In the supermarket earlier this week, two female assistants asked if they could help him, not even noticing I was standing right next to him—on crutches no less. The girl on reception in the lobby of the residences always said hello to him. She'd never even looked in my direction. Even Margo blushed when they shook hands, even though she was at least twenty-five years his senior. Joshua Luca was a pussy magnet.

"I don't adult well."

"You're a doctor," Joshua said. "That's pretty much the definition of adulting."

Joshua didn't get it. Doctoring was my safe zone. I knew what I was doing when I had a child in pain in front of me. I knew how to soothe, examine, and do what I needed to do to make a diagnosis. And I knew how to heal. Outside of the hospital, all bets were off.

"Here we are." Gerry came toward us carrying a glass in each hand. "Two Old Fashioneds."

"A favorite of mine," Joshua said, beaming at Gerry.

Gerry grinned. "Mine too. Some men prefer straight whiskey but I love me an Old Fashioned. Especially after a game of tennis. I feel I've earned it when I come off the court." He chuckled to himself. "Do you play, Hartford?"

I shook my head. I couldn't even offer him an alternative —*No, sorry, tennis isn't my game but I love squash/netball/golf.* Nope, sport and I didn't exactly mesh. Dance had kept me fit. Now, it was being on my feet all day at work.

"I like to pretend I can play," Joshua said, interrupting my awkward non-reply. "I offered myself up for some charity game at Queens a couple of years ago and got thrashed by Andy Murray. Stopped pretending after that."

I started to laugh. That had to be a joke, right? Surely not even Joshua Luca could have had a game of tennis with Andy Murray.

"It was a thrill all the same though, being beaten by one of the best."

"I bet it was." Gerry's eyes were wide. He was clearly impressed, but who wouldn't be? "I love the game. Always played. Keeps me young."

"I should get you to come to the charity game next summer. Maybe you'd be able to beat Andy."

Joshua was completely comfortable in this environment —dishing out compliments and invitations to the tennis like Gerry was an old friend. At this rate, Joshua would get promoted ahead of me, despite him not having any medical qualifications.

"I'd be completely delighted, young man. Any excuse to get my racket out or watch others play. Margo and I are debenture holders at Wimbledon. Go every year without fail."

"I'll arrange it," Joshua said.

"And you should maybe teach Hartford to play. I'm a big believer in balance." Gerry turned as Margo tapped him on the shoulder and pushed another Old Fashioned into his hand. "Cheers," he said, lifting his glass.

"Balance," Joshua repeated. "Absolutely. Keeps you fresh."

Almost imperceptibly, Gerry shifted closer to Joshua. "Not being one hundred percent about the job actually makes you more efficient, more perceptive, *better*. So few people get it. They just want to bank more and more hours. Having a life outside the hospital is a key performance measure when you come to practice under me." He nodded in my direction. "I'll be expecting you to show me the balance in your life, not just prove you can help patients."

What the hell did that mean?

"I'm a devotee of Alex Soojung-Kim Pang's approach to business," Joshua said, not skipping a beat. "I never have my best ideas behind a desk."

Alex who?

"Good man." Gerry gave what I'd come to recognize as his trademark sharp nod to Joshua, then turned to me. "If you've just come back from Medicines Sans Frontiers, you're going to have to work at balance. That kind of environment consumes you. But it's not sustainable. Learn from Josh here." He clapped his hand on Joshua's shoulder like they were old friends.

For a moment I wondered how much Felicity, my boss back in Yemen, had talked about me to Gerry. She'd tried to encourage me back to London for months before I broke my leg. Told me I needed to date, take up knitting, work somewhere a siege wasn't imminent. She'd told me it would do me good to go home. But I loved what I did over there. I was really helping people, and it was so busy the weeks and months just flew by. When I broke my leg, I had to leave. I was a burden if I couldn't work, just taking up a bed and food. So I was forced back here. It wasn't a choice I'd have made willingly.

"I like to be busy," I said. "And I have loads of energy. I suppose I'm just lucky like that."

"You need rest." Gerry's face was stern, like an overbearing Victorian schoolmaster. "That doesn't mean lying on the sofa watching God-knows-what on the Netpix. It means time away from the hospital spent engaging in meaningful activities that bring you joy. It means caring for yourself, investing in the people in your life, and creating a life outside the hospital."

Gerry sounded a lot like Felicity. I guess it wasn't surprising—Felicity had worked with him and recommended me for the position. But I couldn't help wondering whether she'd warned him about me.

"I tell everyone who works with me the same thing," Gerry continued. "How much you heed my advice will reflect in your appraisals. I'll expect you to report to me every two weeks with what you've been doing *outside* of work, as well as what's been going on in the hospital."

He couldn't be serious. I mean, people talked about balance and self-care, but as long as I was being a good doctor, what did it matter?

"During your time with me, I want you to become not a *good* doctor, but a *great* one. And you can't do that if you're always working. It sounds counterintuitive, but you have to trust me on this. You can't be great if you don't give your mind and body time to recuperate from the intensity of your work."

I could see Joshua nodding out of the corner of my eye. He was a bloody gazillionaire. There was no way that happened by taking every Friday off.

"Space for thinking and time to let your mind expand is the only way to be truly successful," Joshua said. I tried not to roll my eyes.

"I'm so pleased Hartford has got someone to encourage her down this path." Gerry nodded to me. "Think on what I've said. We'll talk again soon. Like I said, I'll expect updates every two weeks starting at the end of next week." He glanced at Joshua. "You're going to have to watch her for me. Excuse me. I'm just going to help out Margo."

I pulled my face into a smile as Gerry turned on his heel and left.

"So thanks for taking my side," I said under my breath.

"Sounded to me like we were all on the same side—yours. He's trying to help. So am I."

Of course Joshua wouldn't get it. I *enjoyed* being busy. I didn't want to veg out on the sofa and watch cooking shows.

"Were you always this . . ." He narrowed his eyes as he looked at me and . . . I couldn't look away. I couldn't tear my eyes from the flecks of gold sprinkled across the blue of his irises, the sweep of his eyelashes, the strong, raw jut of his chin.

He didn't finish his sentence so I did it for him. "Stubborn? Opinionated?"

"I wasn't going to say either of those things." He pushed his hands into his pockets in a way I'd seen him do a thousand times. "But your boss is telling you what he wants from you. He's giving you a roadmap to impressing him. I thought that was your aim?"

He was right but it didn't make him less irritating. I didn't want a hobby. Cut me in half and I was medicine all the way through. "How would you like it if someone said you had to change the way you were at a fundamental level and work for the rest of your life behind a desk, doing data entry?"

He had a funny habit of pausing before he spoke. I couldn't decide if he was trying to draw things out to torture me or he was thinking about what he was going to say. Either way, it made me want to fill the silence. "I'd do it if that's what it took to have the career I wanted," he said.

Urgh. When he put it like that, it sounded so obvious. It wasn't so easy for me, though. I didn't know what I would do if I wasn't working.

"It might help you settle into London and find new friends. You never know, he might even be right, and it might even make you better at your job." Joshua looked at me, and it was as if he knew I wasn't buying what he and Gerry were selling. "You understand physiology, right? It's like running. No one would say that running all day every day would make you faster. Your body would just give up in the end. All athletes cross-train and have rest periods. With work, it's the same. You need time to do other activities and time to do nothing at all. It will make you better at work. I promise."

I did want to impress Gerry. Even if I didn't stay at the hospital forever, a good reference from him could make my career, while a mediocre one could blow it. If doing less was the way to get the career I'd always dreamed of, then I suppose that's what I'd have to try to do. It wouldn't be easy. The idea of free time was like a thundercloud blocking out my sun. I didn't want to think about who I was when I had time to do something other than obsess about medicine. I liked the busy, productive, focused me much better. "I have no idea where to start. I've never had a hobby. Don't even suggest tennis—I'm hopeless." I didn't have any interests outside of medicine. Not since before university. Not since the accident.

"You like to cook. What about taking some lessons?"

"Cooking isn't a hobby. It's a means of survival. If I didn't cook, I wouldn't eat."

"So make it into one. Start making cakes or preparing sushi or something."

Would it be that easy to placate Gerry?

"Baby steps," Joshua said, reading my mind. "Maybe you can give me a cooking lesson or two. And then when you're cooking, I bet you find something else to do. That's the way creativity works—it needs space to expand."

"I'm passionate about what I do. I'm a good doctor. What's the harm in that?"

"There's no harm in that unless it's all you do. He's right that if you have other things in your life, you'll get better at your job."

"I disagree. Look at Bill Gates. Does he have hobbies?"

"I hear he likes to play bridge. And Jack Dorsey is a hiker."

"Who's Jack Dorsey? Your mate or something?"

"Just the guy who founded Twitter. And Foursquare. And—"

"Okay, I get it. I'll take up knitting or something." I knocked back a gulp of the Old Fashioned and winced. I didn't like whiskey almost as much as I didn't want a hobby. But with Gerry and Joshua on my back, I was going to have to try. Maybe Joshua and Gerry were right, and time away from work would improve my skills. What they didn't understand was the reason I liked to work hard wasn't just to get better at my job. Medicine had been my balm—the ultimate distraction—for a long time now. It was easy to forget the life unlived when you were focused on saving other people. Nothing save medicine had the power to distract me from considering *what could have been*, and that was just the way I liked it.

SEVEN

Hartford

I wondered how long it would take for Joshua to notice I wasn't wearing my cast. Until he did, I was going to try to figure out what the array of kitchen equipment I'd just unpacked was for. I hadn't a clue how to use ninety-eight-point-three percent of it. The sieve was familiar. And the mixing bowl. But the rest was way over my paygrade.

"All this was in your kitchen?" Joshua looked as baffled as I felt. I'd dragged him in from next door, where he was "busy" relaxing in his boxers, to help me bake. If he was so adamant that Gerry was right about doing stuff outside of work, then he shouldn't mind helping me.

"Some of it. I mentioned to Alice on reception that I was going out to shop for ingredients for baking, and when I got back, a huge box with all this in it was sitting at my front door."

"So we're here to bake?"

"Yes. You will be pleased to know that I'm not operating on you with a sieve."

"But why?" He pushed his hand through his hair, looking thoroughly confused.

"Because the sieve isn't sanitized for surgery, of course."

It took him a beat to process what I said before he speared me with those blue eyes. "Not why aren't you operating on me, but why are we baking?"

"Gerry and I had our first meeting on Friday. He was very cross that I couldn't tell him how I'd been spending my time out of the hospital. He said he wants to speak to me on Monday to see what I've done over the weekend. Can you believe it?"

"He's a man who means business," he said.

"The only thing I like to do, outside of medicine, is eat cake. So I'm extrapolating." I pulled the mixing bowl and scales to the side. That would be a start. "I bought ingredients for a chocolate sponge cake. And I'll take the finished cake into the hospital to share among the staff so Gerry is faced with *evidence* of me having a hobby."

I handed him my iPad then rolled up my sleeves. "The recipe's on there. If you measure out the sugar, I'll put the oven on."

"Right." He prodded at the scales. "Do you know how to work these?"

"No idea. You're the business whiz." I turned on the oven and set about clearing a space for us to . . . bake. This was crazy. All those years ago when I fantasized about Joshua, never did my fantasies include flour.

"What have measuring scales got to do with being a business whiz?" He lifted one eyebrow—a maneuver central to his flirting technique since he was sixteen, from what I could make out. "I mean, obviously, I *am* a business whiz." He narrowed his eyes at me and I couldn't help but smile.

"You have a badge or something?"

"Do you doubt me? Because yes, for your information, I have a badge *and* a matching tattoo."

"A tattoo?" I scanned his fully-clothed body as if I had x-ray vision.

"A tattoo." He caught me looking and grinned. "And wouldn't you like to know where?"

It was as if he'd set my cheeks on fire. The one time I hadn't been fantasizing about him, and he thought I was. "You are full of shit," I said, grabbing back the iPad and pretending to read the recipe.

"Maybe I'll show you one of these days."

Stand down, heart rate. It wouldn't matter if Joshua were Herman Munster's ugly cousin; his confidence would bewitch every woman he ever came near. I needed to power up my forcefield.

"Maybe I'll have to gouge my eyes out with a spoon first," I replied. There was no way he was going to get even an inkling of what his flirtatiousness might be doing to me.

I had to keep a clear head and remember that he couldn't help it. It wasn't personal; Joshua suffered from a chronic condition: incurable flirt.

I set out our ingredients onto the side along with the equipment I thought we'd need: cake tins, greaseproof paper, spatulas, mixing bowl. This seemed a lot more complicated than I'd thought it would be when I had this idea this morning.

"I think it's great that you're going to be embracing life outside of medicine." Joshua had worked out how to use the scales and was spooning sugar into the bowl.

"Why do you care if I want to work long hours, anyway?" I asked.

For a second, he looked flustered. "I just . . . you know. I told my mum I'd make sure you settled in okay."

"Right." Why else would he be interested in what I did? He hadn't even noticed I wasn't wearing my cast. I dumped the butter into the sugar. "We need to whisk this, apparently."

"The butter? Is that even possible?"

I re-read the recipe. "That's what it says. With an electric whisk, which I guess is this." I held up a machine like the one my grandma had. "I think maybe you should do it."

I plugged in the mixer and Joshua began to whisk. We both watched in silence as the ingredients begin to combine. Joshua looked intently into the bowl like his entire future hung in the balance. I looked away so he didn't see in my eyes how utterly adorable I found it. I couldn't remember seeing him trying hard at anything. Everything seemed to come so easy to him. Not baking, apparently. Well, that made two of us.

Joshua switched off the machine and I handed him an egg, being careful to keep my hand from touching his. My forcefield didn't need further testing today.

"Now we have to crack in the egg and whisk again." So far so good. "Here's me getting us both elbow deep in butter. What are your hobbies?"

"I prefer whipped cream over butter." He shot me a wickedly sexy smile, his dimple shifting into fifth gear. My forcefield creaked and groaned and I turned away, busying myself at the sink. I'd let go of my crush on Joshua a long time ago and I wasn't about to go backward. No matter how tempting that grin and that bloody dimple might be.

"But seriously . . ." He glanced at me as I came back to the counter. The mixture was starting to take on a glossy sheen—we were baking! "Outside of work, I have a tight circle of friends who I spend a lot of time with. I like to use the gym and . . ."

"And what?"

"And, nothing specific. Just, that kind of thing. You know, spend time with human beings. Outside of the people I work with."

"How long have you been single for?" I tried to think whether or not I'd ever heard about Joshua having a girlfriend. "Didn't you almost get married once? What happened there?" My mother had mentioned it the summer after I applied to medical school, but I hadn't wanted to hear anything about it. I didn't even want to *think* about Joshua after the accident.

"I spend time with women." His voice was clipped and tight and the normally laid-back Joshua I was so used to turned sharp-edged and defensive. "I don't need a girlfriend to complete me. Or a wife."

"I'm sorry," I said, almost flinching at the way he spat out his words. "I just meant—you have a lot of—and I thought—" I hated that I'd said the wrong thing and didn't even know why. This was why I shouldn't be allowed to *people*.

"I'm happy as I am." As quickly as his mood had turned sour, it flipped back again. He smiled. "I have a very full life. And I don't lack female company." Just like that, his dimple was back.

"Good." I smiled, relieved that familiar-Joshua was back.

"You're glad I'm getting laid regularly?"

I laughed as I shrugged. "Sure. Why wouldn't I be?"

We worked in happy silence as we combined the ingredients, poured the mixture into cake tins, and put them in the oven. I set the timer on my watch for twenty minutes as the recipe instructed.

We both leaned against the countertop, watching the

opaque oven door like we expected something clawed and snarling to emerge from it. "It's weird," I said, breaking the silence finally. "I've never had more free time than I do at the moment. I have working-hard muscles but not life-outside-of-work muscles." One of the things I enjoyed most about medicine was there was a lot to learn. Lots of exams. Lots of stuff to think about. It meant I wasn't thinking about things I wanted to forget.

"Didn't you used to do a lot of ballet when you were a kid?" My stomach roiled as he reached up to his head. "You used to wear your hair up a lot. Like all the time. I remember an omnipresent bun. Have you thought about doing some adult dance classes?"

I wanted to erase the past ten seconds and pretend he'd never asked, but life didn't work that way. "I haven't been able to dance since I broke my leg the first time," I said, as quickly as I could get the words out. "Not properly. Not how I'd want to." Memories tumbled into my brain about the night of the accident—the way I'd been so determined that driving in a thunderstorm was no problem. The way I'd been so sure I'd be able to rescue Joshua and Patrick from where they were stranded at a New Year's Eve party. It had seemed like a great idea in my teenage head, even though I'd only just passed my test. I'd have done anything to get Joshua to notice me. I had my heart pinned on the idea that if I drove to get them both, he'd suddenly realize I wasn't just a kid sister anymore. If only my seventeen-year-old self could have seen what laid ahead—the black windscreen that was impossible to see through, the water-soaked roads the tires couldn't grip. The turn I'd taken too late.

The ditch.

The paramedics.

The broken bone poking through my skin.

And months later, the bitterness when I lost my place at ballet school because I just couldn't dance like I used to.

The alarm went on my watch, pulling me out of my memories. I swiped it to turn it off. Saved by the cake.

I pulled in a breath and focused on what was in the oven.

"You okay?" Joshua asked.

"Fine." Reminiscing did nothing to turn back the clock. It just reminded me why it was important to stay busy and keep my forcefield intact.

"You don't seem fine."

I ignored him. The mixture in the tins didn't look any different to how it had when it went in. Wasn't it supposed to rise or something? I glanced at Joshua to see if he knew what he was doing, but he was just staring into the oven.

"If you don't want to take lessons, what about going to watch the ballet?"

Hadn't he gotten the hint that I didn't want to talk about it? "Why? So I can spend the evening jealous of all the dancers who didn't break their leg?" I couldn't think of anything worse.

"So you don't get any pleasure out of it if you're not dancing?"

I'd used to love going to the Royal Opera House and seeing the Royal Ballet perform. I'd gone every chance I'd gotten. For me it had fired up my drive and ambition. But now? It would just be a reminder of what I didn't have. Of the stupid decisions I'd made. "I don't think so."

He pushed his hands through his hair in that way that suggested he was a little coy. "Luca Brands have a corporate box at the Royal Opera House. One of my important clients loves the opera. But no one ever uses it when the ballet is on. You should go." He pulled out his wallet from the back pocket of his jeans and then slid a business card onto the work surface. "Just call my PA if you want to go. Take a friend. Go by yourself. Anytime."

I took a step away from the counter and closer to the oven. "Thanks." I'd perfected the art of not thinking about ballet and now Joshua was here saying I could attend the performances of one of the best ballet companies in the world whenever I wanted. For the old me, it would have been the perfect gift. But I wasn't the old me anymore.

"I guess I should take it out," I said, pulling on the oven gloves. "You think it's done?"

"I have no idea. I've never baked a cake in my entire life. Apple pie prep was as far as my cooking education went."

"It's the blind leading the blind." I pulled down the oven door and took out the first tin. Well, the mixture didn't move like it had when it was going in. I took out the other tin and then referred back to the recipe. "We need to turn them out onto the wire rack."

"I'm not sure they look right. Aren't they supposed to get bigger?" Joshua reached out and poked one of them, his face contorted like he was considering an important chess move.

"I'm going to follow the recipe and turn them out." I did exactly what the recipe said and turned out the sponges onto the rack.

"They've not risen at all," Joshua said. "We must have missed something."

"No, I checked. We did what it said." He was right though. The cake didn't look right and it felt heavy as I'd turned it out.

"Stella is a good baker." Joshua rubbed his jaw with the palm of his hand as he stared at the flat discs like they were a problem to be solved. "Maybe you should give her a call and she might give you some lessons."

Now he was being ridiculous. "I don't even know Stella."

"Two birds with one stone. You can get to know her *and* learn how to bake. Maybe you end up being friends. Maybe you don't. But your baking can't get worse."

"Hey," I prodded the sponge again to see if the cool air was loosening it up any. "You were right here alongside me."

"Shit!"

I spun around to find Joshua holding his arm in the air. A quick assessment of the still-hot tins on the side told me precisely what had happened.

"You burnt your arm?"

His screwed-up face was all the answer I needed. I pulled him over to the sink and turned on the tap. "Put it under here." The skin was angry and red. I held his arm under the cool water, reaching to add a little more hot to ensure the water wasn't too cold.

"It's fine," he said, trying to pull away.

"It's not fine. We need to keep it under here for longer than you think." I wasn't about to tell him how long. If he was impatient after ten seconds, he'd be climbing the walls after ten minutes.

"Honestly, I'm fine."

"That red welt would say otherwise. I'd forgotten what a bad patient you are." Joshua was usually so cool and calm; if he wasn't in pain, it would be funny to see him so irritated. "Did I ever tell you that you inspired me to become a doctor?" I adjusted his arm to make sure the water was covering the entire burn and continued my story in order to distract him. "You and Patrick were playing tennis when you were home from uni for Easter and you sprained your ankle."

He frowned at me, clearly not remembering the moment that had so completely transformed my life.

"You went for this crazy shot and fell." I could still see the awkward fall and the way his foot had given way as he went down.

"When I sprained my ankle and had to go to hospital? You were there?"

I gave a half-laugh at the idea that he didn't even remember my presence, let alone that I'd nursed him straight after the fall. It had happened exactly nineteen weeks after the accident, when pining after Joshua had changed my life forever. I'd been a shadow to even myself. No wonder he didn't remember.

That afternoon had been another turning point for me. I'd barely eaten or spoken since my accident. My crush on Joshua had been dead nineteen weeks. My place at ballet school had been lost. The only reason I'd been watching Patrick and Joshua that morning—and not lying in my bed, staring at the ceiling—was because it was mildly less annoying than listening to my mum and dad argue about whether I should be sent to counselling. My father had been firmly against it, said I'd snap out of it. My mother had been trying to help. I knew counselling wouldn't make a difference. Nothing would. My own stupidity had lost me my future, and I'd never be the same again. I was content to lie in bed for the rest of my life.

"Yes, I was there. I elevated your ankle. Cleaned the cuts with my water bottle. It felt good to look after someone. After that, I decided to become a doctor." I probably sounded silly to Joshua—like I was a child pretending to nurse its teddy. But it wasn't like that. The entire time I'd been tending to Joshua, I hadn't thought about the accident and my lost future. It was like helping Joshua wiped my mind blank of anything else. I'd made a difference to someone in pain; I'd been useful.

Patrick had been next to useless—he'd told Joshua to walk it off. I'd been the one who knew what to do. I'd told my brother to get my parents and talked to Joshua about football to distract him. I let him lean on me so he could hop to a bench, then elevated his foot on Patrick's equipment bag. It wasn't until after my parents arrived and loaded Joshua into the car, my brother along for the ride, that thoughts of the accident rushed back in. And that's when I knew I had to become a doctor. It would save me. The universe had given me a second chance. I took it, and had been running with it ever since.

"I thought I went to hospital?"

"You did. My parents took you." I'd stayed behind. It would be months before I got in a car again. Even now, I didn't drive.

"Yes, I remember that vaguely. But it turned out to be just a sprain." A sprain that had changed the course of my life. "No hospital visits today," he said, nodding at his arm that I was still holding under the water.

"You'll live. Doesn't look like it's going to blister." I released his arm and turned off the tap.

He leaned against the kitchen cabinet as he watched me dab his arm dry with paper towel. All of a sudden, the air shifted and I became very aware of just how close we were, how Joshua's muscles bunched under his t-shirt, how when he flexed his arm, it tripped the switch on my galloping heart rate. He grinned down at me and I stepped back. Where the hell was my forcefield when I needed it?

"Where's your cast?" Joshua said, glancing at my leg like

I must have forgotten to put it back on when I went to the loo. "And you're walking without crutches. When did that happen? How do you feel?"

I laughed. He'd finally noticed. "It came off yesterday. And I feel good. A little weak but I might venture into the hotel gym later."

He stepped back, still focused on my leg as if it was incredible that I still had a limb under all that plaster. "Wait a minute. I have something you need."

No, you don't, I thought to myself. *You absolutely do not.*

He disappeared out of my flat, leaving the door on the latch as he left. Where was he going?

I set about cleaning up the mess we'd left. As I flipped up the door on the dishwasher, Joshua appeared behind me.

"Come and sit." He put a hand at the small of my back and led me to the sofa. "Put your leg on my lap."

I screwed up my face. "No, Joshua. What are you doing?"

He set a small bottle of something on the side table and pulled my leg onto his knees, rolling up the bottoms of my scrubs trousers. I braced my arms behind me, waiting for something dreadful to happen.

"I bet your skin is really dry from being in that cast." He reached for the bottle and tipped it over, pouring cream into the center of his palm. "This stuff is the best. The eucalyptus is healing. The aloe vera moisturizes."

Before my brain had time to process what was about to happen, I squealed as his hands smoothed up my leg.

He grinned. "It's a little cold right? Just wait, this is going to feel really good."

The screech of an alarm sounded in my head: *Emergency. Forcefield down. Forcefield down.*

"Relax." Joshua lifted his chin. "Put a cushion behind you. You need to learn to take care of yourself. This cream is transformative. You'll see."

"Thank you, Estée Lauder." I looked out of the window, trying to distract myself from the feel of Joshua's firm touch. Despite myself, my body began to droop. It took everything I had not to sigh—his hands just felt so good. Too good. This was such a bad idea. It was as if he knew about my force-field and had made it his mission to disable it.

"You're a little dry, but the leg looks really good." His voice was soft and he bent forward for closer inspection. "You can't tell it's been in a cast for weeks." He stopped rubbing suddenly and I knew he'd seen my scar. "Did you cut yourself?"

"It's from where I broke my leg the first time," I said, gazing out of the window so he wouldn't see how much it still hurt.

"That's why you gave up dancing?"

I nodded.

"That must have been difficult. I remember it was important to you."

I tried to pull my leg away, but he tightened his grip. When I relented, he continued to massage the lotion into my skin. The movements became deeper and slower and my entire body started to buzz. "Maybe you need a bath."

"No thank you. I don't take baths." What was there to do in a bath but lie back and think? It sounded like complete torture. Although, I would have said a massage from Joshua would have been hell up until a few minutes ago. I closed my eyes in a vain attempt to block out some of the Joshua Luca sensation floating into my body.

"Maybe one day I'll convince you," he said, pushing his thumbs up one side of my tibia and dragging them down the other. If he continued like this, I wouldn't just have a crush on Joshua—I'd be pregnant with his child.

"Do something for me?" he said.

Anything, I thought. I shook my head, remembering who I was with and trying to get back in the moment. I opened my eyes to find him looking at me as if he were about to say something important.

"If I inspired you to become a doctor, I should be able to inspire you to call Stella." I half-opened my mouth to say something but couldn't find the words. "That cake really does look hideous."

I smiled. "Okay." I gave him a small nod and shifted my leg from his lap. I couldn't help but be slightly disappointed that he let me go.

EIGHT

Hartford

I opened the lid of the white cardboard box and slid the cake onto one of the canteen plates. A couple of nurses stopped on their way out of the break room.

"You made this?" The one with the high ponytail asked.

I winced. "I bought it. I tried to make it, but failed."

"It looks amazing," a man said behind me.

"Help yourself, Jacob," I replied to the doctor who'd just swept into the break room, taking every woman's attention away from my cake. Jacob was the hospital heartthrob. It was easy to see why. He wore his pale-blonde hair as short to his head as possible, giving maximum impact to his blue eyes and sharp jaw. "I brought some paper napkins because I had to promise Mabel in the canteen my first born just to get one plate."

"This is really nice of you. You made it?" Jacob asked.

I shook my head.

"Hartford! I was looking for you," Gerry said as he sauntered into the break room. He glanced between Jacob and me. "Have you got a minute?" He didn't wait for an answer before heading back out of the door he just came from. I dashed to keep up.

Gerry's office looked like it might have been an old storage cupboard. It was tiny, with a folded-up wheelchair behind the door and a distinct lack of windows.

"Take a seat." He closed the door behind me and pulled out a stool from under his desk.

"You brought in some cake." He checked something on his computer as he spoke. "That's nice of you."

"I tried to bake but failed, so I bought that cake but I'm going to try again. I'm getting some lessons from a friend of Joshua's, actually. You know, trying to get a life outside of the hospital, as you suggested."

He turned to me and frowned. "It's a good first step. And it's nice to see you're making friends. You said you and Joshua weren't dating. Is there anyone else?"

Before I could answer, he shook his head as if to chastise himself. "I know I shouldn't ask, but I see my junior doctors as my children. I like to see them happy. Fulfilled. Margo says I'm an interfering old man and I suppose she's right—"

He was interrupted by a knock at the door.

"Come in." His voice was all stern authority.

Jacob stuck his head around the door. "That research you asked for." He handed Gerry a faded, red paper file.

"Have you got yourself a girl, yet, Jacob?"

Jacob cleared his throat. "Not at the moment, sir."

"Good, good. Then you'll take Hartford out to dinner."

Humiliation climbed my limbs. Had my boss just asked someone out on my behalf? Gerry seemed lovely but I really didn't need him setting me up.

I started to object but Gerry put his hand up to silence me. "Jacob thinks I'm just as interfering as you do, but humor me." He turned to Jacob. "Hartford hasn't known me as long as you have. She's still getting used to my foibles. Perhaps you can catch her up over dinner."

Jacob gave Gerry a relaxed salute as if he'd been in the same position a thousand times and didn't find it awkward at all. "No problem. I'll tell her exactly how to avoid you."

Gerry chortled and then jumped when his phone started to ring.

"Saturday night?" Jacob asked me.

I shook my head. "Honestly, I'm sure you have better things to be doing—"

"It'll be fun. I'm on shift, so shall we meet at eight thirty somewhere? I'll text you the name of a place."

I shrugged. I could hardly say no in front of my boss, who'd just set me up. "Okay. Let me know and I'll be there." I tried to sound enthusiastic, but I was a terrible faker.

Gerry put down his phone and Jacob swept out, pulling the door closed behind him.

"So," he said, and cleared his throat. "We got side-tracked last week talking about what you're going to be doing outside the hospital. Tell me, are you enjoying yourself?"

"Everyone has been very welcoming and I feel like I've been here longer than I have." I wondered if I should mention he looked like he hadn't slept for a week. "The extracurricular stuff is a challenge. But I'm working on it."

"I see you are. Keep at it. I'll need updates every two weeks. In the meantime, I could use your help with some-thing. But I don't want it to interfere with you settling in or finding yourself a life outside work."

That sounded intriguing. I nodded, urging him on.

"I mean it, Hartford. It's the kind of project that can consume you. You have to promise me you're going to keep up with the good work you're doing outside the hospital."

"I promise," I replied.

He pushed back in his chair and exhaled, nodding. "What I'm about to tell you is highly confidential and you must repeat it to no one under any circumstances." Gerry's expression turned from jolly to steely.

"Okay, I won't tell a soul."

"I used to teach at Harvard Medical School and have many wonderful friends in America, many of whom were students or faculty from my six years in Cambridge. One of those friends now works for a major pharmaceutical company over there and has shared some very disturbing news indeed."

He paused as if he wanted me to say something, but I had no idea where he was going with this.

"My friend has come to me because the company they work for has had a change of strategy in order to boost sales in respect to certain drugs currently in development. They have an entire division tasked with developing drugs that can be sold over the counter. That doesn't sound controversial, does it?" He didn't wait for a response, though I shook my head anyway. "But they have teams of people looking at the rules and guidance so the drug gets through loopholes and patchy legislation. By all accounts, they're bribing regulators left and right."

I could feel the hairs on my arms stand to attention. Drug companies held so much power and could do so much good, but three steps to the left and they could do so much harm.

"Merdon are angling for over-the-counter approval on a number of their new drugs, which are close approximations of formulas currently available exclusively on prescription.

What's worse is that they're targeting medicines for children first. They hope they can take advantage of parents wanting the best and quickest help for their children."

I could feel the bite of his words in my sternum. "That's disgraceful. Do you think they'll get away with it?"

"Well, I'm doing my best to ensure they don't. But I have to be careful because I don't want my friend to risk her job and reputation."

"You said you wanted my help. What can I do?"

Gerry sighed. "They're starting in America. With a drug for ADHD called Calmation."

"Calmation? I've read about it in the journals. There's got to be a mistake." There was no way a drug so powerful could be sold *without a prescription*.

"No, they're just weeks away from filing. When they get regulatory approval in America, they'll use it to put pressure on the British regulator. They intend to spread their rot this side of the Atlantic."

"So—" I started then paused, my mind ringing with the sound of internal alarm bells. This was *bad*. "No one can expect parents to make medical decisions about children that could cause lasting damage. A child with such a serious medical condition should be monitored by a doctor." My fury was snowballing. "You're telling me Merdon is going to try to sell a drug *that alters a child's mood* over the counter, like it's a lollipop or something?"

"They're sinking tens of millions into it apparently."

"What can we do? Sign a petition. Create some kind of lobby. Has anyone spoken to you about it? You're the best consultant pediatrician in the world."

He shrugged. "Of course not—Merdon just want to make money and the regulators are a bunch of pen pushers. They don't actually have to deal with the consequences of their decisions." Gerry pulled open an old-fashioned metal filing cabinet and took out a file, which he handed to me. "I need fresh eyes to look at the issue and come up with some kind of plan. I thought as you're not afraid of working in a warzone, you might be just the woman for the job."

This could be a travesty for a generation of children. Something had to be done, and I was just the person to do it. This was just the kind of problem I'd been eager to sink my teeth into.

"I want to help. And I promise, I'll keep baking and have dinner with Jacob, but we can't let this happen."

Gerry gave a weary smile and nodded. "I knew I was right to hire you."

We had to stop Merdon before this strategy was out of the gate. I had no idea how, but I was determined to do whatever it took.

NINE

I was exhausted after a week spent researching Merdon and Calmation. To my surprise, I was actually looking forward to a break. My goals for today were simple: learn everything I needed to know about dating in a single afternoon from an almost-stranger, and try to bake a cake that didn't taste like it belonged on the surface of the road. And, if possible, try to forget about work for a few hours.

Stella flung open the door to her apartment and held out her arms like I was a daughter coming home from the army. "Hartford—it's so great to have you here. We're going to bake up a storm!"

Stella's positive energy seemed to saturate the air around her in sunshine. I just hoped she didn't mind me picking her brain about men and dating while we baked. I'd considered cancelling on Jacob a thousand times. But there were two good reasons why dating someone—anyone— would be a good idea. First, it would keep my boss happy. But second, and maybe more importantly, it would keep my

forcefield against Joshua intact. My defenses had been like
bad WiFi recently—patchy and at some points nonexistent.
After he gave me that massage, I'd avoided him for a few
days while I tried to block out the old crush hammering at
the door. Dinner with Jacob would therefore serve a dual
purpose. And since I hadn't dated since way before I started
with Medicines Sans Frontiers—and even then, I hadn't
amassed a particularly impressive track record—I needed
some help.

If I impressed Gerry with my array of outside interests
and bubbling social life, I hoped he'd see I was serious about
my career and completely dedicated to medicine. Counterintuitive? Yes. Possibly the key to securing a reference from
the most famed pediatric specialist in the UK? Also yes.

"Hi." I tried to look relaxed and happy as I looked over
Stella's shoulder to see Autumn and another girl sitting at
the kitchen island. Asking dating questions in front of an
audience would be daunting, but better that then making a
complete fool of myself with Jacob.

Stella ushered me into the apartment, but before she got
a chance to introduce me, the girl I didn't recognize jumped
from her bar stool, bounded over, and wrapped me in a hug.

"I'm sooo excited to meet you! I'm Hollie." She stepped
back. "Joshua!" she said inexplicably.

"Actually, it's Hartford," I replied, well and truly
confused. I'd only been inside for thirty seconds and already
I felt out of my depth.

"Yes, Joshua's new . . . *friend.*" She grinned at me as if
she and I were in on some kind of secret.

Stella guided me to one of the bar stools and I took a
seat, slightly nervous about what I'd walked in on. It was
only noon. Had they been on the breakfast wine?

"You'll have to excuse us. Joshua's never introduced us

to a woman of his before, so we're all a little giddy," Stella said.

A woman of his? Had I slipped into some 1950s soap opera?

"It's not like that between us. I've known him since forever. Our mums are best friends." Private fantasies of mine aside, Joshua was as likely to see me as a romantic interest as he was to date a slice of toast with that awful marmalade he'd always loved as a kid.

"Hmmm," Hollie said, narrowing her eyes.

"So you've not had sex with him?" Autumn asked.

I laughed. "No, definitely not. Not in real life, anyway."

Stella's eyes widened. "So in your pretend life . . . ?"

I sighed and glanced around the kitchen, wondering when the baking lessons were going to start. When I turned back to the island, three sets of eyes stared at me. Nothing for it than to tell the truth. "I was a fifteen-year-old girl, filled to the brim with hormones, when Joshua was a tall, tanned, impossibly good-looking eighteen-year-old. Of course I've had fantasies."

"We need mimosas," Hollie announced. Stella jumped off her stool and began to pull out glasses.

"Is drinking and baking a good idea?" I asked.

"Of course," Stella said, pulling out a carton of orange juice from the fridge.

"Tell us everything about eighteen-year-old Joshua. Did you ever kiss him?" Autumn asked.

Within a couple of minutes, Stella had poured four mimosas and pulled baking materials onto the counter.

I shook my head. "Never. I mean, he had his pick of girls. And when he was round at our house—which was all the time—if he noticed anyone, he noticed my sister, Thea."

"Stop." Autumn put up her hand. "Of course he noticed you. Look at you."

Bloody Americans and their over-the-top positivity about everything.

"Quite. And think about how I looked with a monobrow and braces."

"Awww. How adorable," Hollie said. "This is even better than I thought. You blossomed into this beautiful butterfly and now Joshua has seen what was under his nose all along."

These girls were crazy. Like, batshit. I needed to change the subject or they were going to start planning my wedding to Joshua. And as much as that sounded like a dream come true to my fifteen-year-old self, I was pretty sure we'd all end up in prison if that was the road we started on.

Stella might have more ability to read the room than I gave her credit for, because she promptly changed the subject. "Some basic baking tips: start with all your ingredients at room temperature, including eggs. Put your oven on and grease your pans and tins first thing. Even before measuring any ingredients."

From my bag, I pulled out the notepad and pen I'd brought and jotted down the two instructions before setting my pad down. "Actually," I said, hoping to steer the conversation into more realistic territory, "as well as baking, I was hoping you could help me out with a few tips and pointers on dating? Because—"

"We'd be delighted," Stella said. "Anything we can do to help. Joshua is a great guy and it's about time he found someone special rather than ricochet between Miss Tuesday Night and the model of the week."

Miss Tuesday Night? Did I even want to know who that was? I shouldn't have come here. These women thought I was here to bond because they were all wives and girlfriends of the group of guys Joshua was friends with. Hadn't Joshua explained who I was? I was just going to have to talk really fast and get out my side of the story. "I'm not Joshua's girlfriend. Or soon-to-be girlfriend. I'm just the daughter of his mum's best friend. I hadn't seen him in over a decade before last week. But I do have a date at the weekend and I haven't got a clue what to wear or talk about or anything. Any tips would be much appreciated." I exhaled. I got the feeling if you didn't talk fast in this group, you didn't get to say anything.

Hollie and Autumn exchanged a glance. "It could work," Hollie said.

"Make him see what he's got to lose," Autumn replied. "We don't want to play games, but sometimes men like Joshua need a little nudge."

"That's what I said to Beck," Stella said.

Oh God. They weren't getting it. "I'm not looking to nudge Joshua. I just got back to England. The only things I own can fit into a backpack. I just want to start work, impress my boss by having outside interests, and date someone to prove I'm not an antisocial workaholic. And at some point, I need to find somewhere to live. Joshua isn't on my list of things to 'do'."

"Here, measure out two hundred and twenty-five grams of this butter and put it in with that sugar I've measured out in the bowl already," Stella said, then added casually, "So you're not interested in Joshua?"

I hopped off my stool and got to work. "More like I'm not into masochism."

Stella's eyes grew wide. "Joshua is into kink?"

How did this conversation just keep getting worse? "No! Maybe? I don't know. I meant that I'm not into pain.

I'm not a teenage girl anymore. I know better than to pine after men like Joshua."

"Good for you," Autumn said. "But you're baking cakes with him and hanging out together. You don't think there are flirty vibes?"

I shook my head. I didn't want to hesitate and give these girls a crumb of something that wasn't there. I tried to suppress the memory of his hands massaging my leg, his thumbs digging into the muscles of my calf. If I so much as blushed in front of this crowd, I'd never hear the end of it. Joshua had to flirt like he had to breathe—he was made that way. Always had been. So if there were flirty vibes between us, it was nothing to do with me. "And then I use the whisk to cream them together?"

Stella nodded and held the bowl for me, clearly understanding I needed all the help I could get.

But not even the loud whir of the electric whisk could stop these girls and their effort to matchmake. "Well, doesn't mean we can't have hope," Autumn said. "I mean, you're beautiful. He's beautiful. You've known each other since you were kids—it's like a fairy tale waiting to happen. But in the meantime, tell us about the guy you have a date with."

There wasn't much to tell. I didn't know anything about Jacob other than we both worked in pediatrics and he was gorgeous. "We're meeting on Saturday at eight."

"This is perfect," Stella said. "Much less pressure because you're colleagues, so if there's no spark, the dinner is just an opportunity to get to know each other better."

That was true. We could always talk about our medical backgrounds and where we went to university. "Any advice? Dos and don'ts?"

"Just be yourself." She slid me a carton of eggs. "Add

one egg then whisk. Repeat four times. Never add all the eggs at once, or the batter will get uneven and gummy."

I followed her instructions. Soon, the batter took on the rich, creamy texture I recognized from my failed attempt with Joshua. So far, then, it seemed we hadn't come to the part of this process I'd screwed up so royally. "Is it okay to focus on work as a topic of conversation?"

"Of course," Hollie said. "What do you talk about when you're with Joshua?"

Luckily, the baking overtook the need to answer Hollie's question.

"Now measure out two hundred and twenty-five grams of self-raising flour and sieve it into the bowl," Stella said. "Self-raising has the baking powder mixed in already, but sometimes you need extra. Always check the recipe."

"Jacob's coming right from the hospital. He's not picking me up, so I'm assuming I wear something casual?" I paused to make the note about flour and then did as instructed.

"Yes," Autumn said. "Some nice jeans will be fine."

What counted as *nice* jeans? I had no clue.

Under Stella's guidance, I added the vanilla and lemon zest, poured the mixture into the pre-greased pans, and put them in the oven. It looked just the same as when Joshua and I had made it, but hopefully this time, the cake would rise.

"Great job." Stella raised her glass. "Here's to cake, dating, and waking Joshua up to what he's missing."

I raised my glass despite the ludicrous toast. This afternoon might produce a good cake, but it had been scant on dating advice. Their obsession with Joshua was a little weird. Their obsession with Joshua *and me* was borderline uncomfortable. Couldn't they see that Joshua and I weren't couple material? For a start, we couldn't be more opposite if we tried. He always looked like he'd just stepped out of a photo shoot and I always looked like I'd just stepped out of a hospital. He could charm the birds from the trees, while I needed help to get through a drinks party with a room full of my professional peers. He lived in a hotel in Mayfair, while I was googling Rightmove for studios in Borehamwood. We weren't compatible. Not in any way. The only thing we had in common was neither of us could bake, and given how the sponges were rising in the oven, even that common ground wouldn't last long.

TEN

Joshua

As I waited for the lift to the penthouse, I typed out a message to my PA, instructing her to go ahead and submit paperwork so that Luca Brands took a corporate box at the Royal Opera House. When I'd told Hartford we already had a box, I might have been exaggerating a little. Or it might have been a complete lie depending on how you looked at it. But the box would be useful for client entertaining and I hoped Hartford would use it. I'd remembered she liked ballet but not understood that she had to give it up after her accident. From the way she'd acted when I brought up taking some classes, she was obviously still sad about it. Hopefully having access to the box would encourage her to go. If nothing else, it would give her something to tell Gerry.

I stepped out of the lift onto the penthouse floor and found Hartford slumped against the front door. She wasn't wearing scrubs. Something must be up.

"Joshua!" She bounced to her feet like she was a puppy who'd been left alone all day. Her enthusiasm tugged in my stomach. It was surprisingly good to see her. We'd not caught up since our baking disaster. And she looked good. I wasn't sure I'd ever seen her in jeans. Her hair was down again, like it had been for the dinner with Gerry and Margo.

"Should I ask why you're sitting on the floor outside your flat?"

She shrugged. "Somewhere between here and Liliana's, I lost my key."

"The cocktail bar? You meet up with one of the girls?" I opened my door and invited her in with a nod. As she followed me inside, I messaged the concierge, asking them to bring up a new key.

"No, I had a date."

The tug in my stomach pulled a little tighter. "A date?" I tried not to sound shocked. Why had I gotten the feeling that Hartford's world was small, consisting of little more than the hospital, her family and . . . me? I'd obviously been wrong.

She came in and hopped on my sofa, tucking her legs under her. "A doctor from the hospital. Gerry set it up."

"Right, and how was it?"

She groaned. "He seemed like a nice guy but . . . I'm just so hopelessly awkward in those situations. Or any situation, really."

"What was the problem, he didn't want to talk about cake?"

She laughed and that pull in my stomach just wouldn't let go. "Any chance of a coffee, or do you have to order up for that?"

"Very funny," I replied, moving behind the kitchen island. I switched on the espresso machine and brought out two cups.

"And do you have any cake?"

"I can order something in. You want me to?"

She scrunched up her nose, making her freckles bunch. "Maybe half a cupcake."

"Hartford, are you eating your feelings? Tell me what happened tonight."

I quickly ordered cupcakes, pulled two espressos, and sat down beside her on the sofa. She obviously wanted to talk, and I was here to help her settle in. This was all part of my promise to my mum—nothing more.

"I'm hopeless at dating," she said. "And I'm okay with that. I really am. It's just that Gerry set it up and he's so adamant about this whole work-life balance thing that I feel like I should give it a shot. And Jacob is . . ." She scrunched up her nose and twisted her mouth as if she were about to sneeze. "He's good looking," she said. "Everyone else at the hospital swoons when he walks into a room."

"Not you?"

She shrugged. "I don't know. I suppose I'm just not . . . comfortable with him." She paused like I was supposed to say something. But what?

Hartford always seemed one hundred percent, relentlessly herself when she was with me. In contrast, I'd witnessed her discomfort at the cocktail party firsthand. I'd assumed it was the number of people in attendance that had forced her into her shell, or maybe the pressure to impress Gerry. Once again, my assumption proved incorrect. "I'm not sure I'm the guy to advise you on stuff like this."

"Right. The girls say you don't date. You just get laid by Miss Tuesday Night—whoever that is." She shrugged. "Getting laid would be good, I guess. Not sure I'll earn marks from Gerry for that, though."

It irritated me that my mates' girlfriends were talking openly about my sex life. I'd learned by now that if I tried to tell them it was none of their business, I would just sacrifice thirty minutes of my life I'd never get back while I listened to them lecture me on why I needed to be in a relationship.

"They shouldn't be talking to you about me. They don't get it. My sex life isn't a joke. It's a choice." I pulled in a breath and tried to soften my jaw. I'd tried the relationship thing and it hadn't worked out. I was happy with my life now. What did anyone else care what I did? They didn't have to walk in my shoes.

"A choice?"

"Never mind. Anyway, getting laid is always good. It's an excellent stress reliever."

She laughed and kicked my leg like we were teenagers again. "Wouldn't it be good to get laid by someone I'd like to talk to afterward? I have no idea. I kinda missed the whole 'relationships' thing. It passed me by when I was studying. I'm not a virgin or anything. I'm just not . . ."

I tried not to smile. Whatever she was thinking seemed to fall from her mouth when she was with me. She had zero filter and was arguably *too* comfortable. Understanding I was the exception to the rule lifted my chest and my stomach settled.

"So, how do you pick the women you sleep with?"

I groaned. I didn't want to get into this with Hartford. "You make it sound like there's a catalog."

"But is it only physical? You don't want to talk and stuff?"

When had this become about me? Weren't we discussing her?

She didn't wait for my answer. "And the women you're with don't want to talk either?"

"I don't insist on silence, but you know . . ." I'd never been embarrassed by my sexual relationships with women.

They were entirely consensual and mutually satisfying, and I didn't play games or pretend I was interested in something more than I was. "We don't spend time together because of each other's scintillating conversation."

She looked at me, trailing her gaze over my face, down my neck, to my chest, my waist, my cock. "You like each other for your bodies." Her voice was softer now. Like it had been when I'd seen her emerge all done up before dinner at Gerry's. Then, the room around us seemed to disappear. Now, there was nothing here except Hartford and me. "So, you just undress and . . ."

I allowed my gaze to travel down her body in response. I took in her parted lips, her tongue darting out to wet them; I enjoyed the sight of those full breasts she'd pressed against me at the airport a couple of weeks ago. Her cinched-in waist, her legs. What was between them.

"It's just physical," she whispered.

"Right."

Our eyes locked and I couldn't help it, I leaned forward and kissed the juncture between her neck and her shoulder. Just once. Once wouldn't hurt, would it? Or twice? I kissed her delicate skin again.

She tilted her head to allow me more room and my cock pushed against my fly. Fuck, when had a woman I'd barely touched got me so wound up like this? My heart was jackhammering against my ribs and I was having to work to control my breathing as if I'd just come off the Peloton. I pressed another kiss farther up her neck and inhaled her sweet, cinnamon scent. Cupping her jaw, I leaned my forehead against hers and tried to steady my pulse.

"Joshua." My name came out on a sigh. Her hand slid up my chest and I groaned. Even though I knew I should stop, I just didn't want to. I wanted her to touch more of me. All of me.

Our lips were almost touching. All I wanted was to taste her. Just once. Before I could process what was happening, she opened her mouth and her hot breath snapped the tether on my self-control. I pushed against her, pressing my lips against hers in soft, hot, wet kisses. She opened her mouth slightly, and I took her bottom lip between my teeth, sucking the sweetness from her as if it had been denied me too long.

Christ, what was the matter with me?

A small moan escaped from her and ricocheted to the root of my cock.

A loud knock on the door sounded, and Hartford jumped ten feet in the air as if I'd electrocuted her.

She put her hand to her mouth. "My key."

She scrambled to answer my front door while I tried to will away my hard-on. Fuck. I tipped my head back on the sofa.

Shit. What had I just done? I couldn't be kissing Hartford. Perhaps it was some kind of misplaced sense of ownership that made me cross a line tonight. I hadn't been expecting her to announce she'd been on a date, and we'd been spending so much time together . . . I was a bloody idiot.

She sidled back into the living room. "I got my key and I'm not sitting back down on that sofa," she said. "It's . . . no . . . not a good location."

I chuckled despite it smarting a little that she was clearly regretting our kiss.

"Did I cross a line?" I asked.

"*We* crossed a very important, shouldn't-be-crossed-under-any-circumstances line. I mean . . . it's . . . you're . . . I'm . . ."

Jesus, she was making it sound like I was toxic. But she was right. Any kind of *anything* between us wasn't going to lead to anything but trouble. I nodded. "It was just a kiss, Hartford." Liar, I thought to myself. "No big deal. Let's pretend it didn't happen."

She nodded enthusiastically, which I tried to mentally brush off.

"You should date," I blurted. "You can't give up after just one guy." If she got herself a boyfriend, she'd have way less time to spend with me. And there'd be another good reason for me not to cross the line again. Yes, Hartford finding a boyfriend was an excellent idea. The quicker the better. "I'll help you so you don't feel awkward. I'll pick your dates. I'll find you someone you want to talk to *and* fuck."

She scowled at me like I'd just assigned her a week of detention. "Only if I get to pick *your* dates."

I laughed. "My dates? What are you talking about?"

"If I have to date, I don't see why you shouldn't."

Where was she going to meet the kind of women I wanted to date? Easy. Nowhere, because I wasn't interested in dating anyone. But I could go through the motions so that Hartford actually dated. That way, the pull in my stomach when I saw her, the way my heart stumbled sometimes when she touched me, and the buzz at the base of my dick when she laughed would all disappear.

"You got yourself a deal," I said. "I set you up on three dates. I coach you through each one, and by the end of it, you'll be able to fly into a fully-fledged dating life."

"Three dates?"

"You've gotta kiss some frogs."

A smile curled around her lips. "I have ground rules."

"Name them."

"No date should be longer than two hours. No sex. And we split the bill."

"You know this isn't *us* dating, right?" I asked.

"Right. But you're expecting me to change things up and force myself out of my comfort zone. I don't see why you shouldn't have to do the same. You're not interested to see if you can just talk to a woman for two hours?"

I hadn't spoken to a woman outside my immediate circle one-on-one for two hours in ten years. Unless it was business related. Hartford was the only exception.

"Come on," she said. "It's six hours out of your life. I'll coach you through it." She grinned at me like she was doing me a favor rather than the other way around.

She held out her hand. As we shook to seal the deal, a frisson of heat travelled up my arm, confirming I'd made the right decision. In three dates, Hartford was sure to have a boyfriend, and I'd be able to stop telling myself how she wasn't my type once and for all.

ELEVEN

Hartford

A week after we'd made our bargain, Joshua had clearly put our kiss out of mind. I'd taken my cues from him in the days afterward, and he'd planted us firmly back in the friend zone. It was a relief. When he'd offered to accompany me to Borehamwood to view a flat for rent that I'd found online, I'd been delighted. We pulled into what looked like the forecourt of a fish and chip shop and Joshua killed the car engine and leaned forward to see where we were headed. He didn't need to spend his weekends helping me flat hunt, but he'd offered and I'd said yes. He knew a lot more about London and property than me. Plus he had a car, which meant I didn't have to worry about dodging the thunderstorms that had been threatening all morning.

"I don't think we can park here." I rifled through my bag, trying to find my phone. I was sure the outside didn't look like this on the estate agent's website.

"You think they were kidding when they put the big P and the white lines here?" Joshua asked.

I glanced up and sure enough, saw the parking sign. "You think parking comes with the flat?"

"I think the aroma of fish and chips comes with the flat."

"Don't worry." I nodded toward the dash. "You have your halved lemon so it won't ruin your interior." I nodded at the lemons I'd placed on the dash of his car and opened the door. "Come and witness how the rest of the world lives, Joshua Luca. We can't all be living in penthouses on Park Lane." It was six weeks until I left the flat next door to Joshua's, but I needed to kick-start my search for a new place. I had no idea how long it would take for me to find something.

"There's a happy medium."

"Don't judge a book by its cover. You might love it when we get inside."

Joshua slid his sunglasses to the top of his head and gave me a not-on-your-life glance. I wasn't going to be deterred. The agent had said this was about a hundred square foot bigger than what I'd normally get for my budget, and it was a five-minute walk to the station. I couldn't wait to see what was inside.

I pressed the slightly grubby buzzer and without anyone answering on the intercom, the door released. Joshua nodded for me to go in first and I stepped into the green carpeted hallway. He was right, you could definitely smell fried food in here. Hopefully it wouldn't be quite so strong inside the flat.

"It's on the second floor." I started to climb the stairs.

"Two flights up and no lift?"

"Right. That's good. It could have been four floors."

The carpet on the stairs was worn and stained, but I was sure it was due a clean soon. A good scrub was bound to breathe some fresh life into it.

As we got to the top of the second flight of stairs, I came face to face with the agent.

"Jas?" I asked.

"Hartford," he said. "Good to meet you. Welcome to your new home." He stepped to the side so I could go in.

"Right," I said, nodding at the living room that had a small kitchen space at one end with just a couple of units, a sink, a cooker, and a fridge-freezer. What else did I need in a kitchen? At the other end was space for a two-seater settee, and in the middle, a small table with two chairs would fit under the window. That was a bonus I hadn't expected. I'd have somewhere to eat and set up my laptop.

"The fish and chip shop is immediately below us?" Joshua asked.

"No," Jas replied. "The owner of the shop has the flat immediately below you and the shop is on the ground floor. Very convenient when you come home late from a shift at the hospital."

"That's just what I was thinking," I replied, shooting Joshua a grin before wandering through to the bedroom. I could tell he was horrified, although he hid it well. "Oh yes. This is compact but perfectly doable."

"There's no bath in the bathroom," Joshua called out.

"Doesn't matter to me. I always have showers anyway. I think it's great, Jas."

"Would it be both of you on the tenancy?" Jas asked.

I couldn't help but laugh at the idea of Joshua Luca—Mr. Park Lane—living above a chip shop in Borehamwood. "No, it will be just me. Joshua already has a place."

"Like I said, you're lucky to get a one bedroom for the price. In your range, it would normally be a studio."

"What's your budget?" Joshua asked, looking confused.

"Mind your beeswax," I said, tapping my nose. "It's got

a nice feel to it." I wandered the three steps to the window and looked out over the rooftops. "And I like that it's unfurnished. Means I can put my own mark on it." I turned back to face the room. "Yes, I really like it. Do I have to decide quickly?"

"Even though it's not available for five weeks, it will be rented by Friday. Like I said, it's a steal. So if you're interested, you need to let me know as soon as possible."

I spent a couple of minutes going from the bedroom to the sitting room and then into the bathroom, trying to imagine myself in the space. It was very different to a tent in Yemen. For a start, it would be my own private space. I got to close the door and spend time by myself. That was a luxury I'd forgotten I enjoyed before I came back to London. Joshua and I had very different ideas of what indulgence was. To me, this flat was everything I needed.

The only thing missing was Joshua next door. It was nice to have him so near, even though my forcefield kept taking hits and had suffered a severe malfunction when we kissed. When I moved, I couldn't imagine why we'd have reason to see each other. We hadn't been friends before Yemen and like he said, he had a busy, full life. I doubted I'd have a place in it once I was out of his immediate vicinity. Even though I knew it was for the best, given my faltering forcefield, the thought curdled my stomach every time it surfaced in my brain.

We said goodbye to Jas and I promised him I'd call by the end of the day.

"Well, that didn't take long," Joshua said as we got back into the car.

"It's a three-hundred-and-fifty-square-foot flat. How long did you want to spend in there?"

He laughed, that damn dimple appearing out of

nowhere to give me a ripple of God-knew-what between my thighs. "I don't get it, Hartford. We're in the middle of nowhere—I mean, is this technically still London? And it's tiny. And not that great. You have money. You're a doctor, for goodness' sake."

"Right, but I don't want to spend my entire salary on a place just for the sake of it. I've spent the last year on a fold-up bed. This place will be fine for me." I liked to save. You never knew when there was a rainy day down the road. I'd learned that lesson the hard way.

"But surely you could afford somewhere the bed isn't pushed up against the wall and you don't have to spend your life smelling of fish and chips."

"You think it's worse than the smell of Yemen?" I was completely serious. I didn't want to put off my patients by coming to work with an off-putting aroma.

"I think that's why it's a knockdown price."

Maybe I could invest in some perfume or something. And anyway, the smell would probably wear off by the time I got to the hospital. "I'm going to think about it. It's a good option."

"Thank God I'm setting you up with these guys before you move in. The smell of fried fish can be a turn-off."

I laughed. "You're such a snob. If he's the right man, he'll want me, chip fat or no chip fat." I wasn't sure about that, but I'd be two floors up. How bad could the smell be?

"You're ridiculous," he said. "But speaking of your dating life, I've picked out your first lesson in love."

It was like someone had unexpectedly bumped me on a crowded train platform, and I had to take a second to regain my balance. *He's being nice. He's trying to help me impress Gerry.* Maybe I'd even find someone to fall in love with.

"His name is Tom. And he's a photographer."

I groaned. "Tell me he's not used to being surrounded by Kendall Jenner and Gisele the entire day."

He flashed a grin at me. "Nope. He takes pictures of food. See, this is a thoughtful setup. You like cake. He likes to photograph cake. It's a match made in cake-heaven."

"How do you know him?"

"He's my secretary's brother."

That seemed like a tenuous connection. Had he put up a poster at work or something? *Wanted: Single man for a two-hour, strictly no-sex date with a frumpy doctor who at least doesn't have a monobrow anymore.*

"Have you even met him?"

"I insisted on seeing a photograph. He seems like a nice chap. Doesn't live with his mother or, from what I can tell, torture animals in his spare time. You're seeing him this Friday at seven thirty at Liliana's."

He was obviously excited. But there wasn't one cell of my body that could muster up any kind of enthusiasm. I didn't have the energy to make small talk with a stranger. "*This* Friday?"

"Yes, this Friday. So, who have you lined up for me?"

"Are we double dating?" That particular thought was horrifying. Being friends with Joshua was fine. Nice even. But it didn't mean I didn't think he was handsome. It didn't mean I didn't secretly hope the occasional flirtatious touch or grin was intentional. I didn't want to have my inadequacies under a spotlight as I watched Joshua *very intentionally* flirt and charm the woman sitting next to me.

"No, I mean, we could if you wanted to." He shrugged. "Could be fun. At least if you were there, I wouldn't be bored."

"Well, I'm glad I don't bore you, but the woman I've

lined up for you is not available on Friday. Unlucky for you, you'll have to spend the evening without me."

We stopped at some lights and he held my gaze with a grin. "Okay, so tell me, who is this woman?"

Truth be told, I'd not found anyone yet. But I would do. I'd just have to arrange it for Sunday. "I'm not telling you anything. But you better be nice to her. And no showing her your penis, like you promised."

"You think I'm a closet flasher?"

"Who knows, Joshua. You and my brother were forever pulling down your shorts."

"We were in the paddling pool. And we were, what, eleven?"

"Once a flasher, always a flasher."

"I'm really not comfortable with you teasing me about being a sex offender, Hartford." Joshua frowned, all mock hurt and seriousness.

I laughed and it seemed to be catching as he started to chuckle as well. "I take it back. I'm convinced you save your penis for private showings. But no sex is a rule, Joshua Luca. Let's see if you can comply."

We might only have a couple more months of friendship to look forward to, but I was going to enjoy it while it lasted.

TWELVE

Joshua

I'd spent the entire week going through the Luca Brands pitch for Calmation. It was good, but something was missing. Maybe it was because I was used to luxury goods, but there was a lack of sparkle and originality about our approach that had me concerned. I didn't want the Calmation campaign to be anything other than fantastic—for the sake of Luca Brands, but also because I wanted this campaign to reach as many parents as possible. The more people who saw it, the more children would be helped.

I leaned back on my dining chair and looked over my laptop at the cityscape, trying to garner inspiration. The team had looked at what was going on in the over-the-counter children's drug market and essentially given Merdon more of what was already out there. I wanted something different. Something better. Something that proved they should appoint us *because* our experience was in luxury brands, and not despite it.

Even a long stint of Genius Time in the bath this

evening hadn't produced any breakthroughs. That couldn't have anything to do with the fact that Hartford hadn't come home from her date with Tom. Her tardiness was bothering me. And it bothered me that it was bothering me. The two-hour mark had passed over an hour ago.

Why did I care if she stuck to the rules?

I kept telling myself it was because I wanted her advice about a tiny nugget of an idea I had about the Merdon pitch, which was true. And I wanted to see how she got on with Tom, because I was her friend, right?

After all, I was supposed to be coaching her through these dates. I'd promised.

Before she'd left, she'd tried on three outfits and given me a demonstration of how she looked standing up, walking, and sitting down in each one before I was able to give my final judgement. She looked good in all of them. But the pale blue top looked best with her skin tone, and the neckline showed off just the right amount of cleavage.

I'd suggested she wear the green.

And *that* bothered me the most. Why didn't I want her to look her best for Tom? Yes, I found her attractive. Yes, my body seemed to have some kind of visceral reaction whenever she was too close. And that kiss? It had been spectacular. But none of that changed the fact I wasn't a man who got serious with women. Hartford deserved better.

A knock at my door pulled me back out of my own head. I needed to think less. And I needed to call Kelly. I'd not seen her for a few weeks. I'd been busy and . . . I'd just not had the urge to call her.

I swung open the door to find a grinning Hartford. I'd not heard the lift.

"Do you have cake for our debrief?" she asked, grinning at me.

God, she was pretty.

"Is that what we're doing? Debriefing? Now?"

"Of course we're debriefing."

That's what I liked about Hartford. Most other women would apologize for bothering me or ask me if it was okay to stop by this late. She was unapologetically in my life, and it was refreshing.

I made two espressos and slid one across the counter. "I did cookies and cream," I said, pulling out the cake box that had been delivered earlier.

A smile unfurled on her face, and I tried to dismiss the feeling of being slightly proud I'd brought her joy. "From Dragonfly bakery? Are you kidding? I've heard about this place. It's meant to be the best in London. Did you get these for me?"

"Yes, but I'll warn you now—I have an ulterior motive." I knew she'd love this cake. It looked like a heart attack on a plate but I'd been assured it was the best you could get. "I have some questions I want to ask you in a professional capacity, in exchange for the cake."

"No problem. God, it looks amazing. And look—chocolate sprinkles. And what is—holy buttercream. Are those sugared violets?" She picked up one of the purple stone-like decorations and popped it in her mouth. "Oh dear sweet sponge, I've not had one of these in so long."

She looked so happy. All at once, it struck me that it might have been her date with Tom that had put her in a good mood.

"I might have to eat this entire thing," she said, gazing lovingly at the cake. "It's the most beautiful thing I've ever seen." She looked up at me and her pale blue eyes drew me in like a Tahitian pool straight out of *Conde Nast Traveler*. Yup, I definitely needed to call Kelly.

She picked up the knife and plunged into the sponge.

I watched as she carefully portioned out two slices and helped herself to dessert plates and forks. "Here." She slid a plate to me. "If you treat Mavis like this, you're going to have her proposing before the evening's out."

I watched as she slid a forkful of cake into her mouth and stilled, closing her eyes as if she was blocking out the world so she could focus on savoring the flavors.

And then my brain caught up to what she'd said.

"Mavis? Who's Mavis?" I rounded the island and took a seat next to her. Our stools were turned at an angle so we were almost facing each other.

She opened one eye and then the other. "Your date on Sunday night."

"You set me up with a woman called Mavis?"

"Joshua, did anyone tell you not to judge a book by its cover or a woman by her name? I was named after a town in Connecticut where my parents banged. I mean, if people judged me by my name—" Her sentence was interrupted by a second forkful of cake.

I wasn't bothered about Mavis. It didn't matter who she was, it was just two hours. I was pretty sure I could get through one hundred and twenty minutes with just about anyone. I was more interested in Hartford. And her date with Tom. And of course, the Merdon pitch.

"So, how was Tom?"

She leaned her head to one side. And then the other. "Okay."

That was it? She'd been nearly an hour past our agreed time limit. Surely that meant it had been a great date? What didn't she want to tell me? "What does *okay* mean?"

"Just that he was nice enough. No urge to rip his clothes off, but it was a nice way to spend an evening."

I tried to push away the memory of her hand on my chest just before we kissed. Had she wanted to rip off my clothes? "But you were late."

"I was talking to the guy behind the bar. He was telling me about a food bank around the corner. I think I'll stop by this week."

"You're going to a food bank?" First the dreadful flat in Borehamwood, now Hartford was visiting food banks? Did she have a crack habit I wasn't aware of?

"Yeah, I might volunteer. All in the name of expanding my horizons and impressing my boss. I figure volunteering is a halfway point between spending days at the spa and spending time at the hospital."

I was beginning to realize that Hartford liked to be busy. But she took it to the extreme. "I suppose it is."

"What's great about that place is that you don't have to commit for the same time every week, like most places. I can volunteer around my shifts, which makes so much difference."

"You're a good person, Hartford." There was no doubt about it—objectively, any stranger looking at how she spent her time would say the same thing. And that was an inspiration for me to do better at the Calmation campaign.

"That's a nice thing to say. You're a good person too."

Was I? I wrote checks for charities but I couldn't remember when I last spent time doing something altruistic apart from helping my friends, which didn't exactly count. But there was no doubt Hartford was truly good. And clever. And beautiful. "I'm trying to be. Actually, you've been a bit of an influence on me, truth be told."

She straightened her back. "I have?"

I nodded. "Yeah, my client has bought a pharma company and want me to pitch."

"A pharma company?" She looked concerned, like I'd just told her I'd be wrestling with alligators.

"Yeah, and instead of being pissed off that I have to try to understand something that's not luxury brands, I'm really enjoying it. It's refreshing to be able to try to help people. It's energizing."

She frowned. "Big pharma doesn't have a reputation for being altruistic."

"Right? That's what I thought, too. But the company I'm pitching for is all about trying to make medicines more affordable for people who need them."

Her frown seemed to have set on her face. "Which pharma company are you pitching to?"

I shook my head. "It's totally confidential, but these are the good guys. And it feels great to be on their side."

Her frown melted into a shy smile and she took another forkful of cake. I watched as she chewed and swallowed. "I like that I'm a good influence on you." Her voice had softened, bringing to mind her breathy whisper just before I'd kissed her.

I shook my head, trying to refocus. "Can I take up some of your free time and pick your brain about kids taking medicine?"

"What do you need to know?"

"As a kids' doctor, you must have to prescribe medication. Do you have a problem with getting the children to actually take it? What happens if they refuse?"

A grin unraveled on her face like I'd just paid her the biggest compliment. "It can be a problem. Obviously, a lot depends on their age. If they're old enough, it's best to discuss it and tell them what the medicine is for and explain that it will make them better. But sometimes that doesn't work or they're too young. In that case, medicines can be mixed in with food or drink and disguised."

"Does that ever change the effectiveness of the drug?" I asked. The idea I'd had was to change the current form of the drug from a pill to a sweet—some kind of gummy bear or something. The drug was there to help children, and they should feel good about taking it.

"Depends on the drug." She paused and sliced off a forkful of cake. "You'd have to talk to your client. What kind of drug is it?" I didn't get a chance to answer before she rolled her eyes. "I suppose you can't tell me."

"Sorry."

"I don't think pharma companies should have brands and marketing," she said. "The government should ban it. Medicine should be medicine."

"That's probably true. At least this company and drug we're pitching for is genuinely trying to do good," I said. "It's not the typical big pharma."

She rolled her eyes. "I hope not."

Eric had sent over a ton of background on Merdon and on Calmation. What they were doing was really impressive. Luca Brands was a step closer to helping them help children and parents. Talking with Hartford confirmed my suspicion that my task now was to make the drug appeal to children, and by extension, the parents who no longer faced a fight to get the medicine down. It might just be the sparkle we needed to make Eric realize Luca Brands could handle the Merdon account.

Hartford's phone buzzed on the counter between us. "It's Tom," she said, her eyes lighting up. She was excited to hear from him. And that was good, right? I just had to ignore the churn in my gut.

She read the text and laughed.

"What?" I asked.

"He says, 'Would love to see you again. Perhaps we can share some cake sometime soon?'"

"Well, he knows how to impress you."

"What do I say?" she asked. "We didn't negotiate our deal beyond first dates."

"This isn't just about our deal. It's about you . . . extending your social circle. If you like the guy, say yes."

Our eyes locked and for a second, I wanted to tell her to text that she wasn't interested. I wanted to sweep her up into my arms and kiss her over and over.

Which was exactly why a second date was an excellent idea.

"I'm not sure if I liked him. I mean, yes, he was nice enough. I'm just not a people-person. You know?"

"No, I don't know. You've made friends with the people on the desk downstairs, with some guy who works at a food bank. You attract all sorts of people. Is Tom someone you want to attract?" I'd not picked Tom with any intent. I'd promised to find a date for Hartford and my secretary's brother was available. But now we were talking about it, I wondered what kind of man Hartford would be happy with. Probably someone who did lots of altruistic things. Someone who worked for Greenpeace, or another doctor maybe. Even if I did do relationships—which I didn't— Hartford should be with someone better suited to her.

"It's been a long time. What if he wants to kiss me? Sleep with me?"

"You don't do anything you don't want to do."

"You're an excellent kisser," she said, her eyes flicking down to my lips and then back up again.

My jaw tightened and I tried to mentally bat away the images I had of holding her, pressing my lips to hers, breathing in her sweet scent. Every time I thought I'd created some space between us, she said something like that. "What can I say? I like to set the bar high."

"Don't go using your dimple on me. You know what it does to me."

My dimple? "No, I don't know, but I'm thinking I'd like to."

Her fork fell to her plate with a clatter and she slid off her stool to stand in front of me. Was that an invitation? "Good, God, Joshua. No wonder women worship you. Everything you say suggests hot, sweaty sex."

I laughed. "It does?"

Before she answered, she headed to the door. "I'm going to have to leave now. If I stay another five seconds, I'm going to be dry humping your leg and trying to kiss you."

I watched as she gave me one of her exaggerated waves and left.

I was grateful she'd gone because I'd been hoping she'd stay.

THIRTEEN

Joshua

The restaurant in Covent Garden wasn't one I'd been to before. Hartford had picked it, though it didn't seem like a place she'd choose for herself. It was modern industrial, with exposed poles and pipes crisscrossing the ceiling, metal chairs, and a concrete floor. I imagined Hartford would be more comfortable in a restaurant with oak beams, exposed flagstones, and a roaring fire. Given that my date was the model Hollie had been trying to set me up with, no doubt Hartford had picked the restaurant on a recommendation from one of the girls. It was like they were all conspiring to get me to fall in love.

Wasn't going to happen.

I scanned down the menu and quickly made my choices so I could focus on my date. And then I pulled out my phone.

Food better be good or as punishment, I'm going to bring you back here, I texted Hartford.

Quick as a flash, my phone buzzed.

All food is good food. But I'm sitting here hoping the food is not up to your usual standards so I get a free meal.

Her reply was typical. Unfiltered but vaguely wise. In the places she'd worked, I imagined she was used to seeing people who would have thought eating in a restaurant was one step away from heaven. Her worldview forced me to look at everything and everyone in a new light. It was unsettling. Unnerving. Uncomfortable.

But for some reason, I craved it.

I enjoyed hearing what she thought about things. About everything.

When I saw a tall, very thin blonde coming toward me, I knew this must be Natalie—or Mavis, as Hartford had nicknamed her. I stood and grinned. Then turned down my smile, conscious of my dimple.

"Nice to meet you. I'm Joshua and . . . you're beautiful."

Her eyes darted to the floor and she looked up at me from under her eyelashes. "Thank you." She was a model with all the attributes you'd expect: long legs, clear skin, big eyes, and a pout she knew how to use. She reminded me a little of Kelly, except with strawberry-blonde hair. "This place seems nice. I've never been before."

We both took our seats and exchanged small talk. After we'd got our drinks and placed our dinner order, we found common ground in a couple of photographers we had both worked with—her in front of the camera and me for campaigns.

"It's a small world," she said.

"Especially London. You wouldn't think we'd cross paths so often in a city of nearly nine million people."

"I have to admit, I've heard things about you. I think you've dated a couple of my friends."

We were at a fork in the road; the evening could go

either way. Either she'd grill me about my relationships with her friends or not.

"London's more of a village than a city," I replied. "It seems you have some insider information. That seems a little . . ." I held her gaze for a couple of seconds before she looked away. "Imbalanced. What should I know about you that would put the scales back into equilibrium?"

Her smile took ten years off her. "You mean what would my exes say about me?"

I wasn't going to ask that exact question, but if she was offering me the answer, I wasn't going to say no. I sat back in my chair, waiting for her to elaborate.

"I suppose it depends which one you ask." She paused and pulled her eyebrows together. "Most of them were complete shitheads." Her tone hardened and she pursed her lips.

Yikes. Maybe the menu had a lid I could order for the can of worms I'd just opened.

"So maybe tell me what your best friends would say about you instead?" I couldn't help but wonder what Hartford would say about me.

Natalie seemed to soften at my question and her smile reappeared. "They'd say I was beautiful, obviously. And a bit extra. And I always know where the sample sales are. I'm the first one in the queue."

Out of all those attributes, the one that sounded the most interesting was the second. "Why would they call you 'extra'?"

"Oh you know, I'm always the one who loses a shoe at a party. I guess I'm just a little wild."

Hmmm. "What kind of wild things do you like to do?"

"Party. Travel. Swim in the sea naked. A party on a

yacht combines all my favorite things in life. You like yachts?"

I'd met girls like Natalie before. They were nice to spend an evening with but difficult to recall in any detail two days later. "Sounds fun. I've been on a few yachts in my time."

"Super fun, isn't it?"

I don't remember having a bad time on a yacht. But I couldn't quite recall what exactly had made it a good time. "Sure."

"Will you excuse me while I go to the loo?" She headed off to the ladies and I pulled out my phone.

No messages.

What are you doing? I messaged Hartford.

Your two hours aren't up. Why aren't you talking to your date?

I grinned. *She's having a wee. Do you have cake for our debrief?*

What was I going to tell her about Natalie? She was nice enough. But tonight seemed a bit pointless. No, I had to stop thinking like that. I was here because it meant getting distance from Hartford. Which was good for me. And it meant Hartford agreed to date, which would be good for her. Good for her career. She'd disappear from my life as quickly as she'd entered it and I could get back to normal.

She texted back. *I've got something better than cake.*

An image flashed in my brain of Hartford standing at the window, facing London, naked, looking over her shoulder back at me.

Shit. She didn't mean it like that. Knowing Hartford, she probably meant she had two cakes.

Those are fighting words.

I watched as Natalie sauntered back to the table in the

way only very tall, willowy women could. "Those toilets are so cool." She sat back down. "You should try them."

I nodded, trying to think of something witty or flirtatious to say in response to commentary on restaurant loos.

Our main courses arrived and we fell silent as we dug into our food. Except that Natalie didn't eat. Not really. She had salmon on watercress but other than a few leaves of watercress, she just seemed to stir the items around her plate.

"Not hungry?"

"I have a shoot tomorrow. Don't want to bloat."

"Right." We should have just come for drinks rather than dinner. My phone buzzed against my thigh and I wanted desperately to see what Hartford had said. I resisted. I'd agreed to this date to create distance, not to create something to talk to Hartford about—an excuse to spend more time with her.

"So, you know Hollie, too, don't you?" I asked, scrambling for something to say.

"Yes. She's so nice. Her jewelry is absolutely gorgeous. I'm all about stacking pieces but making one thing stand out. You know?"

I nodded as I chewed my steak.

"Some models don't know how to wear jewelry, but I think I have an eye for it. In fact, I'd like to design one day."

"That's interesting," I replied. "I'm sure Hollie would be happy to talk to you about it."

"I'm so busy at the moment. I want to build up enough of a brand that I can do something with mass appeal—maybe get some kind of deal with Tiffany or something."

Sounded ambitious. But ambition was good.

"I just want to make the world prettier. Some of the designs you see are so bloody ugly. I want to bring the pretty back." She grinned. "I like that. Bringing the pretty back. Like, bringing the sexy back but . . . you know, *pretty* instead. My mind just thinks of these things. All the time. I'm full of ideas. I'm very creative."

I swallowed down another bite then put down my knife and fork. I was done here. Natalie was meant to be distracting me from Hartford, but sitting here, all I could think about was getting back to the penthouse to share cake with my next-door neighbor.

FOURTEEN

Hartford

I'd celebrated my sixth week in London by baking a cake.

Not only had I baked, but my sponges had risen, the buttercream had reached the perfect consistency, and the entire thing looked edible. Okay, maybe I'd had to call Stella twice to check stuff, but she wasn't actually here supervising me. I'd done this by myself.

As I took a step back to admire my creation where it stood on the countertop, I had to admit, I'd outdone myself. Joshua would be impressed.

If he ever got to see it. I'd looked up a picture of his date tonight and honestly, I wouldn't have blamed him if he'd broken our no-sex rule for her. She was beautiful. Tall and thin and romantic looking. Every inch a supermodel.

But I'd baked.

A banging at my door made me jump, and I couldn't contain my grin. It had to be Joshua, right? No one else would be banging on my door at . . . I checked the time on my watch. Wait, it was only eight forty-five. The date was meant to go until nine thirty.

"Who is it?" I called out.

"You better have cake," Joshua replied.

I pulled the door open. "I knew you couldn't last two hours just talking to a woman over dinner."

He groaned and pushed past me, then stopped when he spotted what was on the kitchen side. "Nice work," he said and I swear, I might have grown an inch.

"It's a triple sponge," I said. "Broken up Flake on the outside stuck to the vanilla buttercream."

"Very nice," he repeated, peering closer. "What's the filling?"

I scrunched up my face. I was going to burst; I was so excited for him to see. "You'll never guess."

He glanced at me like he was Miss Marple, having discovered the murderer. "Hand me a knife."

I headed to the utensil drawer. "Hey, you need to explain why you're back here so early. You signed up to two hours."

"Believe me, it felt like three. I need cake first."

That was a fair trade. I handed him the knife. "Wait, don't cut into it yet. Let me get plates and forks first." I scurried round, getting everything lined up.

"Right," I said. "Now."

Joshua looked at me, shaking his head like I'd completely lost the plot. "You know, you've built this up now, I'm expecting something mighty special."

He had no idea what was about to hit him. This was a step up from special.

He sunk the knife into the sponge and it click-click-clicked as it hit what was hidden inside.

"What have you hidden in here?" He pulled out his

knife and measured out a wedge, pushing his knife in again. "Okay. If there's something alive in here, I'm suing you for emotional distress."

"You're a coward. Pull it out."

Balancing the slice on the flat of the knife, he pulled it from the rest of the cake, revealing the best thing I'd ever seen in my life.

"Wow," he said as the candy-coated chocolate sweets poured out of the middle of the cake and onto the cake stand.

"Mini eggs! They were selling the last few bags at the supermarket."

"So cool," he said.

"Totally. I saw it on a TV program and found a recipe. Are you impressed?"

He laughed. "Very. I hope it tastes as good as it looks."

"I'm getting better at baking, thanks to Stella. Should be edible at least."

Joshua cut another slice and we took our plates to the sofa.

"So, tell me about Natalie," I said. "Hollie said she's totally your type." Knock-out gorgeous and amazing in bed, no doubt.

"It's good," he said, his mouth full of cake. He pointed at what was left with his fork.

I swallowed down my first bite. "Really good." The Flake and the Mini Eggs thrust the cake into hyperdrive. "But tell me about the date."

"Natalie was nice enough."

"But not someone you'd want to settle down for?"

He sighed and put down his plate. "Not at all."

"I can imagine you're not looking to change too much.

Shagging supermodels and living in a hotel is a fairly solid routine."

"I don't shag supermodels." He paused. "At least I haven't shagged one in a while."

I laughed. "Well, you don't have to go through dates two and three if you don't want to. You've proved me right—you can't hold down a conversation with a woman for two hours."

"Not true," he said. "You're a woman. And I can talk to you for two hours."

My heart jumped and dived into my stomach at the thought that I was something unusual, something special to Joshua. I needed to get a grip. He'd been very clear about not wanting me. Yes, we'd kissed, but it had been a momentary loss of control. We'd just spent too much time together. My forcefield had malfunctioned and he . . . he'd just acted on instinct or something. Because I had a vagina and he was an out-and-out player.

I picked up a mini egg from the collection on my plate. "Yes, but I don't count. I've known you since—"

Joshua's phone buzzing interrupted us. He glanced at the screen. "It's from Natalie. I better get it."

I shrugged. "Show me how it's done, Coach."

He slid his fingers across the screen and jerked his head back at the message. He didn't look impressed.

"Is she name calling you? Were you rude to her?"

He started to laugh. "I wouldn't call it name calling. And no, I wasn't rude."

"What did she say?"

He glanced at me as if he were contemplating how to answer. "She didn't exactly *say* anything. She chose to communicate through pictures."

I sat up straight. "Really? Like naked pictures?"

He laughed again and nodded.

How typical that a woman he'd only just met would be sending him naked pictures. But that was the effect Joshua Luca had on women. "What bits?" I leaned over to try to see.

"Hey, no. There's no way I'm going to show you." He swiped and prodded at his phone. "There. I deleted it."

"That's very gentlemanly of you," I said, slicing another mouthful of cake. My forcefield wasn't prepared for him to be quite so . . . I wasn't sure if *polite* or *grown up* was the right descriptor, but his sense of decorum was more touching than I'd anticipated.

"I'm not a fifteen-year-old boy who needs to impress his friends with pictures of naked women."

Every time I thought my forcefield was back up and running, Joshua had to go blowing holes in it. But I was getting better at patching them up. I just had to hope that one day the entire thing wasn't going to collapse in a heap. "What are you going to say in reply? What does anyone say when they get an unsolicited naked picture from a relative stranger?"

"Maybe I shouldn't say anything. It's not like I'm going to see her again. And I don't want her to send any more."

"You don't? Hollie said she was beautiful. Maybe she'd be up for becoming your Miss Thursday Night."

Joshua grumbled something under his breath but I didn't catch the details.

"You have to say something in response."

"Maybe I should just tell her . . . thank you?"

I kicked him in the shin and tried not to laugh at him being so delightfully clueless in this position. A part of me had assumed that Joshua was batting away boob-pictures on a regular basis. "I thought it was me that needed a dating coach. You cannot tell a woman 'thank you' after she sends you a picture of her boobs, without sounding like an arsehole."

"You're right."

"Of course I'm right."

He typed out a message on his phone and then held it up to me. *Great to meet you tonight. Good luck in the jewelry designing. Take care.*

"You're a pro," I said, genuinely impressed. He'd made it clear he wasn't interested without being rude. "I would think you were a nice guy but we just didn't vibe."

"I *am* a nice guy. And we *really* just didn't vibe."

Joshua was nice. To me. But if we were romantically linked, I wasn't so sure I'd feel that way. I imagined the women who slept with Joshua couldn't get enough of him and always wanted more. Hell, I had to fight that feeling and we hadn't gotten naked together. Thank goodness.

"Like you said to me, you need to kiss some frogs before you find the one."

"Give me some more cake or I'm going to set you up with a model for your next date."

"Sounds good. I've always had a thing for pretty men. You ruined me forever."

He turned his head to look at me, unable to hide his smirk. "Excuse me, I did what?"

"Ruined me." I let out a dramatic sigh. "Everyone knows that your first crush creates a blueprint for all future lovers." I scrunched up my nose. Why couldn't I keep my inside thoughts from spilling out of my mouth?

"I was your first crush?" He looked genuinely surprised. Like this was new information to him. I always felt like it radiated out of me in neon. Maybe I'd been better at hiding it than I thought.

"A crush the size of Everest." The fact I could admit it was more evidence I was a different person now.

The dimple was back and so was that sexy smirk he should patent and sell. "I like that idea."

"*Had*," I replied. "I *had* a crush on you. Past tense." I couldn't bear the thought that I still fantasized about him. A woman's forcefield couldn't remain intact *all* the time.

"Oh," he said, faking a wounded look, as if he cared whether a woman like me would have a current crush on him. Maybe he just assumed every woman wanted him. And he probably wasn't so far off.

"I'll have to do better for your next date," I said, desperate to change the subject. "I'll find your perfect woman."

"If you say so." He let out a sigh. "Make sure she's interesting. Or funny. Or ridiculous. I hang out with you for two hours and it's never strained like it was with Natalie."

My cheeks heated at his compliment. He really knew how to make women feel good. Maybe I could set up a business on the side of doctoring where I hired him out to women who were feeling a little bit shitty.

"Yeah, but it's different with us," I said. It was always easy between us. Not that I didn't say the wrong thing in front of him and embarrass myself regularly—just that I knew it wouldn't affect how he was with me. Our connection was deeper than some silly faux pas because our families were so inextricably linked. "We have that brother-sister thing going on."

"We do not," he spluttered. "That's . . . disturbing. Especially since we've kissed and you just confessed to a crush on me."

That kiss . . . "A past-tense crush. I've known you such a long time now . . ."

"Come on, Hartford. Do you really think of me as your brother?"

I thought about it. Joshua would always be too impossibly handsome for me to think of as my brother. He still made me shiver when he looked at me a certain way. I was still mesmerized by his hands, his chest, that dimple. Now I knew him a little better, it wasn't just the flirty confidence, the charm, and the good looks that were attractive. He looked out for me and wanted me to succeed at my new job. He could laugh at himself and question himself too. On top of being gorgeous, I really enjoyed his company.

"Well, not brother exactly. More like . . . friend who's really good at leg massage and isn't a bad kisser?"

The dimple was back. "Don't kid yourself. I'm a great kisser."

That was for sure.

FIFTEEN

Joshua

The department store was teeming with people. I fought my way through the crowds to the jewelry displays at the far end of the store, where I knew Hollie would be. I'd happily agreed to lend her one of my top stylists to help her arrange her new concession at Harvey Nichols. Little did she know, she was going to be repaying me for that favor sooner than she thought. I'd nearly tried to kiss Hartford again last night. Even now, thinking about her having a crush on me had my dick hardening. I needed to take action.

"Joshua!" Hollie said as she spotted me. "What are you doing here?"

"I came to see your fantastic success. How did Camilla get on?"

"Oh my God, thank you for lending her to me. She's so creative and really helped me make the most of the range." She stopped and put her hand on my shoulder. "Can you believe I'm in Harvey Nichols?"

"Absolutely I can. Your stuff is great." I could see why

Vogue made such a fuss about Hollie. She was really talented.

"I know, but I'm two rows over from Dior and Chanel. It's crazy."

"You do have a very good spot here. It's going to be a roaring success." I glanced down into the glass counters where her jewelry was displayed against a sea-green background. "It all looks very fresh. Not too much."

"Exactly," she replied. "That's exactly what I was going for. I'm only here for a trial in the beginning so we'll see what happens. But I swear, I'm happy to come and work behind the counter if it means they keep my stuff here. I can't think of anything better."

"You've done brilliantly, Hollie. It's well deserved."

"Thanks, Joshua. And I appreciate your help. Now tell me why you're really here?"

Yeah, she'd seen right through me. I didn't usually just drop by Harvey Nichols, but after last night, I needed her help to find Hartford someone she'd really like.

"I think you know that I've been setting up dates for Hartford—you know, to expand her social circle a little. I'm looking for someone for her second date. I was wondering if you knew anyone?" Hollie met a lot of people between her business and attending functions with Dexter, and I was hoping she'd know someone who'd be a good fit for Hartford. I'd spent far too much time with her recently. The lines had gotten blurred. I needed to redraw them.

Hollie leaned her hip against the counter and crossed her arms in front of her chest. "Let me get this clear." She paused. "You *think* you want me to suggest someone Hartford could go out with?"

Her question was worded strangely. "Erm, I'm not quite sure I follow you, but yes. I need help getting her a date.

You like Hartford, right? She's funny and interesting and so passionate about her work."

God, I'd been so close to kissing her last night. In the moments after she'd stood to leave and before she'd moved to the door, it was all I could do not to grab her by the hips and drag her closer, fitting my mouth against hers. I couldn't make that same mistake again. We'd agreed. And it was clear she didn't want me like that anymore than I wanted . . .

"She's all those things," Hollie agreed.

"Right, and I need to find a man worthy enough to date her. You must know someone. Someone *you* would date if you weren't married to Dexter. Someone worthy of you."

She paused, narrowing her eyes at me. "I do know someone, actually."

"Oh yeah? Tell me about him." I took a steadying breath, preparing myself to believe the best about whoever Hollie had in mind.

"Sure. He's gorgeous—could have been a model if he wasn't so busy running a company of his own and making big money. He's kind, funny, smart as hell. Hasn't been in a long-term relationship for a long time, but I think he's ready."

I cleared my throat. "Right, well . . . he sounds great. How do you know him?"

"Met him after I moved here, actually." She paused, reaching for something under the counter. In her hands she held a flat, black oval—maybe a picture frame. Hollie beckoned me closer, then flipped the item she held: a mirror. "It's you, you big dummy."

A chill raced down my spine. "Absolutely not. I don't . . . get involved with women."

"But you like Hartford," she said.

"Of course I like Hartford." I couldn't imagine anyone not liking Hartford. She was one of those people who just made everyone instantly comfortable. Another reason why I needed to get a bit of distance. I was too comfortable hanging out with her.

"So why don't *you* take her on her second date?"

I snorted. "I told you I don't do relationships. I need a guy she might like who *does* do relationships. Someone who might turn into a second date. Maybe even give her mother the grandchildren she's so desperate for." I wasn't about to share the fact that I'd kissed her or that Hartford *used* to have a crush on me. I'd never hear the end of it.

Hollie's look said she had already given me the answer I was looking for. But she hadn't.

"You must know someone," I said. Maybe I was looking in the wrong place. Perhaps I should speak to my mate Nathan. His brothers were all doctors. One of them might take her out. A doctor would more likely understand where Hartford was coming from—her need to help people and the dedication she had to her career.

"I'll have a think about it. But you should consider taking her to dinner."

Hollie wasn't getting it, which surprised me; she was normally pretty switched on. "We have dinner all the time because we live next door to each other."

Hollie laughed. "How the six of you guys managed to make your billions, I have no idea. Y'all can be dumb as rocks at times."

I frowned at her. "Oi. Less of the abuse, thank you."

"Joshua, you like Hartford. It's obvious. And that's great. I know it's not your usual M.O. but it's good. Take her out. Make her swoon. I have it on very good authority that she's fantasized about having her way with you."

Hollie's smirk told me I hadn't managed to pick my jaw up off the floor fast enough. "It's not like that between us. We're friends. And like I said, I'm not interested in a relationship."

She looked at me like I might be the most stupid person on earth. "Joshua, Joshua, Joshua. I'll try to think of someone *else* I think might be right for Hartford, but I suggest you have a big think yourself about whether or not you actually want someone else taking her out. When you come to your senses and realize what's right in front of you, she might not be available anymore."

That sounded perfect. The sooner Hartford wasn't single, the better.

SIXTEEN

Hartford

I was on a mission: fulfil Gerry's "Life Outside the Hospital" requirements for the week *and* find Joshua a date. Today's guided tour of the National Gallery would hopefully accomplish both.

I stood on my tiptoes, trying to get a glimpse of the large painting the guide had ushered us toward. A man in front of me noticed me straining to see and shuffled to the left to give me a better view of the naked woman lying on a blue bed. She had her back to us and her bottom out, and was looking at herself in the mirror. It was exactly the kind of picture you'd expect to see if you came to an art gallery.

"So obviously, this is Venus," the guide said.

It was obvious? I was way out of my depth.

Our guide was in her thirties—perhaps thirty-two or thirty-three. She was about the same height as me but her hair was sleek and glossy and her make-up expertly applied. The pale gold lanyard strung around her neck said her name was Janet.

Joshua might like her. Their names would sound cute together. And as one of the curators at the gallery, she would be clever. Joshua deserved someone who could keep up with him.

Yes, she was a definite candidate.

"How do we tell?" she asked our group of twelve eager gallery-goers.

Holy buttercream, a Socratic method teach-in, now? It felt like I was back in med school. I hoped she wasn't going to pick on me because I didn't have a clue. "If we want to cheat, we can look at the title." She laughed to herself (sense of humor—important for Joshua). "We call this painting *Venus with Cupid, The Toilet of Venus* or *The Rokeby Venus,* but we also know who we're looking at because Velázquez gives us a large clue. Can anyone tell me what that is?"

Someone muttered something and she nodded enthusiastically. "That's right—*Cupid's* presence tells us this isn't just any woman, admiring herself in the mirror. This is the goddess Venus."

How do we know it's Cupid? I wanted to ask. But I kept quiet. It was probably obvious. Our guide went on to tell us about Velázquez, and how the painting had been attacked by a suffragette.

"What I love about this painting," Janet said, "is that despite Velázquez—a man—painting it for men to admire, to me, Venus has all the control in this picture. She's admiring herself in the mirror. She's seeing her own beauty and power reflected back to her. Some people argue that at that angle, she wouldn't be able to see herself, but this isn't a photograph. It's a depiction of self-love. For me, this is a portrait of female confidence and power."

I looked again at the picture. At the reflection in the

mirror. At the bed clothes draped over the bed—voluptuous, just like Venus herself. She wasn't the flawless model in magazines and on catwalks, but she was proud of what she saw in the mirror. She was pleased with who she was on the outside. But something told me she felt good about who she was on the inside too.

Any woman who felt like that about herself held real power.

Since the accident, my body had been a constant reminder of what I couldn't do, of what I'd lost. I couldn't help thinking I'd quite like to be Venus, to feel that good. That powerful. That free.

I pulled out my phone and took a picture, wanting to capture the feeling to come back to later.

After Janet answered questions, we moved on. I made sure I kept up with the group and managed to get into the front at the next painting.

"This is Bacchus and Ariadne," Janet said. "Painted by Titian. It's a great example of the diagonal composition of the baroque period and one of the most important paintings in the gallery. I can give you more facts about this painting, but what does it say to you? What do you *feel* when you look at this picture?"

"He's in love with that girl," I blurted out. "Crazy in love."

Janet's eyes lit up. "Exactly. Here Titian depicts the first moment that Bacchus sees Ariadne and falls in love right there and then. It's the greatest depiction of love at first sight that's ever been painted."

But Ariadne didn't look convinced. "Is Ariadne running away?" I asked, looking at the woman who was the object of Bacchus' affection. "Is she . . . rejecting him?"

Janet turned to look at the picture. "I suppose I've never

seen it like that before. The conventional reading of her posture is that she's looking out, dismayed, at Theseus' ship as he sails off, abandoning her." She pointed at the barely-there brushstrokes indicating a ship on the far left of the picture. "But that's the beauty of art—so much of it is open to interpretation. Maybe this is the moment Bacchus sees and falls for Ariadne, but it's the moment *before* Ariadne returns his affection."

The moment before she returns his affection. I took in a breath, drinking in the concept of love having some kind of linear evolution: a before, a during, and sometimes an after. It made sense. And I liked the idea that Ariadne didn't like Bacchus just because he liked her. Okay, maybe it hadn't taken her long to catch up, but she made her own decision about him. I pulled out my phone and took another picture.

"Art is as much about feeling as it is about seeing." Janet grinned enthusiastically at her audience. "You don't have to know about art to enjoy it or to learn something about life from it."

The next picture was a depiction of Samson and Delilah by Rubens, just after they'd had sex. It was so raw and so real it made me blush. Samson's tanned, muscular arms reminded me of Joshua. And from the look on Delilah's face and the way her hand settled onto the satiated, sleeping Samson, I couldn't help but think that she liked him more than she was meant to. I needed to pull her to one side and tell her to get her forcefield up pronto, or she was going to have trouble ahead.

By the end of the tour, I'd gone from thinking that each of the paintings we looked at on our tour was just some stuffy old picture to wondering when I could come back.

As Janet wrapped up the tour, I pulled out my phone to bring up a picture of Joshua. She may think I was a little weird when I tried to set her up on a date, but hopefully she'd have a change of heart when she saw him. I scrolled through my pictures. The last one I had was of him with my triumphant cake. He looked so goofy as he gave me his best shocked face. I grinned as I found a picture of him driving back from the flat in Borehamwood. We'd stopped at some lights and I'd captured him just as I was teasing him about being such a snob, not wanting to live above a chip shop. I hadn't examined the picture in any detail before today—it had just been one of those snaps you take and don't think too much about. I wasn't sure if it was just because I was trying to find the most flattering picture of Joshua or whether focusing on the paintings today had encouraged me to look closer, but I swear I hadn't noticed the look he was giving me before. It wasn't irritation I saw in his expression. And it wasn't the exasperation I was so used to either. It was . . . affection maybe. Or something else I couldn't quite figure out.

"Did you have a question?" Janet asked. I looked around to find the rest of our tour group had disappeared. Janet would make a great date for him—she was pretty, interesting, clever, and funny.

I paused, taking in the picture of Joshua one more time.

I shook my head. "Just wanted to thank you for a great tour," I said. "I really learned a lot."

Before I found Joshua his next date, I really wanted to figure out what it was that I'd captured in that photograph.

SEVENTEEN

Hartford

After a whirlwind week at work, I wanted to crawl into bed and sleep. But Joshua had arranged my second date and I wasn't going to cancel. Especially as I felt bad that I'd not even organized his second date yet. Was I procrastinating on purpose? No. But I wasn't *not* procrastinating, either. Tonight, I wanted to remain open to meeting someone who looked at me like Bacchus looked at Ariadne. From where I was sitting at the bar, I glanced over to the entrance to see if anyone new had arrived. Tonight was a drinks-only date with a client of Joshua's. And he was a little late.

I picked up my phone and scrolled through the pictures I'd taken in the National Gallery the previous week. I needed to channel Venus' power tonight.

"Hartford?" a man said behind me.

I turned to come face-to-face with someone who looked like Michael Fassbender's twin brother.

I grinned. "Hi, yes, I'm Hartford."

He gave me a weird, almost forced smile and nodded as

he took the seat next to me. "I'm David." He didn't shake my hand or even kiss me on the cheek, but greeting someone sitting at a bar was awkward, I supposed.

David picked up the drinks menu and seemed to examine it like it was evidence in a murder. "You live around here?" he asked, without looking up.

"Yes, next door to Joshua." I smiled but David didn't see because he wasn't looking at me. "This is the Piña Clara." I held up my drink before I took a sip. "My first ever. It's delicious if you need a recommendation."

The barman appeared in front of us.

"I'll have a Hudson Manhattan Rye," David said.

I was poised to tell him that I didn't need another, even though my glass was almost empty. Despite the fact I wasn't seeing patients tomorrow, I wanted to be sharp.

But David still hadn't even looked at me since that first moment, let alone assessed the level in my glass.

Maybe he was nervous.

Or he'd just forgotten.

"So," he said, turning to face me at last. "How do you know Joshua?"

"Old family friend," I replied. "What about you?" Even though I knew the answer, I was desperate to break the ice that seemed a meter thick at the moment.

David's drink arrived and I breathed a sigh of relief. Maybe he just needed a bit of alcohol to loosen his lips and help him relax. I was sure the next two hours couldn't be this . . . awkward.

"I'm a client of his."

I nodded, willing him on. But nothing. My date began to check out what was behind the bar and then what was behind me. "What sort of work do you do?" I asked. He didn't seem to want to be here at all.

"I'm in marketing. For Mulberry." His words were clipped and cold.

"Do you enjoy it?" I asked him.

He looked at me, having exhausted every available line of sight save the one immediately in front of him, and sighed. "Can I be honest with you?"

Here it was. He was going to confide that he'd had a shit day and was having trouble mustering enthusiasm for our date. But that would put us in an excellent position, because I could be a wonderful listener while he relayed all his troubles. "Of course," I said. "Be as honest as you like. It's the only way to be, as far as I'm concerned."

He slid off his seat and downed his glass of rye. "This isn't going to work out. You're just not my type. I go for . . . sexy girls and . . . you're . . . This feels like a waste of an evening. I'm going to go." He pulled out his wallet, left thirty pounds on the bar, and walked out. Just like that.

Heat crawled up my skin. When it reached my face, it was as if I were on fire.

Oh God. Oh God. Oh God.

I focused ahead, hoping stillness would help me disappear. If I made eye contact with another person, and saw confirmation that there were witnesses to what had just occurred here, I might never recover.

As the heat on my face mellowed, I realized I was gripping my glass a little too tightly. Slowly, I slid my almost-finished cocktail onto the bar. People around me seemed to be chatting, and I couldn't swear to it, but no one seemed to be staring.

I sucked in a breath and tried to figure out what to do.

I hadn't even had the chance to respond. Even if I had, I wouldn't have known what to say. The guy couldn't stand to make a bit of small talk and have a drink with me? Was I so hideous? Boring? Ridiculous?

I longed for the ease of the hospital, where social interactions were easy and low-stakes. Where I knew my role, thrived with purpose. I'd not felt as utterly hopeless as I did in this moment since the paramedics pulled me out of that ditch over a decade ago.

The barman came over and asked if I wanted another drink. What I wanted was some kind of magic button that could transport me from my stool to my bed. I settled on asking him for the bill. There was no way thirty pounds was going to cover both our drinks in a place like this.

I willed the barman to move at warp speed so I could leave as soon as possible.

But where would I go?

I was only two streets away from home. What I wanted to do was crawl between my sheets and eat cake, but Joshua would surely hear me come in. I couldn't face him, couldn't tell him what just happened. Maybe if I was quiet enough, I could slip in unnoticed. I could text him at the two-hour mark and tell him I was too tired to debrief. In the meantime, I could slip into bed with Netflix, a cupcake, and a lifetime's humiliation.

EIGHTEEN

Joshua

There were only two flats on the top floor of the residences, and so the light footsteps in the outside hallway were most likely Hartford's.

Except she shouldn't be back for another hour. I checked my phone. More like an hour and a half. There was no way she'd ditch a date so quickly. I stalked toward my front door and pressed my ear to the wood. Nothing. It must have been a cleaner. Or a staff member checking something.

And then I definitely heard the grind of a key going into a lock. I flung open the door to find Hartford letting herself in across the corridor.

"You ditched a date after half an hour and thought I wouldn't catch you creeping back in?" I shook my head, gleeful at the thought the shoe was firmly laced up on the other foot now. "I don't know, Hartford, you can't even hold down a conversation for two hours with someone."

She didn't turn around as she opened the door. "Actually, I'm not feeling very well. I'll catch you later." She slid inside and closed the door.

Confusion and shame mixed in my gut. I'd been joking. Had I offended her? I took my phone and typed out a message.

Sorry for assuming the worst. Hope you're okay.

After five minutes, she hadn't responded.

But that was understandable if she was throwing up or . . . stuck on the loo.

After fifteen minutes, she still hadn't responded and I got worried. I texted again.

Can I get you anything? Or send for a doctor?

I'm fine, she responded.

At least she was alive. I ordered some cupcakes from Dragonfly and then instantly regretted it. If she had an upset stomach, buttercream wasn't going to help.

I paced. Hartford hadn't mentioned anything about not feeling well when she was waiting for David to arrive. In fact, she'd texted me to say she couldn't believe the bar was charging thirty-five pounds for a cocktail. That meant either the cocktail had made her sick . . .

Or her date had.

Patience had never been my strong suit, and I wasn't about to change now. I wanted to know what had happened.

I slipped out of my flat and across the hall. I resisted the urge to bang on her front door. Instead, I tapped out another text. *Want some company?*

No response.

Well aware I was being a pushy bastard, I knocked on the door.

I waited. And waited. But I heard her come to the other side of the door.

"What do you want, Joshua? I'm going to have an early night."

I could hear the sadness in her voice. It wasn't the Hartford I knew, and I wanted to know what was going on. "Tell me what happened?"

"Nothing," she said. "Really, it's absolutely not important—" Her voice caught and she fell silent.

Dread twisted in my gut at the tone of her voice. Something terrible had happened. I'd never seen her like this. "Did he hurt you?"

"God, no. Nothing like that. All I have is a bruised ego."

Thank goodness she wasn't physically hurt. But I didn't like the idea that any part of her was bruised. "I'm sorry."

"Don't be. I'm fine. There are people worse off—I'm just feeling sorry for myself."

"Stop," I said. "You're allowed to be sad, Hartford. If you can't be upset because there are worse off people in the world, then by your logic, you can't be happy unless you're the happiest person in the world. Your situation might not be tragic, but it doesn't mean you don't need a shoulder to cry on and a piece of cake to eat."

The urge to pull the door from its hinges and wrap my arms around her was close to overwhelming.

I just wanted to hold her.

"I'm okay, Joshua, but thank you for checking on me."

What could I do? I wanted to take away whatever it was that was making her sad. But I couldn't beat down the door and demand she smile. Could I? "Okay, well, I'm going to stay here for a while and if you want to talk, I'm just the other side of the door. If you don't want to talk, I'm still just the other side of the door."

I leaned against the wall, ready to stay for a while. I needed her to know I was nearby if she needed me.

"I'm being ridiculous," she said eventually.

"Impossible."

"He didn't do anything. In some ways he was kinder to just . . . you know." She sighed. "I just need a dose of Bravo and a good night's sleep."

The lift doors pinged open and one of the porters from the residences appeared, holding a box of cupcakes. "Well, I could add a cupcake to that mix if it helps?" I took the box and nodded a silent thank-you.

"You have cake?" Her voice was still flat but she answered a little quicker than she had done before.

"I do. You want me to leave them in front of the door?"

After a bit of rustling, the door creaked open. "Come in," she said. Her eyes were puffy and red rimmed. She'd definitely been crying.

I'd kill David when I found him.

I caught the door before it swung closed and followed her into the sitting room. "You want plates?"

"I need water. You want a glass?"

I followed her to the kitchen and slid the tray of cupcakes onto the island. "Water would be great."

She handed me a glass and her gaze slid to the cakes. "Is there a cookies and cream one?"

I pinged open the lid. "Looks like there are three."

She climbed up onto a bar stool, which brought her almost to the same height as me. "That should do it."

I didn't think I'd ever seen her actually finish a whole cupcake. Things must be bad if she was thinking about eating three. I pulled in a breath, trying to rein in my need to find out what the hell was going on.

"I don't want to make a big thing about this." She reached for a cake and turned it around in her hands, as if trying to decide which bit she was going to eat first.

"Okay." I leaned on the counter next to her seat, bracing myself for what came next.

She scooped a tiny bit of frosting from the cake and popped it into her mouth and sighed. "He arrived, ordered a drink, then after about two minutes, said he wasn't interested and left."

I clenched my fists and did my best to keep my thoughts to myself. What. A. Twat.

At least he hadn't touched her. The guy was an idiot for not being interested in Hartford. But that had to be his loss. I wouldn't let it affect her. "Tell me everything from the beginning."

I stayed as still as I could, trying to keep my face blank and my breathing steady while she told me the entire, very short, story.

"He did me a favor, really. At least I didn't waste my evening."

No, it was far worse. That arsehole had ruined her evening *and* her confidence. "He's a dickhead."

"He was just being honest." She was trying to let him off the hook but I could tell by her sad eyes that cake wasn't enough to erase what he'd done.

"He was rude," I replied. "He could have stayed and had a drink."

"What, and faked an emergency after an hour? Would that have been better?"

"I don't know." What was the matter with him? Couldn't he see how amazing Hartford was? Not that he'd had a chance to get to know her. "He should have realized he was bloody lucky to go on a date with you. You're clever and funny and beautiful. He doesn't deserve you if he can't stick around long enough to find out how bloody great you are."

She looked from her cake to me and scrunched up her nose in a you-have-to-say-that expression. "You're excellent BFF material. Did anyone ever tell you that?"

"I'm serious. You have so much going for you, and he wasn't man enough to stay and find out. So that's his loss. And fuck Mulberry. I'm going to drop them as a client."

Hartford laughed and the sound tugged at the corners of my lips. "You are not going to drop Mulberry as a client."

She was probably right. "I'll find a way to make him pay."

"He didn't break my heart, Joshua. You're very sweet, but really, I think you're more upset than I am at this point. I've had two mouthfuls of cake and I'm feeling a lot better."

"You are?" I asked. She seemed to have brightened up a little. "Well, at least I can make you laugh."

And then all of a sudden, those sad eyes were back. "It's my own fault. I didn't exactly put in a lot of effort. I assumed a bit of mascara and something other than scrubs would be enough. But I guess most guys are looking for contouring—whatever that is. And a fake tan and eyelash extensions. I'm never going to be that girl who looks like she just stepped out of a magazine. My arse is always going to be slightly too big, my hair unwieldy in the rain, my smile a little sideways. When it comes down to it, I just don't care enough to do anything with make-up that takes more than five minutes."

It was true that Hartford didn't spend time or effort on make-up or some of the other glamorous things certain women did, but that didn't make her any less stunning in my book. And whatever she wore wouldn't make her any funnier, kinder, or more interesting. Those were the things I appreciated about her most, liked about her most . . . All things about her that I didn't want to lose.

"What are you talking about? Your arse is perfectly . . ." I didn't know a good way to finish that sentence without sounding like a dick. And her hair was gorgeous whenever I'd seen it down, which wasn't very often.

She tilted her head. "Joshua . . ." she said, her tone warning me not to bullshit her.

"I mean it!" How did she not see I was being completely serious? I put down my glass and turned to face her. "You don't need bloody contouring or any of that . . . stuff." For a guy who was meant to be smooth, I couldn't find the words to convince her.

She rolled her eyes. "He was just being honest and—"

Before I could overthink it, I stepped closer, closing the distance between us, cupped her face in my hands and pressed my lips to hers. My heart raced like it was free-wheeling downhill from the top of a mountain, and my fingertips buzzed like I'd brushed a live wire.

And then a firm hand at my chest pushed me away.

"Joshua." Her expression was stern. Fuck. I'd made things worse. "I don't need a pity kiss from you."

I took a step back. A what? "What are you talking about? That wasn't pity."

She rolled her eyes. "Really? We agreed that this . . ." She circled her finger between the two of us. "Is a bad idea."

"I know," I said. "I know. It's just . . . I want to kiss you. And I think you want me to kiss you too."

Her pale blue eyes widened and I stepped forward.

"If you don't want this, just tell me. But I don't do pity kisses." I scooped my hand around her neck and pressed my lips to hers again, this time, easing my tongue past her soft lips and kissing her properly. I didn't spare a second thought for what this was, or wasn't, or might be. Consequences be damned—I was kissing Hartford.

She pushed at my chest and reluctantly, I pulled back. "Joshua."

I didn't want to stop. I wanted more. All the reasons *more* was a bad idea seemed to have stayed behind in the corridor and now, in this moment, all I wanted was Hartford.

I pulled at her shirt and began to undo the buttons. She could stop me if she wanted, but all I could think about was how her skin would feel next to mine and how her breasts would taste in my mouth.

"I'm okay, Joshua. You don't need to do this."

I looked up at her. "I want to. I want *you*."

"But . . . is it a good idea?"

I pulled off her shirt, pulled her bra strap off her shoulders, and placed a kiss on the indentation the strap had left. Her skin was soft and smooth and oh-so-hot. "It feels like a good idea."

She sighed as I traced my fingers up her spine. "There are a lot of reasons why it's not."

"We're friends," I said. "This. Tonight. It doesn't have to change anything if we don't let it."

She stared at the top of my chest and I paused, waiting for her reaction.

She slid her hands up my chest and began to unbutton my shirt. "And tomorrow it will be like it never happened." It wasn't a question and I wasn't about to argue. "Yes. I can make up for the fact that I've only done six thousand steps today."

I chuckled and pulled off my shirt, stripped out of my trousers. "That sounds like a challenge. Let's see if I can make you sweat, Hartford." I snapped open the buttons of her jeans and pushed my hand down into her underwear to find more heat. "Let's see if I can make you pant." My fingers found her clit. I caught her moan in my mouth as I kissed her again. It was more passionate this time, less careful. Needier. Dirtier.

Her hips began to sway as my fingers pushed and circled. Her body was so responsive. But, God, it wasn't enough.

I stepped away and yanked her jeans down, impatient for more.

"I don't know where to start. My mouth on your pussy, your breasts in my hands, or my cock as deep as it will go."

She transferred her weight onto each leg as I pulled off her jeans, her fingers threaded into my hair to steady herself.

Staying on my knees, I pulled her toward me and pushed her underwear to one side.

"Joshua," she gasped, stumbling back until she hit the sofa and sat. Perfect.

I pushed open her legs, my hands on her thighs, as I dipped forward to taste her. Fucking delicious. Her clit pulsed under my tongue as I greedily licked and sucked and pushed and rounded her. She was wet so quickly, my hardened cock reared in eagerness at the idea that soon I'd be buried in it. I was impatient for her slick heat and pushed in two fingers.

Her hands tightened in my hair and she bucked off of the cushions. "Joshua. It's too much. I'm going to come."

I pulled my mouth away from her pussy with a pop. "That's right."

Circling my thumb over her clit, my fingers working into her, I watched as she climbed higher and higher and higher. She called out as I felt her vibrate around my hand.

Fuck, I couldn't wait to get inside her.

As she floated back down from her orgasm, she gave me

a small, shy smile.

"You're so sexy," I said and held out my hand.

"I'm not sure if I can walk."

I chuckled as I pulled her up from the sofa. "And we're just getting started."

As we got into her bedroom, I spun her around and unclasped her bra. "I've been wondering what these might be like to hold since the day I picked you up from the airport."

"You have?" she asked.

I stalked around and cupped her breasts. Soft and firm, they almost overspilled my hands. I brushed my thumbs over her nipples and groaned. I wanted to see how they moved as I fucked up into her.

The bed was high, like the one in the penthouse. I'd always wondered what it would be like to fuck in my bed. It was the perfect height. I guided Hartford over and lifted her onto the top of the sheets, pulling her legs apart and settling between her legs.

"Condom," she said.

I nodded. Fuck, where was the closest one I had?

"I'll have to go back to my apartment."

"In the drawer next to my bed."

I frowned. "Really?"

She shrugged. "It's good to be prepared."

That was for sure.

I grabbed a condom, tore it open, and slid it onto my almost-painfully hard cock.

"This won't be awkward tomorrow, will it?" she asked as she glanced down at where I was positioned at her entrance.

"Not if we don't let it be." I pressed my crown forward, tightening my jaw as I resisted the urge to ram into her.

"Oh God," she said, falling back onto the bed. "Joshua!"

I pushed into her, sliding, slowly deeper and deeper until I could barely think. The sight of the bare breasts I'd thought about too often since she'd come back into my life, the tightness of her pussy, the warmth in her ice blue eyes— I'd barely moved and already I wanted to come and come and come.

She was a fucking goddess.

She shifted her hands up my arms and drew her legs up either side of my hips. The scent of cinnamon washed over me. "You okay?" she asked.

"I'm more than okay. You feel fucking fantastic." I began to move. Softly at first, trying not to bubble over too soon. I breathed in the sound of her gasps and moans. I gorged on the sight of her undulating breasts. I closed my eyes to dive into the feel of her hands, her hips, her sweet, sweet pussy.

A sharp twist of her hips and the panic in her eyes told me she was close. I smiled. Fuck, I liked that I could make her come. I liked that my body fit so well with hers, that I could make her feel so good. I hooked my arms over her shoulders and thrust harder and harder as she convulsed around me. I slowed to allow her to recover until she called out my name in a soft call of surrender. Something in her timbre cut through my self-control like a blade. I couldn't hold back. My orgasm crashed through me, violent and urgent, like my body was fulfilling a primal need to give this woman everything.

Shit. What was that?

Sweaty and confused, I rearranged us so we lay spooned together, my arms around her waist. "You okay?" I asked, once our breathing had returned to normal.

She nodded, her long, soft hair gliding against my chest

like a sheet of silk. "I've heard it was possible, but I've never had two orgasms like that before. Do most women you're with do that?"

As much as I loved how straightforward Hartford was, now wasn't the time to be making any comparisons. "Let's just focus on—" I caught myself before I said *us*. There was no such thing. "Let's focus on you."

I shifted her leg back and over mine and slid my hand between her folds. "This is so good. I love how wet you are."

"That's a turn on?" she asked.

"Of course," I answered, a very willing teacher. "I did this to you. My cock made you this wet. It makes me feel powerful." Her hips circled, grinding her arse against my cock. In seconds I was harder than I had been the first time.

She reached back and clenched my length in her fist, squeezing and releasing as I strained under her fingers. "Yeah. I get that."

A growl reverberated in my throat. I wasn't sure how we'd got here but I wasn't sorry. She felt better than I could have possibly imagined.

I reached for another condom, and when I'd covered myself, slowly pushed into her from behind. This time I didn't stop. As if we shared a mind, both of us made small, perfect, restrained movements that drew out each other's pleasure.

"It's so good," she said. "Less but more at the same time."

I let out a small groan. I knew exactly what she meant. I tried to keep my pace steady and my movements smooth. I wanted to stay like this for hours—her skin against mine, my heartbeat against hers. It was as close as we could ever possibly be.

It was fucking perfect.

NINETEEN

Hartford

I squeezed my eyes shut in a long blink. *Focus*, I said to myself. I was about to have an important meeting with Gerry. I couldn't be thinking about the delicious way Joshua's thumbs pressed into the space next to my hip bones, the way his tongue felt against my skin, his expression when he came. I had to *focus*.

I pulled back my shoulders and knocked on Gerry's office.

"Yes," Gerry's tone was uncharacteristically snappish. "Hartford." He glanced up at me. "Good, good. Come and sit down."

I'd been working on trying to find a way to stop Merdon from launching Calmation as an over-the-counter drug. But there were limited things we could do when we couldn't talk about Calmation publicly.

"What do you have for me?"

I slid across an article I'd written about the dangers of

ADHD drugs for children being available over the counter. "This one is the right length for Health Service Journal. This one," I said, handing him another piece of paper. "is a little longer and more specific, which will be right for the BMJ."

I paused while he read them both.

"If only we could mention Calmation by name—call them directly to the mat." He scratched his chin.

"We lose a lot of power because it's not specific. There's no target we can go after. If we could talk about Calmation itself, we could get you on news programs, go on social media—really make it a campaign. I think we need to start fundraising, so we'll be ready to legally challenge the regulator's decision. We need to get signatures from top pediatricians all over the world saying what a bad decision this is."

He sucked in a breath. "It's difficult. I don't want to get my contact in trouble. Big pharma can be . . . tricky."

"I just don't think we have much firepower without talking about Calmation directly."

"Let's put a plan together—one we can put into action as soon as Merdon files in the US."

I nodded and handed over the folder I'd been clutching. "This is what I have."

Gerry shot me a suspicious look and opened the file. He flicked through the launch plan I'd been working on.

"I was thinking that as soon as we can go public, I might be able to get Joshua's input—you remember Joshua Luca, who I brought to dinner? He's in PR and marketing. I'm sure he would help us if I asked him. I know he's doing some work for a pharma company at the moment. He might have some good insights."

"This is all excellent work, Hartford. I'm impressed. But it must have taken you a great deal of time to do all this without any help. Have you still managed to create some balance in your life? Have you managed to properly get away from thinking about medicine?"

I wasn't about to confess to Gerry all the things Joshua had done to me the previous night that had caused my mind to go entirely blank and my limbs entirely weak. "Absolutely. I've been taking those baking lessons, I went to the National Gallery the other day, and . . . I've been dating."

Gerry smiled. "Well, then this is a good day. We can only deal with what we can control and my goodness, you are doing exactly that." His tone was like a warm hug. I couldn't help but be proud that he was pleased.

"Do you know when Merdon are going to file for approval in the US?"

"I don't have exact dates," Gerry said. "I just know it's imminent."

"As soon as they do, I can get Joshua's input on my plan and see if there's anything we've missed. But there are things we can do the day they file."

"I agree. Let's hold off on these articles until we can name names. Excellent work, Hartford. Not just on your planned crusade against Merdon, but also trying to create a life for yourself outside of medicine. I'm proud of you."

"Thank you." I smiled and stood, pulling his office door closed as I left.

I was proud of myself too, and grateful to Gerry for pushing me. Finding things to do outside of the hospital hadn't been as horrifying as I'd expected it to be. I'd thought that if I wasn't consumed with medicine, I'd go back to how I was before I'd found it. I'd go back to being a girl who couldn't dance anymore. But I'd kept busy and not found my thoughts sliding to the past any more than usual. The regret I'd thought would flood in about what my silly infatuation with Joshua had cost me just hadn't materialized.

Maybe that's why I'd shut off my forcefield last night and kissed him back. The fear of what he could do to me had dimmed. I knew him now in a way I hadn't done when we were teenagers. Things were different now.

TWENTY

Hartford

As I stepped out of the lift, my entire body buzzed with excitement at seeing Joshua. He'd said sleeping together wouldn't change anything between us, and I hoped that was true. I really wanted to talk to him about Calmation. We could strategize together—a pastime bound to be more successful than baking together. That wouldn't happen tonight because of having to keep Gerry's contact confidential. But soon.

I paused at my front door to find my keys. Joshua's door opened behind me.

"Good evening," he said, in that relaxed, gravelly tone that usually meant he'd just woken up or had been deep in thought. "How was your day?"

I turned and smiled at him. God, he was pretty. "Good. Busy. Gerry's pleased with my extracurricular activities."

Joshua's eyebrows lifted. "I hope you didn't go into too much detail."

I laughed and tried to ignore the flush of heat creeping up my neck.

"Well, I'm going to show you another way to spend your time outside of the hospital tonight." Joshua picked up my bag and held out his hand. I took it, and he led me into his flat.

As I followed him inside, I spoke to his back. "We should have a conversation before we get naked again. You only do the casual sex thing, and I know that. Like, I *really* know that."

"We can talk, but first, I'm going to let you in on a secret of mine." He guided me to the kitchen island, dropped my bag on the side, and pulled out a glass from the cupboard and a bottle of wine from his fridge. He poured, but instead of handing it to me, he picked it up in one hand and held out the other. I didn't question him. All my energy was being channeled into curiosity about what he had in store for me.

I followed him into the bathroom, where he placed the glass on the inset marble shelf and pressed some buttons on a pad on the wall; water started pouring into the bath. His bathroom was like something out of a hotel—walls of marble and mood lighting. Which fit, I supposed, as we *were* in a hotel. Sort of. He pulled towels and a robe off the shelves at the far end of the room and placed them on the bench opposite the bath.

"Okay," he said, turning his attention back to me. "Do these scrub things have buttons, or do they just pull off?" He tugged at the hem of my top and I pulled away from him. What was he doing?

"This is your secret? This is how you seduce your women? You bathe them?" Now that we'd slept together, was this what was going to happen? I was going to get the full Miss Tuesday Night treatment?

"No, this is a bath that I ran for you. And if you're going to get in, you need to be naked. I'm going to sit the other side of the door and we can talk about anything you want."

I felt like I'd skipped a chapter. "And this is your secret?"

He nodded. "Baths. They're the key to relaxation, creativity, and taking care of yourself. Or in this case, me taking care of you." He withdrew a wooden box from a drawer under the sink, and inside were tiny bottles of who-knew-what. "We need some frankincense, chamomile, and of course, lavender." He selected what he wanted and set about dripping the contents of each into my bath. "And some plain bath oil." He reached for a bottle that sat next to my glass of wine and added a generous dose to the water. "It's all organic."

The man had lost his mind.

"Right, get in. You can put this in your biweekly report for Gerry."

Next he'd be teaching me how to meditate.

"Save the skeptical glares, Hartford, and take off your clothes. I can't tell you how many solutions I've found to problems in this bath. This tub has provided everything from breakthrough ideas for pitches to solutions for profitability issues." He turned to me and fixed me with a smoldering look. "And I've never shown anyone this. Not any other woman. Not my best friends."

I pushed him out of the door so he didn't see my widening smile. That bath was looking pretty inviting right now.

"Are you in?" he called. "I'm going to get a cushion and a beer; I'll be back."

I pulled off my scrubs and stepped into the first bath I'd had in over a decade.

"I put the towels and a robe on the bench," Joshua called from the other side of the door.

Was the bench here so someone, or a couple of people, could talk to the person bathing? Were the business set taking meetings in the tub these days?

"You want music on?" he shouted while soothing, classical piano music drifted through the speakers.

"I don't think so," I called back. The concerto stopped abruptly.

"I forgot to switch on the candles. The ones around the bath are battery operated. The switch is on the base."

Candles were the last thing on my mind.

"Are you in yet?" he asked.

"Just sitting down." How had he convinced me to do this? I felt ridiculous. But this water felt like sliding between silk sheets.

"I hope the temperature's right. It will be thirty-eight degrees exactly. That's how I usually take my baths."

I let out a small laugh. "Joshua Luca, I bet if you surveyed the entire British population, you and the Queen would be the only two people in the land who would know their preferred bath temperature." As I lowered myself into the water, I had to acknowledge that the guy knew what temperature to run a bath.

"The essential oils in there will help you relax. And also, it might help lift the smell of Yemen."

"Hey. I do not still smell of Yemen." But hell, this bath smelled delicious. Like a garden full of flowers. I took a deep breath and allowed my body to sink deeper into the water.

He laughed. "No. Not anymore. So, let's talk."

A ripple of anxiety circled in my stomach. I didn't know what I wanted to say. I liked Joshua, there was no doubt about it. Could my forcefield handle casual sex with him? I knew he couldn't give me anything more.

"I really enjoyed last night," he said, his tone low and gravelly again.

"Me too," I replied. "But let's not talk it to death, okay?" I didn't want some awkward dance where he had to tell me that he didn't do serious relationships. Or that once was nice and everything but there wouldn't be a repeat performance. My forcefield had taken hits last night and I needed to power up before I could handle a relationship talk. I just wanted it to be *us*. I didn't want last night to have ruined anything. "We're still friends."

"Right."

"I'm well aware you only do the casual thing, so let's be casual about this. If it happens again . . ." If it happened again, I'd have to power up my forcefield in advance. That way, it wouldn't feel so full of holes the way it did now. "Then it happens again. If it doesn't, it doesn't."

"Right," he said. "The casual thing."

"Right," I replied.

"Right. Can you stop saying *casual*?" he asked.

"Can you stop saying *right*?"

Despite him being the other side of the door, I could feel his grin between my thighs.

"Whatever you say, Hartford. So if we're not going to talk about . . . last night, do you want to talk about work?"

I'd love to chat through the whole Merdon and Calmation thing, but it would have to wait until everything was out in the open. Then I'd pin him down and make him give me input into my plan. "Not really. There are things brewing I might want to talk to you about in a few weeks, but not now."

"How's the leg?"

I lifted it out of the water, watching as the water slid from my decade-old scar. "It's okay. I think it will always be my weak spot, you know?"

"We all have them." I heard his head fall back onto the bathroom door.

"Weak spots?" I asked.

"Yes. And scars."

"But not you. Isn't Joshua Luca completely flawless? Super successful, pussy magnet billionaire."

"Pussy magnet?" I could hear his smile in his words and for a split second I wanted to tell him to come in and join me in this perfectly warm water. To show me what weak spots and scars he had, and offer to wash them all away.

"Where are your scars, Joshua?"

Silence settled between us like the steam on the mirrors. We were at a crossroads in our relationship—he could make some quip about his bone never having broken, or we could dive deeper.

"I'm not sure I have scars exactly. But I'm not flawless either."

"Really? Tell me something you're not good at. Something you've failed at. Something you want but can't have?"

"I've had my share of challenges. Work is . . ." He paused, and I imagined him doing some mental gymnastics about what he should say. "I suppose Diana breaking things off was a low point."

Diana. Was she the woman he'd wanted to marry? I remember there being a lot of phone calls and hushed conversations around the time of the wedding, but I didn't recall any specific details. I supposed I'd assumed it had been Joshua's decision.

"Looking back, it was completely the right thing for both of us. We were far too young and didn't have a clue what we were doing."

"Do you still miss her?"

"No, I don't think I ever did. I just wish she'd told me rather than just not turn up to the ceremony, you know?"

I sat bolt upright and water sloshed over the sides of the bath. I'd had no idea he'd been jilted. I'd been deep in my I-don't-want-to-hear-about-Joshua phase at the time, which seemed to have lasted about ten years. "That must have been rough." I wanted to get out and comfort him, but the last time the subject had come up, while we were baking, he'd shut me down. I couldn't help but think that the only reason he'd opened up now was because there was a closed door between us.

"Yeah. I suppose I had life planned out in a certain direction and all of a sudden . . ."

Plans changed.

I knew that feeling.

"Did it happen before you set up Luca Brands?"

"Yeah, just before."

"So you channeled all your energy into creating a successful business."

"I suppose."

It made sense. It also explained why Joshua didn't get serious with anyone, although I wasn't sure he saw it as clearly as I did. His scars were well hidden and after all this time, unlikely to heal. Without a marriage, Joshua had wedded a casual-relationship lifestyle, and I needed to respect his boundaries. I could keep my forcefield fully charged, keep the feelings that always managed to rage out-of-hand for him in check. It was the only way to let myself have more of what we'd shared last night—and every moment I spent with him, it became clearer that more of Joshua was what I wanted.

TWENTY-ONE

Joshua

It was a normal Sunday night get-together with my five closest friends. As I looked around, I was reminded how these guys had been here for me. When I'd first started my business, these nights in the pub had been invaluable for brainstorming ideas or discussing problems. And before that, when my engagement ended, these guys kept me sane. Stopped me drinking and helped me channel my hurt, anger, and frustration into my business—and the tennis court, of course. These men were the reason I'd gotten through. Since my conversation with Hartford through the bathroom door, my brain hadn't switched off, and I couldn't quite figure out why. I needed to talk it out.

"Who's this Hartley I keep hearing about?" Andrew said as we sat at the round oak table and watched Dexter and Beck argue at the bar over who was putting their card down for the tab. "She important?" He never minced his words. Never gave into platitudes or overstatement. And he had an uncanny ability to zone-in on the crux of an issue.

"It's Hartford," I said, nodding. *Hartford Kent.* "She's fine. Moving out in a month." Her time next door had gone quickly, at least for me. I'd thought I'd hate having her as a neighbor, but it had been better than expected. Much better. "She's become a good friend." A friend that I shared things with I'd never told anyone.

"What are we talking about?" Gabriel asked as he took a seat.

"Nothing really. I was just saying that Hartford is moving out soon. She's become a good friend. Last night she was in the bath and we were talking—"

"Talking in the bath?" Gabriel asked.

"Who are you taking baths with?" Tristan asked as he sat down, quickly followed by Beck and Dexter.

"Joshua was talking to Hartford while she was in the bath," Andrew replied, and I didn't need to look at Tristan to know that his eyes were popping out on sticks.

"I was on the other side of the bathroom door. We weren't in the bath *together*. We're friends. I was encouraging her to relax and take care of herself." I wasn't clueless —I knew I wanted her to be happy and I knew that meant I liked her a lot. As much as Kelly was a great girl, I wasn't encouraging her into the bath after we'd had sex. Hartford was different.

Around the table, all my friends were exchanging pointed glances. I got it. It was the same kind of confusion I'd felt internally for a while now.

"Right," Beck replied. "You like her, and she's a great girl. Attractive, seems to know how to handle you. Clever, obviously."

"Yes of course she's a great girl. And I don't need to be handled, thank you." It made me sound like cattle. But he was right, I did like her.

"It's good that you like someone, finally. We know Diana did a number on you, but she was twenty-two when all that went down. Who's not an idiot at twenty-two?" Tristan said.

Mentioning Diana in our group discussions was akin to talking about Macbeth in a theatre. You just didn't. No one needed reminding of what had happened. It was embedded in our existence. Like foundations of a house that had been dug in a hundred years ago and no one had seen or thought about again. So why had my so-called friends decided tonight was the night to take down the off-limits sign on my ex? Maybe I'd given them some kind of subconscious permission slip.

"You're *still* an idiot," I snapped at Tristan.

"From what I hear from Dexter and Beck, you and this Hartford woman have been spending a lot of time together," Andrew said, thankfully changing the subject. I wasn't here to talk about Diana. "Everyone is cheering you on."

"Will your heads explode if I tell you I kissed her?" I wasn't about to confess anything more had happened between us.

"Good work," Tristan said, holding his hand up for a high five he wasn't going to get.

"Well, that's progress." Gabriel put his hand on my shoulder. "I can tell you from experience that running from pain will only get you so far. Diana left you a long time ago. You were a different man. History won't repeat itself."

Now Gabriel was talking about Diana? It felt like they were in my back garden, digging up my patio. There were no dead bodies there. I wasn't in pain. Or running from it. At the time it had been difficult but we'd all had difficulties in our past. I enjoyed my life now. I was happy.

"You need to move on from Diana, mate," Andrew said.

"The probability of Hartford also leaving you at the altar is statistically insignificant."

They were all piling on now. Is this what they all thought? That I was still hung up on Diana? From anyone else, I would have ignored them, but I trusted these men. If I ever needed to bury a dead body, these men would help me do it. And they'd figure out a burial site more inventive than under my nonexistent patio.

Gabriel cleared his throat. "I was trying to be slightly softer but, yes. What Andrew said."

I needed a button that would transport me back to the penthouse, so I could soak in the bath for ten minutes and think about what they were saying. And then afterward, I could zap myself back here and tell them my conclusions. I was going to have to have my Genius Time on the hoof.

"I don't do relationships," I said as if I were placing the first piece of a thousand-piece jigsaw puzzle down in the middle of the table.

"Right," said Dexter. "After being kicked in the bollocks like you were, it's normal not to want to commit again . . . right away."

The second piece of the puzzle had been put down. I could follow Dexter's logic—I'd not had another serious relationship since Diana. Part of that had been because all my focus was on my job, which, come to think of it, made Hartford's commitment to medicine after her accident all the more understandable. It struck me like a brick to the head, how we'd both reacted to our separate heartache by wholly throwing ourselves into work. What did it say about Hartford that after over a decade, she was still doing it?

"But not forever," Gabriel said. "At some point you have to let that pain go and move forward."

"I don't feel like I've been holding onto what

happened," I said. That's what had brought me here tonight. I liked Hartford. A lot. I liked her complete lack of self-consciousness around me. I liked her smile and her freckles and the way she was so bloody kind. I liked her silence as much as her conversation. But there was something stopping me moving things forward with her. I just wasn't sure what.

Was it possible I had been holding onto what Diana had done for so long that the pain had become like white noise? I didn't often think about Diana or what she'd done—or hadn't done. I had a full and fulfilling life. It wasn't like I was still heartbroken.

More like I still bore a faded scar.

"I'm not sure I know what my life looks like with a woman," I said, laying down another piece of the jigsaw. If I was going to be honest anywhere, it was with the men who'd seen me through thick and thin.

"Maybe you haven't tried very hard to picture it," Gabriel said. "The arrangements you have at the moment don't involve the women you're sleeping with being in your life outside the bedroom. It's like you will only entertain the opposite of marriage. And maybe it helps, but each arrangement seems like a reaction to being hurt."

I didn't feel hurt.

"Bethany's the same way—for ages she wouldn't sleep in her big bed because she fell out of it the first night she spent in there. In the end, she didn't even remember falling. She just knew she didn't like the bed."

I took a deep breath, trying to let his words settle. "You being celibate for a thousand years was you not wanting to sleep in the big bed?" I asked.

He nodded. "I didn't want to care for someone and have my heart ripped out again. A bit like you, I suppose. When

Autumn came along, I knew I had to make a choice between opening myself up and losing her. Opening myself up was the lesser of the two evils."

My invisible, internal scar burned red at his words. My wedding day had been the worst of my life. People talk about their worlds being shattered and most of the time they were exaggerating, but that day? That day, everything I thought I knew about the world went up in flames.

I'd woken up with a sense of certainty of how the day would go—who I was and who I was going to marry. Within hours, it had all gone up in smoke.

I'd replayed all our conversations in my head, searching for clues that she wasn't happy or that she didn't want to marry me, but I'd found nothing. And I still didn't know why she'd left. I'd never had any kind of explanation. I had to start again from the foundations and build myself back up—my confidence, my self-belief, my trust in people around me.

Gabriel continued. "You have a lifetime of experience behind you in a way you didn't last time you fell in love."

In love? It was like Gabriel had just dumped a hundred puzzle pieces on a carefully emerging picture and obscured everything that had been coming into focus.

"I'm not in love. And I'm over Diana. It's hardly like I've been celibate all these years." I laughed, but Gabriel's face was stony still.

"There's nothing wrong with casual sex after a breakup," Dexter said. "We've all been there. But unless the shagging turns into more, it's going to start to feel empty. Surely you must get that."

I considered how I'd been avoiding Kelly. Sex with her was never bad, but it had become . . . a little less than it had been at the start. Our routine was always the same:

A couple of sentences about work or the weather.

Kiss.

Undress.

Blowjob.

Sex.

Orgasm.

A couple more sentences about work or the weather while pulling on our clothes, followed by a goodbye.

Dexter was right. It felt empty. Even though I'd only slept with Hartford once, *being* with her made me feel full. And if I was full, I didn't need Kelly. Or anyone else.

"I like the company of beautiful women," I said. "I'm not going to apologize for that. Most men would give up a limb to spend a night with one of the women I . . . You get the point."

"Who gives a fuck what other men think," Andrew said. "The only person who matters is you. And maybe your mum. Fuck the rest of them. You don't sleep with women to make other men jealous. Or because you've convinced yourself it's the only way to avoid being hurt. You make love to a woman because she makes you happy."

It was like he'd punched a hole clear through my chest and I could feel the wind whistling through.

Hartford made me happy.

Not she's-fun-to-hang-out-with happy, but really miss-her-as-soon-as-she-leaves-the-room happy.

It made me want to pull her into my arms and spend the night swapping stories. And it made me want to lace up my trainers and run.

"God damn you, Andrew. You're always fucking work-ing. Why do you have to be available tonight?" He knew I didn't mean it. It was why, along with the group message, I'd sent him a one-on-one follow-up saying I hoped it could make it. I'd needed him here.

He unleashed a smile. "You're welcome."

"Say in theory, you all are right and I like Hartford and I'm protecting myself. How do I convince her to take a chance on me? She . . . thinks I'm only capable of having casual relationships." I wasn't sure she wasn't wrong. I didn't know where the bloody hell to start. "I'm not going to push myself on someone who's not interested—"

"You coward. You need to pursue her. Convince her," Tristan said.

"What? You think I should be like you and stalk her into doing my bidding? How many women have taken out injunctions on you?"

"Persistence pays off," he said, disappointingly not rising to the bait I was dangling. "And if she's worth it, she's worth a bit of effort. Stoke the fire of desire."

"The what? You know—never mind. I can't convince Hartford I'm the man for her when she probably thinks I'm exactly the opposite of the man she wants."

"Why not?" asked Andrew. "Gabriel used to think he wanted to be a lawyer. Look at him now—covered in sawdust most of the time. People can change. You should at least give her a chance to see the man who is serious about her and let her make up her mind."

I groaned. She probably saw herself with another doctor, a man who saved lives and did other worthy things. "Actually, I need to find her another date. The guy I had lined up went back to his girlfriend. I need someone good. The last guy was a disaster."

"Instead of finding her another date, why don't you take her out?" Tristan asked.

"Have you been talking to Hollie? Hartford would just

laugh and say I was too lazy to find her someone else."

"I've got an idea," Dexter said. "I know a doctor. Good-looking guy. Sporty. Only issue is he's a Chelsea supporter, but if we leave that aside, he's a good catch. I think he actually did that doctors in warzones thing that Hartford did."

It felt as if Dexter was slowly sinking a knife into my stomach. "How is this helpful?"

Dexter continued. "This guy isn't ready to settle down. But you can show her who he is online. She'll be excited to meet him, right?"

"Again, I'm not sure how this is helping," I said.

"You tell her that maybe she should have a practice date with you," Dexter explained. "To make sure things go well for that last date. You offer to give her feedback, tell her you'll coach her so her date with my mate goes well."

"I like it," Tristan said. "Then you can make your move."

"You should be on the date for real," Dexter said. "Pick her up, give her flowers, compliment her, take her to dinner somewhere really romantic, hold her hand across the table. Maybe kiss her at the end of the date. By the time you're done, she'll have forgotten all about my mate."

"Basically, you're saying I should trick her into going out with me?" What I liked most about my relationship with Hartford was there were no games or pretenses. I could be exactly who I was with her because she was exactly who she was with me. Except I'd gone and fucked that all up by catching feelings.

Dexter shrugged. "Not trick her exactly. She'll just get the opportunity to see you at your best. What have you got to lose?"

Hartford. Hartford was what I had to lose. But if I didn't do anything, I'd lose her anyway. It was worth a shot.

TWENTY-TWO

Joshua

It was close to midnight when I found myself pacing at my front door. I'd spent the afternoon giving feedback to the team on the research for the Merdon pitch, and since then I'd been waiting. Waiting. And pacing. Waiting. And pacing. Now that I had a plan, I was impatient. I wanted to put wheels into motion.

Finally, I heard the ping of the lift and I swung open the door.

"Hartford," I said in a tone that said I meant business. She lifted her head, revealing the dark circles under her eyes. She looked tired. And slightly frazzled. "You okay?" I said, softening. Had something happened?

She nodded. "Long day. That's all. You okay?" She yawned, covering her mouth and squeezing her eyes shut. I wanted to scoop her up, pour her some wine, and run her a bath.

But I wasn't going to do all of those things.

Not yet anyway.

"I'm fine. I was just on a call with the US and heard the lift."

"How was your day?" she asked.

"You don't want to hear about that. I should let you go to bed and get some sleep." I'd wait to tell her about her third date and my plan to "help." Even though it might kill me.

"I won't be able to sleep for hours yet. Too . . . wired. It's been a crazy day."

"I have cake." I held open the door. I'd picked up her favorite, cookies and cream.

"That sounds perfect." She collapsed on the sofa, kicking off her shoes. It made me smile because she seemed so comfortable here, as if she'd moved in. It struck me, not for the first time, that I liked having Hartford in my space. From that first week, when she popped her head in to collect me for a grocery run, her presence here had felt natural. Proof enough, if I needed it, that the boundaries I'd set for other women simply didn't apply to Hartford. I set about getting two glasses of water, each with a slice of lemon.

"I'm going flat hunting again at the weekend. There's a new place come up in Borehamwood, a one-bedroom. I think you'd like it. No chip shop below." She pulled out her phone and started scrolling. "Here," she said. "Swap you for a glass of water."

She took the drink and gave me the phone. I took a cursory look at the flat she was considering.

"I could extend on next door if you want me to," I said. "It's not a big deal. You'd have more time to figure out exactly where you wanted to live." Borehamwood was miles away. I'd never see her if she lived all the way out there.

"You're sweet. But you can't get me used to living like

I'm a celebrity. I need to get back to reality eventually."

The thought of her moving out in just a few weeks brought back my sense of urgency. "I had drinks with the boys tonight. I've found you a third date. A friend of Dexter's. He's a doctor."

Her eyes brightened. "Where does he work?"

"I have his full name. Shall I look him up?"

I typed out "Brian Sandford doctor" into my phone and up he popped. Dexter wasn't exaggerating when he said the guy was good looking. For a second, I thought about lying and saying that nothing had come up. But I needed to stick with the plan. And for the plan to work, she needed to be motivated to impress him. I turned my phone and held it up for her. "What do you think?"

"Handsome. Let me see?"

I handed her the phone and sat next to her as she scrolled through his online profile. "He's a few years older. But made consultant already. That's impressive—Oh. He did Medicines Sans Frontiers." A smile burst onto her face. How was I ever going to compete with that? "When's the date?"

"Next weekend." Now was the time when I needed to bring up going out with me. I took in a deep breath and took the plunge. "I thought that after last time, maybe you need-ed . . . I don't know, some kind of trial run."

"What do you mean? Because of David?"

"Just in case your confidence has you off balance. You don't want to be getting your sea legs with a guy like Brian, right?"

"He looks too good to be true."

"Right." I was part horrified that she'd taken such an instant liking to him, and part relieved that his profile was making my argument for me. It would have been nice if maybe even a tiny part of her had hoped that I might decide casual wasn't the order of business when it came to her. But I'd made this bed and now I had to lie in it, which was why I was Googling pictures of Brian. "So, maybe have a practice run before you go out with him?"

"What do you mean, *practice run*?"

"I don't know," I said, trying to sound as if I was thinking up ideas on the spot. "You and I could go for a drink—have a fake date."

"You and me?" She scrunched her brow as she handed me back my phone. I bit back a smile at the way her freckles danced across her nose.

"Yeah. Like we could dress up and pretend it's a date. And because you know me, you won't feel nervous. You'll get your confidence back so you're in strong form for your date with Brian."

She shifted around the sofa and looked at me. I could almost see a thousand thoughts in her head all competing with each other.

I wanted to hear every single one.

"So, we pretend we're on a date and if I'm a disaster, you can maybe give me pointers?" She didn't look horrified by the idea.

"Right. And if I do anything outrageous, perhaps you can point them out and—"

"Sounds good," she said.

The muscles in my neck all let go at the same time. "You're up for it?" Had she understood what the idea was?

"Yeah. But if we're splitting the bill, can we not go to that Heston Blummenthingy restaurant? I just walked by there and the prices are insane."

"What about if I pay?"

"Is that allowed? I mean, doesn't that violate our split-the-bill rule?"

"For the sake of the experiment, let dinner at Heston Blummenthingy's restaurant be on me."

She held my gaze as if she was considering saying something. She looked away. "Okay then, dinner. You and me. What do I wear?"

I picked up my phone again. I'd seen something the other day that I thought would look gorgeous on Hartford. Now was the perfect excuse to buy it for her. "This," I said, holding up my phone.

"Pretty. But how much?"

"What size are you?"

"They price it depending on size?"

"No, just tell me your size."

"Twelve UK. Which is why I'm not eating any of your late-night cake."

I chuckled. She had nothing to worry about. She was perfect. "And shoe size?" If I was going to dress her, it would be head to toe.

"I have shoes," she said.

"Shoe size?" I'd seen some beautiful Lanvins that would work perfectly with that dress.

"Six. Although they might have grown to a size twelve today. They feel like they're busting out of my shoes right now."

"You want a foot rub?" I asked.

A grin unfurled on her face. "You're the best. But I like you too much to do that to you."

I smiled back. "I like you enough to mean it when I offer you one."

"Do you think the neighbors in Borehamwood are as friendly as you?"

I laughed. I hoped not.

TWENTY-THREE

Hartford

There must have been some mistake. I looked at the beautiful black lace dress I'd just uncovered from the clouds of tissue it had been wrapped in. It was the one Joshua had shown me on his phone. I picked up the card that had come with it to read it for a third time.

You'll look beautiful. I can't wait to see you in it tonight. Love Joshua

The man had lost it. What was he buying me clothes for? It wasn't just the dress—he'd sent shoes too. And a handbag. Maybe he was afraid I might turn up to dinner in scrubs and embarrass him. To be fair, it was a distinct possibility. Maybe he had all his hopes pinned onto this Brian and wanted me to impress him so he could feel less responsibility for me. That was probably it. For all I knew, he did this with every date. If so, it was impressive. And a little controlling, especially if he didn't know the woman. I grabbed my notebook from my dressing table and scribbled a reminder. Joshua and I had agreed to give each other feedback on the date and I didn't want to forget. I'd tell him that for a girlfriend, this was an amazing thing to do, but for a first date, a little overbearing. Then again, I could think of a million women who'd be blown away by a guy buying them a dress like this before a date. My seventeen-year-old self would have exploded at the thought.

It was an hour before Joshua said we had to leave, so I had plenty of time. I set to the task of taming my hair just as my phone buzzed.

I'll be there in an hour. Can't wait to see you. xx

A pre-date text? With two kisses? Oh, his charm was in overdrive tonight. I needed to have a quiet word with my ovaries to let them know Joshua was putting on a show and not to get over-excited. I'd been fortifying my forcefield all week, and thank God. Here I was, about to go on a fake date with Joshua, having to remind myself that this situation might have been my teenage dream but it still wasn't real. When did life get so complicated?

I should reply. I had to take this as seriously as he was.

I typed out, *Looking forward to it, Joshua.*

I paused. Should I add kisses? That had never been a thing between Joshua and me on our texts. But if he was Brian . . . I'd probably send a kiss if he had, right?

I added two kisses and pressed Send.

I'd been looking forward to a relaxing evening with someone who was turning out to be my best friend. But if he was going to go all charming-loverman-player on me, I'd have to up my game.

In forty-five minutes, I'd managed to wrangle some mascara and blush, and my hair was actually behaving itself for once. I'd even managed some polish on my toes. The woman in the mirror looked . . . fine. Pretty, if understated. Despite standing in only my underwear, I was sweating like

I was in the Sahara. I padded over to the bathroom and ran a flannel under some cold water, then held it against the various parts of my body that felt like they were on fire. I wasn't made for dressing up. It wasn't in my biology.

When I'd cooled down a little, I returned to my bedroom and stared at the dress hanging in the doorway. It was so beautiful. I bet I'd rip it getting it on. I went back into the bathroom and washed my hands, determined to make absolutely sure that I didn't get any marks on it before I left the building.

My hands were shaking as I took the dress from the hanger and unzipped it. Trying to be as careful as I could, I stepped into the frock and shimmied it over my hips. At least it fit. I slipped my arms in and reached around the back to the zip. The fabric felt beautifully soft against my skin and held me in at all the right places. I stepped into the dressing area to take a look.

Wow. I didn't look like me. I looked like one of the women I saw passing through the lobby of the hotel. I *almost* looked like I belonged on Joshua's arm. At least I wouldn't embarrass him. Now I just needed to channel the power and confidence of the Rokeby Venus.

I slid on the super-strappy sandals. Just as I reached for my clutch, Joshua knocked on the door.

Excitement bubbled in my stomach—something I'd not felt with either of the two dates Joshua had set me up with so far. Probably because I knew I was going to have a great evening tonight and I didn't need to worry about impressing a stranger. It took the pressure off.

"Hey," I said as I opened the door, grinning.

Joshua lifted his chin. "Wow."

"You like?" I did a little spin. "You have excellent taste."

"You're beautiful," he said.

"It took me over an hour to get ready. Can you believe it?"

Joshua laughed. "These are for you." He handed me a posey of flowers in a square bag with fancy writing on it.

"You're too much. You didn't need to get me flowers." I took a deep breath, inhaling the scent of the pink and yellow roses and freesias. "They are beautiful though."

"Your dates should bring you flowers. You're worth it."

I tilted my head and gave him my best don't-be-ridiculous look. "Get out of it."

"If your date brings you flowers, don't tell him to 'get out of it.' Thank him. Got it?"

"Thank you, Joshua." I looked at him, a little puzzled. The dress, the texts, and now the flowers? He really was going above and beyond.

"You're more than welcome. They're in water so will be fine until you get home."

I set the flowers down in the hall and shut the door behind me.

"Let's go." Joshua held out his hand.

I slid my palm against his and it felt like the most natural thing in the world. "I can't remember the last time I held a man's hand other than you." Tonight, and earlier in the week, when he'd led me to the perfect thirty-eight-degree bath.

"Me neither," he said.

It didn't take long to get to the restaurant. Joshua was a gentleman the entire way, opening doors—though he always did that. Paying me compliments—again, a common occurrence with Joshua. He asked about my week, which was par for the course. As much as he was an excellent fake date, he'd been a real friend to me these months. Something in my chest tightened at the thought of moving away in just a few weeks' time. I'd miss him.

We were seated in a small booth at the back of the restaurant. "I'm a little concerned," I said. "I don't think most men I date will be this attentive. If the conversation dries up, what do I do?"

"Do whatever comes naturally. Be yourself." Easy for him to say. Joshua always knew the right thing to say.

I laughed. "You know that's a bad idea."

"No," he said a little more firmly that I would have expected. "It's not a bad idea. You're a great person and fun to be around."

I groaned. "You're meant to be helping me. That's the point of being here. I'm not going to learn anything if you just tell me I'm great." That was the thing about Joshua; when I was with him, he acted like I was the most interesting and funny person he'd ever met. All part of his charm I supposed.

He held my gaze as if he were about to say something, but before he could, a waiter interrupted and Joshua ordered us cocktails. I stayed silent, wanting to hear what he was about to say, but the moment had passed.

"Will a man normally do that? You didn't ask me what I wanted, but you chose the one on the list I would have picked for myself."

"That's because I know you. You can't expect your dates to be mind-readers. But if you like when I order for you, you can make a point of telling your date what you'd like to have. See what he does when the waitress comes by."

"True. Brian is going to have a lot to live up to."

He smiled like I'd just given him the biggest compliment.

"Are you okay?" I asked. He seemed sort of different.

Still the same Joshua I felt comfortable with and loved hanging out with, but somehow a concentrated version. I wondered if this is what it felt like to be taken out by Joshua —to be his girlfriend. The dress, the flowers, the compliments—Joshua wasn't one of those boys who peaked in high school. He got better with age. Damn him.

"Having the time of my life. You?"

The time of his life? He was being sarcastic, right? The fact was, if he asked me the same question, I could answer honestly the exact same way. Being with Joshua had become my new favorite thing to do.

"I got an email from Thea today," I said. "Are we allowed to be talking like we know each other?"

"You want full-on role play mode?" he asked. "If so, Doctor, I've got a terrible ache that needs kissing away. It's right—"

I put a hand over his mouth, barely containing my laughter. "I think I'd prefer it if we were just us. But . . ." I glanced down at my dress. "I have a spare white coat back at the apartment." If he was going to do the sexy-flirty thing, I was going to *try* to give it back.

"Noted—and maybe one of these days, I'll have you dress up and do me a full body check, but tonight I'd prefer it if we were just us too. What did Thea have to say?"

"Just telling me about the classroom politics at the school she's working in. And moaning about mum's interfering. You know, nothing dramatic."

"I guess interfering is part of the job of being a mother."

"My mother thinks so. Obviously, I don't hear from Patrick unless it's my birthday or Christmas. He's off doing whatever it is he's doing in Singapore. How come you two never stayed in touch?"

"No particular reason. University overtook things. We'd

both made new friends, and I didn't go home much so I didn't see him. I suppose I was lazy." There was no doubt that Joshua was charming, but he was also honest. He never tried to pretend he was someone he wasn't and he always underplayed his skills and achievements. Even if I did say so myself, I had pretty good taste as a teenager. I didn't waste an obsession on some badly behaved pop star or over-hyped actor. Joshua was a really good man. Then. Now.

"I guess that's what happens," I replied. "Unless someone's important and you make an effort to keep them in your orbit, they float away." It had only been a couple of months, but I was so used to spending time with Joshua, telling him about my day or hearing about his latest demanding client, that it was going to be a real shift when I moved.

"Are you going to float away, Hartford?" Joshua asked, as if he'd read my mind. He fixed me with a stare that told me he wasn't making a joke. "I want you in my orbit."

My stomach dipped. He sounded so serious, so unusually earnest. If it hadn't been Joshua in front of me, it would have felt almost romantic. Like we were two people who really liked each other on a real date. A man coughing three or four tables away caught my attention. I tried to dismiss the thought that he needed a good slap on the back—I wanted to give Joshua my full attention. I wanted to know why he'd sounded almost pleading.

But then the screaming started.

I was on my feet and across the room in a matter of moments. The screams were coming from the female companion of a man clutching his throat and turning a pale shade of blue.

"He's choking!" she shouted. "Someone help him! Please!"

The balding man had stood and was pulling at his

collar. He was at least a foot taller than me. I needed to administer a Heimlich but wasn't going to be able to get the right angle, even with the added height from my heels. I kicked off my shoes and then jumped onto the chair the man had vacated.

I wrapped my arms around him, clasped my hands together, and *yanked*.

It didn't help, but at least I found the bottom of his rib cage. I jerked my fists in and up again, and something gave; his body released and he gasped for breath. I leapt off the chair just as he plonked himself down.

"I thought my time was up," the man said in an American accent. "Thank you, miss." He took a deep breath and blew it out dramatically.

I crouched down bedside him and took his wrist, wanting to make sure his pulse was steady. "Have some water and rest a while. You should go to hospital. You seem fine, but I can't perform all the checks they can in casualty."

"I'm fine. Breathin', thanks to you."

"I know but—"

"This is the best goddamn steak I've ever eaten." He poked at his plate with a pudgy finger. "I don't say that lightly. I come from Texas—a good steak is a way of life out there. There's no way I'm leavin' this restaurant until I'm done or dead."

I tried not to roll my eyes as I turned to the woman next to him, who I assumed was his wife. "Some food could have made its way into his lungs. He really needs to go to a hospital. I don't even have a stethoscope with me." *Note to self: find evening clutch large enough for necessities.*

"Thank you, honey," his wife said. "But my husband is the most stubborn steak eater you'll ever meet. I'll keep an eye on him."

"Please do. And if he struggles to breathe at all, take him straight to A&E."

"Don't you worry." She patted me on the arm. "Can I write you a check or somethin' to say thank you?"

I slipped my shoes back on. "Absolutely no need. Enjoy your dinner."

I turned to find Joshua staring at me, his mouth slightly agape. I smiled and wandered back over to our table.

"You're Wonder Woman," he said.

I rolled my eyes at his teasing. "Sorry to interrupt—"

"Only you would apologize for saving a man's life. You were amazing. He would have choked to death."

I shrugged. "He didn't." I glanced back over my shoulder at the guy laughing with his wife. "Hopefully he won't develop aspiration pneumonia. But I've done what I can."

The waiters made more of a fuss of me than I was comfortable with. They brought us a bottle of champagne along with our starters.

"This is nice." I picked up a champagne flute. "I feel like I at least contributed to dinner in some way now."

"You being here with me is all the contribution I wanted." Joshua raised his glass. "Let's make a toast."

"To not choking on our dinner?" I suggested.

"To staying in each other's orbits," he countered.

I grinned, a warm feeling chasing down my limbs. Until now I'd forgotten what we'd been talking about. "I'll drink to that." I hoped Joshua and I would see each other after I moved.

I'd miss him.

Too much.

That was why the interruption from the Texan diner had come at the right time. It was as if Joshua had unwittingly been casting a spell over me all evening. I needed to remind myself that tonight wasn't a real date. He didn't see me like that and I had a forcefield around me to make sure I didn't see him like that. We were friends. With a history. That was all.

TWENTY-FOUR

Joshua

The evening wasn't going to plan. Hartford was still dismissing my flirting, and she couldn't take a compliment no matter how many I gave her. I was supposed to be *stoking the fire of desire* according to Tristan, but so far, I hadn't seen evidence of so much as a spark.

"You know, you've got me thinking . . .I know I agreed to all this dating stuff to keep Gerry happy, but I'm coming round to the idea that maybe finding someone to love might not be the worst thing in the world."

I nodded and glanced down to see if my heart was actually beating out of my chest. Had I managed to break through to her? Or was she talking about love in the abstract? Someone she might find in the future?

The attraction I felt for Hartford wasn't anything like what I'd felt for Diana. It felt deeper somehow, despite the fact that Diana and I were going to be married. We'd both been so young and stupid. Hartford was delightfully open and honest, but she wasn't naïve. I'd watched her save a man's life tonight, stop a family's grief before it started. She was phenomenally capable, and although she was a little green in so many ways, it was nowhere that mattered. She was a clever, sensitive, caring woman. I completely respected her. But it was more than that. As I sat holding her hand, listening to her experiences of medical school and Yemen, her theories on death and love, I couldn't look away from the variety of expressions that danced across her face, the way she was so kind to the waiter, the patterns she drew in the air with her free hand as she waved it around to emphasize words here and there.

By the end of the evening, if I'd had any doubts of my need to be with Hartford, they had all fallen away.

"We should go," Hartford said, glancing around. "There's only us and one other couple left."

"I'd stay here all night listening to you."

She tilted her head and smiled. "So smooth, Joshua."

She thought everything I said was a line. But it wasn't. It never was when I was with her because I didn't need to fake anything when she was around. I could just come out and say it, tell her how I was feeling—be as open and honest with her as she was with me. It was a risk, and one I wasn't prepared to take at the moment. I wanted her to know I was serious; my feelings for her weren't going to change overnight.

I nodded to the nearby waiter, getting his attention for him to bring the bill. "Just a hint. You might want to act a bit more impressed by your next date."

"I'm immune," she said, tapping her nose. "Created a Joshua Luca forcefield when my mum said she'd arranged me to sleep in your guest bedroom."

The waiter interrupted with the bill before I got to ask about the forcefield.

"You've been so kind to me with the flat next door and coming to Gerry's for dinner, introducing me to your friends, setting me up on dates, and now so thoroughly preparing me for one."

We'd spent a lot of time together the last couple of months. I might have only realized that I wanted Harford recently, but looking back, the feeling had been coming on for . . . since that first day when I picked her up from the airport. "You've been a terrible burden, Hartford. But I've endured."

"You can't call me a terrible burden! I'm your date for the evening. I presume if Mr. Number Three tells me I'm a burden, I should cut the date short?"

"If anyone ever calls you a burden, you need to give me a call and I can remind you of the time you saved a man's life over dinner."

We locked eyes again. For a moment, I thought she understood what I was thinking, how I was feeling. Did she understand that this date was anything but fake for me, that I wanted her to see how much I liked her? Then the scrape of tables being moved at the other end of the restaurant broke the spell, and she grabbed her bag. I led her out of the restaurant.

I slipped my hand into hers as we headed back to the residences, strolling along in the warmth of the summer evening. Being with her felt so incredibly right—like life was exactly how it was meant to be.

"If he offers to walk me home, what do I say?" she asked me.

"It depends if you like him. It might be easier to take a cab, even if it's walkable. Then you don't have to make a decision about whether or not you want him to come up." The very thought of another man riding up the elevator with her, his hands at her low back, his lips on her— "He'll just see you to the cab door if he's worth knowing, which this guy apparently is."

She nodded as if she was assimilating what I'd just told her. "That way, I don't have to deal with any kind of . . . kissing incident."

"Kissing incident?"

"Yes. Can you imagine if he wants to kiss me?" She made a face like she couldn't fathom anything worse. I hope she hadn't felt like that about our kiss.

"You might want to kiss him," I replied over the dull pang in my gut.

"I can't imagine I will," she said. "He'll be a virtual stranger. And we will have just eaten."

As we continued back to the residences and up to the penthouse floor, she continued to tell me all the reasons she didn't think she'd be kissing her date. I was happy to listen.

When we reached her front door, she turned to me. "I had the best time tonight." She beamed up at me as if she couldn't have wished for better company. "You're a great date." Her bluest of blue eyes sparkled clear and bright.

She pulled out her keys.

"You've forgotten one thing," I said.

She frowned at me.

"The goodnight kiss." I stepped closer to her and circled one arm around her waist. "I mean, we should be thorough."

She gazed up at me, and I wasn't sure what it was I could see in her expression—did she want this as much as I did?

"Okay?" I asked as I cupped her face.

Her mouth opened slightly as if she was going to say something, then she seemed to think better of it and just nodded.

My heart thumped on my ribcage as if it were desperate to be let out. I took a breath to steady myself.

Don't fuck this up, Luca.

Why was I so nervous? I'd kissed her before. We'd slept together, for goodness' sake. I supposed the difference was now I knew what I wanted and what I had to lose.

As if she could sense my anxiety, she gave me a small smile. It was all the encouragement I needed.

I dipped my head and pressed my lips to hers. This time I wasn't trying to silence her. Or calm her down and make her see she was beautiful. I was just doing what felt good. Again. And again. I couldn't remember focusing so much on a kiss before. Usually, I was more interested in what came after the kiss. But all I could think about in this moment were her warm, soft lips and the scent of cinnamon. My tongue glided into her mouth and I had to tamp down the urge to slide my hand up her dress and press her against the door with my hips. Her hands crept up my chest and I sank into her touch. It just felt so right. Hopefully she was thinking the exact same thing.

Eventually, I pulled back and watched as she opened her eyes.

"Right," she said, nodding. "I always think I must have been imagining it, but nope. No wonder."

She wasn't making much sense. "No wonder?"

"No wonder you can have your pick of women when you can kiss like that."

I grinned. That didn't sound like I'd fucked up.

"Can I though?" I asked.

Her eyebrows pulled together a fraction, but she didn't answer. And I knew, beyond the shadow of a doubt, that there was at least one woman I wanted who I simply could not have.

"I should go inside," she said. "That's what I should say now? Even if he's as hot as you and can kiss like that?"

"You're thinking of inviting me in?"

"Goddamn that dimple," she said. "I should definitely excuse myself or I'm going to . . ." She narrowed her eyes as if she were trying to make sense of our ridiculous situation. Instead of finishing her sentence, she pressed her palms to either side of my face and drew me toward her lips. I closed my eyes, expecting to feel her mouth on mine, but instead she pressed a soft kiss just to the side of my mouth, where I realized that goddamn dimple must have appeared. I couldn't help my smile, or the sharp intake of breath that rushed into my lungs when Hartford's soft kiss turned into a gentle bite. Before I could react, she'd kissed the spot again. "I've been thinking about doing that for fifteen years," she whispered, her voice gone husky. "Good night, Joshua."

She scuttled inside as if she'd catch fire if she stayed out a moment longer.

When her door shut, I pulled in a deep breath.

One date wasn't going to be enough to have her see me as potential boyfriend material. But it was enough to tell me she was the only woman I wanted.

I just needed her to see I was the only man she needed.

TWENTY-FIVE

Hartford

I threw open the curtains in the living room to reveal an unusually blue sky for London, even in summer. I needed some fresh air to clear my head, so despite the air conditioning, I pushed open the windows. In the twelve hours since dinner with Joshua, everything had become a little bit fuzzy. Not only was my forcefield faltering, but after our fake date, I wanted to reach for the off switch. Last night was supposed to have been pretend, but there were moments that felt so very real. I was still trying to make sense of it.

The knock at the door had my heart racing. Even though I knew it was just Stella, I was still sort of hoping it would be Joshua.

"Hey!" I opened the door to Stella weighed down by shopping bags. I quickly grabbed a couple from her. Crikey. They were heavy. "What have you got in here?"

"Flour. And other bits. I thought we'd bake some bread."

Stella was taking her teacher role very seriously. Given what an excellent baker she was, I wasn't surprised.

"You think I'm ready for bread?"

"Of course you're ready for bread." We put the bags onto the island and set about unpacking them. "I didn't really bake until I moved in with Beck, but bread was the first thing I made in our new home. The kitchen in our flat is just so bloody amazing, I wanted to use it as much as possible. I didn't have a clue what I was doing."

"I would have thought you'd grown up baking. You're so good."

"Nope. I'm a newbie really." She pulled out an apron and looped it over her head before securing it around her waist, then went to the sink and washed her hands. I copied everything she did like a good student. "Before Beck, I spent a long time with a man I thought I was going to marry. Then he married my best friend, and I met Beck. Life has chapters. Who you were at the start of the story isn't who you'll be at the end. I wasn't born a baker and you didn't come out of the womb a doctor.

"Okay, let's get out the KitchenAid." Stella slid it out of the cupboard, placed it on the counter, and plugged it in. "So how's Joshua? Still being a good neighbor?"

I wasn't sure if my cheeks flushed red as I nodded, but they felt like they were on fire. I couldn't think about Joshua without thinking about last night. And the night we'd gotten naked. And our first kiss. And then all the times in between when I just loved being with him.

"Of course," I replied. "You know what Joshua's like." I tried to put on my best we're-all-friends voice, but something about it didn't ring true. There was no doubt that over the last six or seven weeks, Joshua and I had developed a true friendship. But over those weeks, something had shifted.

"Not really," Stella said. "Normally Joshua is about work or his friends or going to one of a million parties he's invited to or . . . you know, doing whatever he does with whoever he does it with."

Jealousy seeped into my brain and I tried to brush it away with a hard blink. I wasn't jealous of anyone sleeping with Joshua. Because I was immune. Because I still had a Joshua Luca forcefield around me.

Maybe less of a forcefield and more of a sturdy fence.

A velvet rope.

A voile curtain.

"Beck mentioned you two were setting each other up on dates," Stella said.

"Yeah. One more to go. This next one is a doctor. Joshua wants me to be prepared. He's coaching me." I was fairly sure our fake date had ruined me for all other men. I wasn't even certain I wanted to meet Brian anymore. What was the point, really, knowing he'd never measure up to Joshua?

"Coaching you?"

"I don't have much dating experience—too focused on work all these years—so he's helping." Again, more evidence of Joshua being kind. I couldn't think of anything I didn't like about him.

"What does this coaching involve? Lessons in how to . . . what?"

"Not lessons exactly." I was trying to think about the things that Joshua had actually said to correct me last night. "We went to dinner last night. You know, as a practice run."

"Where did you go?"

"Just this place up the road from the hotel. He bought me the perfect dress to wear. So that helped—"

Stella froze, a spoonful of flour hovering over the bowl. "Pause. Tell me how that works. Joshua . . . bought you a dress?"

"Yes," I said. "So I wouldn't be stressed about picking out my outfit. It's totally gorgeous and I can't imagine what it cost him, but it was just so great being able to wear something I knew was going to be appropriate."

"He bought you a dress, took you to dinner. This sounds like an *actual* date."

I swallowed, not quite knowing what to say. I wasn't about to confess to the handholding and the kissing. I hadn't wanted to admit it even to myself, but whispers of suspicion had been creeping up on me. Last night had been one of the most enjoyable nights of my life. And nothing about it had seemed fake.

"If I tell you something, do you promise not to say anything to anyone?"

Stella promised solemnly.

I took a breath before my confession. "I think I might like him. Like *really* like him. I know that's stupid. It's Joshua we're talking about. He doesn't do relationships and he's used to dating supermodels—"

"It's not stupid," Stella said, her tone certain. "The salt can't touch the yeast." Stella handed me a packet of dried yeast. "You need to put them at opposite edges of the flour."

"But they're all going to be mixed together in the end anyway."

"I don't get it either, but I've tried to mix it at the beginning and it doesn't work."

I set about measuring the ingredients and placing them carefully into the mixing bowl, then mixed with a wooden spoon.

"I think you and Joshua make a great pairing. I've seen

Joshua at these parties he throws for work and he's terribly smooth and uber-charming. And then I see him when he's with Beck and the guys and he's smooth and charming but he's also . . . more authentically himself. When he's with you, it's the real Joshua I see. Not some souped-up version. I think he can be himself with you."

I laughed. "But that's because he sees me as a friend rather than . . ." We had slept together but it was just a one-off. Then last night . . . that kiss. I shook my head. I didn't know what the hell was going on.

"A friend doesn't buy you dresses. Next you'll be telling me he kissed you at the end of the evening, *for practice*."

She glanced at me when I didn't respond.

"He kissed you?"

I nodded.

Stella started to laugh. "He might have been telling you the date was fake, but there's no way Joshua is kissing a woman he doesn't want to kiss."

"But if he wanted to date me, why wouldn't he just ask me out on a date? The man isn't shy."

Stella sighed. "I don't have an answer to that."

"Exactly." And in the alternative universe where Joshua Luca wanted to ask me out on a date, what on earth would I say? I'd created a forcefield around myself to ensure that I couldn't make the same mistake as I did when I'd been an infatuated teenager. But I wasn't seventeen anymore. He wasn't a teenage god. I was a doctor who made good decisions every day. He was a generous, loyal man who had showed me—and everyone around him—nothing but kindness.

TWENTY-SIX

Hartford

If Joshua Luca asked me to go to the moon, I'd probably say yes.

Which explained why I'd just stepped out of the shower instead of being curled up in bed catching up on *Made in Chelsea*. It had been a long week at the hospital as Gerry and I continued our efforts to prepare to stop Merdon getting their ADHD drug approved by the regulator as soon as their application was announced. Somehow Joshua had wrangled a promise out of me to go to lunch with him. I should have said no because things were . . . unclear between us, and I didn't want them to get any messier. But despite myself, I'd agreed. He was just so utterly convincing about everything—even that I should accept the parcel I'd found on my doorstep when I got home last night.

The dress packed in the tissue stuffed in the beautiful black glossy box was beyond beautiful. I would never have considered it if I'd seen it in the shop, but given the note he

left with it, he knew that's how I'd feel. It said, "Trust me. It
will look great. Wear it to lunch tomorrow."

More gifts. Another arrangement to meet—even if it
was for lunch. This felt like more than friendship.

I toweled off and unzipped the tiered, floaty, floral
dress. If my mother was here, she'd tell me it looked like
Grandma Green's bedroom curtains. And it did a little bit.
But that didn't stop it from being gorgeous. I stepped into it,
the lining slipping over my skin in the way that only expensive fabric did. I zipped it up and the fit was perfect, as if it
had been especially made for me. Joshua had supplied
sandals, which fit as if someone had made molds of my feet.

I spun in front of the mirror, loving the way the air
caught under the skirt and lifted it up. I wasn't one to
complain, and the outfit was completely gorgeous, but it
seemed a little over the top for a sandwich at Pret.

Right on time, Joshua knocked on the door.

"I feel overdressed for a sandwich," I said as I answered
the door. I swept my hand down my dress.

"Agreed. If you get asked to go for a sandwich, don't
wear this." He grinned at me like he just won an account
from Gucci. I knew he was dying to work with them.

"We're not going to get a sandwich? You said lunch."

Joshua was wearing pale blue-grey trousers and a white
shirt without a tie. The pair of us could be going to a
wedding.

He laughed and held out his hand. "There might be
sandwiches, among other things. We're having a picnic. Just
across the road."

He held out his hand and without thinking, I took it.
We made our way to the lifts.

"We're holding hands," I said, stating the obvious as we
rode down to the ground floor. "Is this another fake date?"

"I thought you needed a daytime date under your belt."

"I appreciate your commitment to my success." I tried to catch his eye but he was focused ahead.

We crossed the lobby and emerged into the fresh air. I couldn't see Joshua as a picnic kind of guy, but it looked like he was serious about eating alfresco.

I resigned myself to feeling confused.

"Tell me about your week. I've barely seen you."

"Nope, you just haven't had to babysit me as much this week." I grinned up at him but he just frowned back. "As well as doing the normal doctory stuff, I'm working with Gerry on a project that . . ." I still couldn't break Gerry's confidence about Merdon getting the over-the-counter approval for Calmation, even though talking to Joshua might help spark some ideas. I didn't want Gerry's contact getting into trouble. I could safely give Joshua the outline without mentioning names. "We're working to stop the health regulator from approving a new drug that's coming out."

"Aren't new drugs a good thing?" he asked.

"I guess it depends. The pharma company is hoping to get this drug licensed for over-the-counter sales. Every pediatrician who knows anything would think it was a terrible idea if they knew."

"Over-the-counter sales? Which drug is it?"

I shook my head. "I can't say. I'm sorry. I wish I could. It would be great to get your help with it."

He frowned. "If it's a bad idea, the regulator will say no, won't it?"

If only life was that easy. "You'd hope so." I wished I could tell him everything. "But we want to make sure that children's interests are being looked after." Gerry and I had started to unofficially lobby against the drug. We'd mined our contacts to see if we could reach people who had influence at the regulator and were briefing them privately. Gerry was also using his high profile to get booked on TV and radio to talk about the effects of the recession on children, and bringing up the importance of mental health and doctor-parent collaborative care. It felt like we were taking action, and it was exciting to be part of something bigger than just treating individual patients. What we were doing could impact tens of thousands of children.

"It's a drug for children?"

I nodded. "Children with ADHD. We're trying to make sure desperate parents aren't taken advantage of." I shouldn't say anything else. I knew Joshua didn't have much experience in pharma, but the world was a small place and I didn't want to get anyone into trouble. "So anyway, I've been researching stuff and planning things with Gerry. We've been busy. So no babysitting duties for you."

Joshua squeezed my hand as he led me across the busy road to the park. "I've never babysat for you, Hartford. You're perfectly able to look after yourself, cast or no cast, as we both know. We just have mothers who like to interfere."

He always knew the exact right thing to say.

"I'm not as green as she thinks I am."

"Having kissed you, I would agree with that."

Before I could ask him what he meant, he dropped my hand and turned me to the left. A patchwork of picnic blankets had been lain on the ground and large, jewel-colored, poufy cushions were strewn around a central, low table. Over a white cloth, plates and dishes and glasses and jugs in gorgeous colors and patterns beckoned us to explore the delicacies they held. "It looks like something out of a photoshoot."

He chuckled. "Funny that. I did have some help from a prop-stylist friend of mine."

"It's beautiful," I said, seeing something new every time I looked. *Was that a cake stand under that muslin cloth?* "No man is going to do something like this for me."

"A man already has," he said, taking a seat on one of the cushions and pulling me down next to him. "Champagne?"

I nodded, still confused about what we were doing here. "What made you think of this?" I asked. "It's so pretty and thoughtful and honestly, Joshua, I'm not sure how you don't have a girlfriend. You're absolutely killing the romantic gesture game." This was the kind of thing boyfriends did. Not neighbors. Not friends. I might not date much, but I knew that. I also knew that if he wanted us to be something more, he needed to say. Joshua wasn't shy. He didn't get to have the business and lifestyle he had by being coy. If he wanted this to be real, he would tell me. And if he didn't, I'd read the entire situation wrong somehow.

He handed me a glass but didn't let go. He looked at me for a long moment before finally releasing his fingers. "I thought it would make you smile. And it's my way of saying thank you."

"What do you mean? Thank you for what?"

He shrugged. "You bring out a better man in me. You need to know that you make a difference, just by being you."

I wasn't sure anyone had ever said anything nicer to me. *Ever.* I was waiting for a but. I kept waiting. It never came.

"Of course, there's cake," Joshua said, pulling the muslin cloth off of the cake stand. "A series of miniatures from the hotel. And then there are strawberries." He pulled a cloche off a bowl full of strawberries speckled with vibrant sprigs of fresh mint. "And sandwiches of course." He revealed another cake stand under another cloth.

"Can we live here?" I asked, scanning the table and trying to figure out which of the delectable treats I was going to start with.

"It's better than Borehamwood." He grinned and handed me a tea plate.

"My lease starts on Tuesday. Who will you borrow a cup of sugar from when I'm gone?"

He froze, the cake mid-air. "You didn't tell me you signed for a place already." He put a selection of mini cakes on our plate and handed me a fork.

"Well, my three months at the residences are up at the end of next week. And this place is nice. It makes sense. Close to the train line."

"I won't visit you out there, you know. No one will."

"That's okay. I'll have my cats. And my knitting. You'll be rid of me."

"Finally," he said. "This babysitting gig is over."

I'd miss Park Lane. Not because of the hotel or the fancy security. Not because of the plush carpet or the windows that overlooked the park. But because of my neighbor. He'd started off as my first love and changed into something even better—a really great friend and a man who arranged picnics in the park and took me to dinner.

A man who kissed me.

A man who'd done things to my body that should be illegal.

"So you have one date left." He set his plate back on the table and shifted so he was cross-legged and facing me.

"Yes, the doctor. Who is going to be *very* impressed with my kissing skills, thanks to you."

"You don't have me to thank for your kissing skills."

"You're right. You don't deserve thanks. I'm ruined after that kiss."

"Ruined? How do you work that out?"

"Isn't it obvious? No man is ever going to be able to kiss me like you did—right out of my shoes. I'm ruined. Every kiss I have from now on is going to be compared to yours and it will come out wanting—I'm sure of that." Just the thought of that kiss had my skin tingling and shivers snaking up my spine.

The corners of his mouth turned to the sky and he gave me one of his trademark smiles. "Out of your shoes, huh?"

Was he genuinely being coy for the first time in his life?

"You know."

He took my plate from me and set it on the table and then kneeled up, took my hands in his, and kissed me again. Out of my shoes.

He pulled me onto his lap and cupped my face in his hands as his tongue worked its magic against mine.

This didn't feel like a practice lunch date or a lesson in kissing. My brain was filled with a faint buzzing I recognized as the sound of my forcefield officially giving up. I wanted this man whose arms I was in. And I wanted to know if he wanted me too.

"I'm sitting on your lap," I said.

He circled his arms around me and nodded. "It's nice."

"Ruining me so I can never kiss another man without comparing him to you wasn't enough? You had to bring me here, with all this"—I indicated our picnic set up—"so the bar will be set impossibly high for future romantic dates. Now you're going to hold me while we watch the clouds pass overhead. Where's the poetry, Joshua? I mean, you've come this far. We should have poetry."

"I agree." He slid me off his lap so I was sitting beside him and then he lay back, patting the ground beside him so I would do the same.

Joshua tucked his arms behind his head and cleared his throat. "'On the Ning Nang Nong all the cows go bong and the monkeys all say boo—'"

I started to laugh. "You can't recite the Ning Nang Nong to me. You're totally breaking the mood."

"Then what?" he said, "Ah. Okay, I have the perfect poem."

"No more Spike Milligan," I said, mockingly serious.

"I promise."

"Then go ahead."

"'The more it snows, tiddley pom . . .'"

I pushed up on my elbows. "That's not poetry." I tried to shoot him a stern look, but my smile gave me away.

He pushed up so we were face-to-face, nose-to-nose, then he kissed me again. I was less stunned this time and more intent on savoring the firmness of his lips and the press of his tongue.

As he pulled away, we rested our foreheads together. I pressed my fingers along his jaw, exploring what it might be like to really be with this man beside me instead of just pretending. A man who'd just confessed to being a better man with me in his life.

We parted and he took my hand in his like we were a couple who'd been together a decade.

"I beg to differ," he went on. "'The More it Snows' might just be the best poem ever. Besides, it's the only one I know by heart. There's one by Keats I quite like but I can only remember one line." He furrowed his brow in concentration. "'Heard melodies are sweet, but those unheard even sweeter.' For some reason, I don't seem to like it as much as I used to. 'The More it Snows' or 'The Ning Nang Nong' is more my style, I think."

"You're still seven years old in your head, aren't you?"

"Not seven but maybe seventeen. Aren't you?"

All I could remember about being seventeen was the accident. It had made me grow up fast. I'd slipped on a cloak of heaviness after giving up what I'd dreamed of, and I'd never been able to shrug it off. I'd been happy since then, of course, never more so than when I was busy. But when I was with Joshua, I could imagine a life that was more than that. A life where I could be happy in the silence.

"This is all beautiful." I wanted to know what was going on between us. I needed to understand whether I was reading something into nothing.

He looked at me and grinned. "I'd call this afternoon pretty close to perfect."

The thoughtfulness, the preparation, the kissing. I needed clarity. I wanted to understand why we were here. I summoned all my courage and took a deep breath. "I'd call it a date."

He pulled me closer. "I'd agree—a perfect date."

TWENTY-SEVEN

Joshua

This might go down as one of the best days of my life.

I squeezed her hand as I led Hartford out of the lift to the penthouse floor.

"It's been such an incredible afternoon, Joshua. Thank you. When you do something, you really go all out."

It had been worth getting up at five to finalize the Calmation pitch so I could have the afternoon off to be with Hartford. I'd only just got it finished with ten minutes to shower and change. I'd left the hard copies printing off on the printer I'd set up on the dining room table, and the team were fully briefed. We were ready to go on Monday, and I was enjoying my time with Hartford before then. Life was about balance. Business and rest. Work and play.

The way Hartford's eyes had lit up when she'd seen the picnic in the park would stay with me forever. She'd looked overwhelmed. Delighted. Like I'd given her the moon. I could have punched the air. I hadn't quite been sure how it would go down. She didn't often relax, so taking her to drink champagne and eat cake in the park had been a risk. It had been worth it to see her expression. And then when she'd called it a date, it was as if the blood in my veins had stopped. She'd figured out this was no practice run for me.

I just needed to know if *she* was still pretending.

We came to a stop outside her door and I leaned against the doorway, taking in her relaxed smile and bright, ice-blue eyes. She seemed to get more beautiful the more I got to know her.

"You're worth it." I took a step closer to her so we were toe to toe, tipped her head back and kissed her. Because that was what a date should do after an afternoon like we'd had. And because I wanted to. I wanted this afternoon to be real. For her as much as me.

She tasted of sunshine and heat, and I couldn't help but let out a groan as I explored her mouth. Her hands dug into my hair and I pushed her against her door, my hands buzzing with urgency and need.

"Joshua," she whispered as I kissed down her neck. "It's not . . . you feel . . ." Her hands trailed down my chest to my belt, her fingers slipping behind my waistband. Christ, I wanted to feel her hands wrapped around my cock. I wanted to feel every inch of her skin under my tongue. I wanted to make this woman orgasm so hard she'd never think of another man again.

I reached and scooped up the layers of her dress, smoothing my palm up her leg, reaching higher and higher. I pulled back to look at her, to ask the question burning me from the inside out. Her face was flushed, eyes hazy with what I hoped was wanting. "Hartford." My eyes dipped to her full, plump mouth.

"What are we doing?" she asked.

Did I have an answer? I wanted to tell her that I'd

thought of nothing but her for months now. That nothing between us had ever been faked. That I hadn't been her teacher but her pupil.

"What do you want us to be doing?" I asked.

She sighed. "You want to come in?"

Yes, I wanted to get naked with her as soon as possible, but I wanted more than that. I wanted her in my place. The place reserved just for me, where I never brought other women. "I want you to come into my flat."

I pulled her toward me with one hand and opened my front door with the other, then stepped us both over the line.

"You're so beautiful," I said. "That dress . . . your eyes . . ."

"Joshua," she said, her voice a mixture of pleading and disbelief.

"It's true, Hartford," I said as I unzipped her dress. "You're as beautiful on the outside as you are on the inside, and that's bloody stunning."

She stood on tiptoes and pulled my mouth onto hers as her dress slid to the floor.

She fumbled with my shirt buttons. I just wanted to rip my shirt off, to get rid of another barrier between us, but I didn't want to risk her thinking she wasn't doing it right. So I waited, watched as she concentrated on my buttons, her delicate fingers pulling at the cotton of my shirt. Once it was off, she smoothed her hands over my shoulders. "You're . . . big." Her fingers trailed down and across my stomach. "And hard."

I smiled, enjoying being inspected and explored. I wanted her to know my body. Know what was inside my heart and soul.

Then she poked my right pec. "Is that even natural?"

I laughed. "You're the doctor."

She tipped her head back. "I guess I am. My diagnosis is that you're an excellent physical specimen."

"Back at you." I snaked my hand down her back and grabbed her arse.

She winced. "Excuse my granny knickers."

"They didn't even hit my radar." The only thing I was interested in was her. "It's not the knickers that have my attention."

Her eyelashes fluttered as if she were blinking away rain. "You know you're ridiculously smooth, right?"

"But you know that I mean it, right?"

She reached up around my neck and I lifted her up, pulled her legs around my waist, and walked us into the bedroom. She stopped our progress with a hand on the doorframe. "Joshua, my forcefield is down," she said, her eyes lined in silver. "I'm not pretending anymore. I can't wake up tomorrow and pretend tonight never happened."

Relief flooded through me and I closed my eyes, trying to focus on what she'd said.

"I can't be a Miss Tuesday Night."

"There is no Miss Tuesday Night. Not for months now. Not since . . . you." I hadn't made a conscious decision not to see Kelly or any of my other regular partners. Having Hartford in my life had filled the holes so completely, there was no room left for any other woman. It had just taken me a while to accept how I felt. "And I don't want to pretend this didn't happen."

She trailed her fingers to the back of my neck and I lost all sense of reason. As we lay on the bed I caged her with my arms, wanting to take her in.

Over the last couple of months, this woman beneath me seemed to have coaxed me out of a shell I didn't know I was living in. Every day since she moved in, I couldn't wait to get home. To her. To hear about her day, to watch as she'd carefully take a slice of cake, to enjoy her teasing and her complete lack of pretention, to revel in her kindness and the way everything was just so easy between us.

There was no denying it. I had fallen for Hartford. Pretending otherwise was pointless.

She slid her hands down my sides. "You okay?" she asked.

I nodded. "Just thinking."

"We don't have to do this if you don't want to."

I swept her hair from her face. How could she think I would want to back out? "I want to. I want to more than it's possible to explain." I wasn't sure I'd ever wanted anyone more. The dates and the kissing had started as something else for her. Even when we'd slept together that first time, we'd agreed it wasn't real. Not irreversible. Now it was different for her. And me.

I unfastened my trousers and kicked them off then knelt back over her, trailing kisses down her throat, licking and sucking and enjoying the taste of her warm, soft skin against mine. She sighed, her body sinking into the mattress. I pulled down the straps of her bra and flicked her nipples with my tongue, bringing them to tantalizingly sharp points. I grazed my teeth over them, and at her moan, a chill of satisfaction snaked down my spine.

I was going to make her come so hard.

I moved lower and stripped off her knickers in one swift movement. She twisted away from me. "Don't you dare," I said, grabbing her thighs and pushing them apart. "I want to taste you."

"Joshua," she said, her legs relaxing.

I reached between her legs and slid my fingers into her

folds, finding her deliciously wet. "This was what I was looking for," I said. I pushed into her silky softness, blinking my eyes shut to try to keep out how good it felt.

How very right and perfect everything about this moment was.

TWENTY-EIGHT

Hartford

Joshua Luca is going down on me.

I was trying to pull myself out of the moment to retain some kind of control over my mind and body, but it wasn't happening. Joshua's insistent tongue was working overtime. His hands were everywhere. When we had slept together the first time, I must have shut a part of myself off, scared of falling too hard, too fast. Now all my senses were on max.

His body was like nothing I studied in anatomy and like everything I'd seen in the pictures in the National Gallery. His muscled back, arms, and shoulders rippled under my fingers like Samson in the painting I'd seen by Rubens. Except I was no Delilah. It was Joshua that had robbed me of all my senses and power, not the other way around.

"You're fucking delicious," Joshua said as he looked up at me from between my legs, his fingers still dipping and pushing and driving me wild.

"Please God don't stop," I croaked out, desperate not to be left on this edge of almost-explosion.

My mind couldn't focus.

Joshua dipped his head down and restarted the rhythm with his tongue that had got me wrung out and writhing on the bed. The stirrings of an orgasm pressed at the base of my spine and I gasped. I wasn't going to be able to be graceful when I came. His insistent fingers and tongue, his hot breath, all pressed into me like fists pounding on a table, demanding my orgasm.

Release shot through my body like lightning. It was as if someone had pushed me off the edge of a cliff and I could do nothing but enjoy the view on the way down.

And it was glorious.

Sex hadn't ever been so all-consuming. So clamorous that there was no room to think. All I could do was feel.

Exhilarated

Enraptured.

Adored.

As my body sank back into the mattress, I was vaguely aware of Joshua's hands sweeping up my body and then his lips on mine. It was as if he kissed me back to consciousness.

He kneeled and rolled on a condom. His dick was upright against his stomach, thick and veined and straining like a dog on a lead. Joshua's tongue was impressive. But his penis? Perfection.

He leaned over me and I hooked my heels over his thighs, pulling him closer. And just like before in the park, he leaned his forehead against mine. For a moment there was no sound but the blood pounding in my ears, no movement apart from the rise and fall of our chests. It was as if we were bracing ourselves, knowing that what happened next would be momentous.

The preamble passed and Joshua pushed into me, achingly slowly, eking out all my desperation and pleasure.

My fingernails bit into his shoulders and I opened my legs wider, trying to let him deeper, closer. His muscles under my hands shifted. I wasn't sure if I would breathe again.

"Hartford," he choked out, giving voice to the shock I felt at how well we fit together.

He moved out of me slowly, like I was made of glass, then pushed in again. This time his eyes were closed and his brow was furrowed as if he were channeling all his energy into one movement. Like he was giving me everything he had.

He gasped as he reached the end of me and his eyes snapped open. "I . . . I." It was almost panic I saw in his eyes. "You feel so good, and I want to take you so hard and fast you won't be able to move for a week."

I reached and cupped his face before he slumped over me. The hulking, fit guy I'd adored as a teenager, who had grown into an even more hulking, muscled specimen of a man, was breathing like he'd just run a marathon—all because of the effort it took not to nail me to the mattress. I nudged him so he turned over and I was astride him.

"Really?" he asked.

I shrugged. "I clearly have more self-control."

Those wickedly naughty eyebrows of his suggested getting me on top had all been part of his plan.

I tucked my hips underneath me, settling on his thick cock as deep as I could. I tipped my head back, relishing that fullness, that feeling that every single one of my senses was turned up to maximum.

I pressed my palms to his chest and began to move, rocking back and forth on his cock in small, intense movements that kept him deep and ensured that this moment right here would last for as long as possible. I didn't want this to be over soon for any reason. I didn't want to break the spell of whatever had happened to get us to this moment.

This was my not-so-fake date.

This was an old, never-forgotten crush.

This was my best friend.

Any moment in the future presented obstacles whichever way we moved, so I wanted to stay here, now, for the rest of time.

He reached around and grabbed my arse and started to move me in the very precise way and exact speed that he wanted. It might have looked like I was on top, but a man like Joshua was always in charge.

"You're going to make me come from that angle," he said.

I slowed to a stop and he pushed himself up so he was sitting, wrapping his arms around me. "No, I mean, I can't watch your breasts move like that. It's like witchcraft. They're fucking perfect."

I was used to Joshua being smooth, but the sheen on his forehead and the slight pant to his voice told me it wasn't just something he was saying to make himself look good or me feel good. Before I had a chance to respond, he'd escaped from under me and pushed me to my back.

He lifted my hips and thrust in. He was impossibly deeper, fuller, *more* than he had been a moment ago, and I cried out his name. He kept pushing into me, hands on my hips burning into my flesh, and hot, soft words falling from his lips with each sharp movement. I couldn't stop the wave of my climax as it approached, fast and furious.

I grabbed at the pillows and bedsheets, trying to find some kind of anchor to help me survive what was coming, but nothing would help. Joshua had taken ownership of my body in that moment. I had to accept that.

I called out, and with a final thrust, felt the force of his climax crashing over both of us, cascading through me into every atom of every cell of my body.

He collapsed over me and pulled me to him as we both fought for breath.

Seconds, minutes, hours seemed to pass.

"What was that?" he whispered in my ear.

My ears rang like I'd been to a twenty-four-hour-long rock concert. I'd lost the ability to move my limbs. I wasn't sure I could even speak any longer, so I just shook my head. Whatever it was, I wanted to hold onto it for as long as possible.

TWENTY-NINE

Hartford

Was it weird to watch someone sleep?

I'd woken up about ten minutes ago. We hadn't shut the curtains last night and somehow Joshua was managing to sleep despite the sunshine spilling through the huge windows. That or he knew I was sitting here watching him, and he was indulging my weirdness by pretending to sleep. I wouldn't put it past him.

I wanted to stay here until he woke and talk all day and do everything naked, but I had to leave for my shift in thirty minutes.

I checked my phone. Correction: twenty minutes. *Shit.* I pulled on my dress and looked around for a piece of paper and a pen to leave a note, but there was nothing. I opened the bedroom door, being careful not to make a noise, and saw a bunch of papers on the dining table and a printer that had overflowed whatever it was printing onto the floor. I'd steal some paper for a note without disturbing what I was sure was organized chaos.

I crouched to gather up the fallen papers and an image caught my eye. I turned it the right way up.

Calmation.

I read it again to make sure I'd not imagined something.

No, I hadn't. It definitely said "Calmation." Heat crawled up my body and I tried to think.

Why would Joshua have papers relating to the very ADHD drug Gerry and I were set to campaign against? My heart began to thunder in my chest as I turned over more of the fallen papers to try to see what was going on. I stood and placed each page on the table. Image after image of packaging with different logos. Some of the packages were regular cardboard pill packets. Others tubs of vitamins. One even looked like a packet of gummy bears.

Every few images there were a couple of pages of writing, which I skimmed in a kind of haze. I read the final page with more intent, my brain stumbling back from the shock that had sent me reeling. I dropped the paper like it was on fire.

It settled at my feet, right side up. I tried to ignore the nausea that growled in my gut.

Luca Brands presents Calmation for Merdon.

I covered my mouth with my hands to stop myself from screaming. There was no way Joshua would do this. He was the king of luxury goods. Why would he work with them?

I clawed at my throat as I tried to take a deep breath, but all I could pull into my lungs was heat and panic.

I tried to piece together the memories of our conversations. He told me he was working with a pharma company that was helping people. He said he was inspired by me to do good. Could he really believe that, or was he just doing the bidding of whoever would pay him?

Yesterday I had told him I was campaigning against a

new ADHD drug with Gerry. With all the insider information he had, he must have put two and two together and realized I was talking about Calmation.

I sank to the floor and tried to think what I should do.

I could wake him and demand that he tell me why he didn't say anything yesterday. I could try to insist that he drop his campaign to help Calmation and join me in the fight against them. And if he refused? I'd have to try to stop him *and* Merdon. Before I could think twice, I was out of his flat and focused on getting to work.

I had to stop Merdon.

I had to stop Joshua.

I had to tell Gerry I might have tipped Merdon off that we were going to oppose the regulatory approval.

What had I done? I'd betrayed Gerry and slept with someone who went against everything I believed in.

For the second time in my life, I'd lost sight of what was important because of Joshua—only this time, I wasn't about to let my carelessness spiral into disaster. Life was a lot simpler when I was focused on saving people rather than flouncing round in silly dresses eating too much cake.

I had a job to do.

THIRTY

Joshua

Turning onto my back, my eyes still closed, I pushed the sheet down to my waist and reached over my head for a full-body stretch. I remembered where I was. Who I was with. What had happened last night. My smile was automatic. I opened my eyes but there was no sign of Hartford. My stomach sloshed with an old anxiety and I mentally brushed it aside. She was just in the bathroom, or getting coffee or something.

I sat and swung my legs over the bed, pulled on some boxers, and went to find Hartford.

The bathroom was empty, so I padded into the living space.

No Hartford.

The churning in my stomach was back. It had been gone a long time and I'd forgotten how it felt—like someone was dancing on my grave and I was about to throw up.

I tried to swallow but my mouth was dry. I needed to

get a grip. I was not dressed in a morning suit. And I didn't have a fiancée.

This wasn't my wedding day.

Where was she? "Hartford?"

Nothing.

"Hartford." My voice was louder this time. I started opening doors in the hallway before racing to the bedroom to open the wardrobe.

After last night, after what had happened, after we'd confessed it was real—she'd just left? No, she must have just gone back across the hall to get something.

I grabbed my phone and dialed her number.

No answer.

I dialed again.

Still no answer.

I turned to face the windows and saw the pitch to Merdon laid out, each potential packaging image sitting next to each other on the dining room table like criminals in a lineup.

Shit. That was a breach of client confidentiality.

Why had she been going through those papers anyway?

I'd talk to her and make sure she didn't say anything to anyone. I remembered our conversation just before the picnic. She must have been talking about Calmation when she was describing the project she and Gerry were working on, surely? It sounded like they were on some kind of crusade against the drug. If it was Calmation, they must have misunderstood what Merdon were trying to achieve. They were trying to help families. Make drugs cheaper and more accessible. I'd talk to her and explain it. She and Gerry might even be able to help with the campaign if Luca Brands won the pitch.

I tried to ignore the sharp twist in my gut. Merdon had

been very clear about the benefits of this drug, but if there *were* downsides, they were unlikely to tell me. It was people like Hartford and Gerry that would see the whole picture.

I wished Hartford had hung around, and I could have asked her what she thought now she knew of my involvement. I hated that she'd just taken off without even leaving me a note or sending me a message. It just wasn't like her.

I glanced at the time on my phone. Two hours and I'd be in front of Eric, presenting Luca Brands' pitch for Calmation. I needed to focus. And now that I thought about it, I needed to prepare some additional questions to make sure I wasn't getting into something I wanted no part of.

THIRTY-ONE

Joshua

I always knew in the first few minutes of a pitch whether Luca Brands was going to be successful in winning an account. Today was no different—Eric wore the decision like a push-up bra with a low-cut blouse. It was obvious. What I hadn't been expecting was Eric to announce the decision to us before we'd packed up our presentation.

"I'm delighted, Eric. You know Luca Brands will work tirelessly for GCVB, Merdon, and Calmation." I tried to stay as stoic as possible, when what I really wanted to do was punch the air. Not only had I saved hundreds of jobs at Luca Brands, we were going to have an opportunity to help children get the drugs they needed.

I couldn't wait to tell Hartford.

"We need to get started right away," Eric said. "Can we talk implementation?"

"Now?" I asked. He couldn't have seriously expected me to work up the implementation plan before I knew if we'd won the account.

"Just a few headline points and I can do some introductions. It will save putting another meeting in the diary. We're filing with the US regulator tomorrow and . . . Let me bring in the team." He scurried out of the room.

I glanced at the four members of the Luca Brands team that sat either side of me. I could tell by their tight jaws and panicked expressions that this was the very last thing they wanted. But we'd won the account. That's what we had to focus on. And it would give me a chance to ask some of the questions that I'd prepared about potential medical opposition to the drug. Before I could voice my reassurance, Eric was back, as if he had a line of people waiting outside.

I stood and moved around my chair, ready to shake hands. I knew two of the six people who had filed in, as they were previously in GCVB.

Two other women—strategy and PR for Merdon, respectively—offered their business cards along with a handshake. The final two people to join the meeting weren't so forthcoming. They gave their names—Jean and Tim—but nothing more.

We all took our seats around the large table. My assistant distributed the Luca Brands team sheet that set out headshots and job descriptions of everyone who would be working on the account. I waited for Tim and Jean to slide their business cards across the table so I would be able to understand their roles in the meeting. It didn't happen.

"Shall we do introductions?" I suggested, wanting to know more about the two new people in the room.

"I think most of us know each other. I'm keen to see what you've got in mind for implementation," Eric replied, his tone a little more tense than usual.

It was a weird reaction. It might be a little time-consuming to go around the table, but completely normal given the size of the meeting.

"We haven't had much time to prepare, but maybe we could walk through the timeline. Everything flows from there." I made sure to keep scanning the room, looking for micro-expressions. Maybe I was paranoid, but I got the feeling something was up. The pitch meeting had been professional but warm. Now a thin layer of ice had settled on the other side of the boardroom table.

Eric glanced across at Tim and Jean, almost as if he was expecting them to chip in. They remained silent. "As I said, we're filing with the US regulator tomorrow and expect approval by the end of next quarter."

"And the supply issues you mentioned before are all ironed out, is that right?" I asked.

Eric gave a brief nod. "We'll have enough stock for launch of Calmation at the time of regulatory approval," he said.

I took a breath, thinking about first steps. I wanted to understand what doctors like Hartford and Gerry would think about Calmation. *And* I wanted to show Eric that we knew what we were doing when it came to launch. "We want to capitalize on the exposure the approval process will bring, particularly among medical professionals."

I spotted a slight wince from Eric's assistant and paused. I needed to know more.

"We might need to amend that approach slightly, but go on," Eric said.

"Amend the approach, in what way?" I asked.

Eric met my eye and took a deep breath. "We're hearing of some disquiet from a group of pediatricians."

My gut curdled, but I stayed silent, wanting him to elaborate. Was the disquiet the unofficial lobbying that Hartford had talked about? Were she and I on opposite sides on this? But Eric didn't say anything. He surely wasn't going to stop there. I needed more information.

"What sort of disquiet?" I asked.

"Some people think parents shouldn't be the ones to decide if their children need Calmation."

Some people? Did he mean Gerry and Hartford?

"The key thing is that we put control back in the parents' hands, rather than the hands of GPs. That's the insecurity that underpins the disquiet about Calmation. We're leapfrogging the doctor's prescription pad. We understand parents know their children best." Eric's delivery was stiff and rehearsed. It sounded like talking points had been circulated internally before our meeting.

Eric might be on-script, but if he was referring to Hartford and Gerry, what he was saying wasn't entirely true. Neither Hartford nor Gerry was a power-hungry control hound looking to make life harder for patients. I knew Hartford cared about children and their health. And she worshipped Gerry, so I was sure he was the same.

I needed to stop fixating on Hartford's viewpoint. The opposition might not be her and pretty much every product and service on sale today had haters. This account would save the livelihood of nearly half my staff. I needed to think about the big picture and not borrow trouble unless it was going to impact the campaign. "And you think this . . . disquiet may impact our timetable?" I asked.

Eric shot a glance at Tim and Jean. "We're putting together some options that should keep the campaign on track."

"Can Caroline help with that?" I asked. Caroline was heading up PR for this campaign and was the best in the business. "We're very used to competitors creating anti-launch campaigns through social media and have some strategies to counteract those. And we have excellent relationships with the press across Europe."

"Thanks," Eric replied. "We're just going to do some basic counterintelligence work."

Counterintelligence? "You suspect some kind of internal leak?"

Tim finally spoke up. "We're reviewing internal practices and procedures."

That was a non-answer. Something was off. Were they thinking about pulling the drug but didn't want to tell us? I much preferred it when I could work hand in hand with my clients. If they kept problems and issues secret, there was less I could do to head off disaster. "We're here to help and support you in any way we can. Please feel you can use our resources and network for anything you need."

Eric gave one of his tight, shallow smiles.

This time it was Jean's turn to speak. "If any of you are approached, or notice anything unusual, please call me immediately at the number on this card." She passed a stack of cards for each member of my team to take. When they came to me, I saw the plain white rectangle didn't provide much in the way of identifying information—just a name, a phone number, and a generic email address. Who were these people, and why were they here?

"Approached?" Caroline asked. "And what do you mean by 'unusual'?"

"Let's keep going through the timetable," Jean said.

I'd spent most of my career working for luxury brands. I was well used to creatives being paranoid about competitors. I was familiar with the importance of secrecy and threats of corporate espionage. I was accustomed to sitting in a room with a stressed-out, overworked team who were doing everything they could to launch their product with a bang. But this meeting was unlike any I'd ever experienced before. It was like they were MI5 and had discovered plans for Italy to start a war.

I didn't like to work blind. It was a sure way to look like an idiot. Eric might not be ready to tell an entire meeting room what was wrong, but perhaps he'd talk to me one-on-one. If I had all the facts, I'd be better at my job. I wanted to make sure there were no surprises.

I had a Google alert set up on all my clients, target clients, and clients' competitors. I also had a junior assistant responsible for briefing me on whatever was in the news that might impact our accounts. Whatever was happening hadn't yet hit the news cycle, but that didn't mean disaster wasn't just around the corner.

I knew one person who might be able to see into the future of Calmation. The only problem was that so far today, she'd refused every one of my calls.

THIRTY-TWO

Hartford

I secured my locker, pulled my backpack over my arm and headed to the hospital exit. I'd spent the last two hours of my shift catching up on paperwork, waiting for Gerry to finish his meetings. I still hadn't managed to confess to him what I'd done.

At least by the time I got back to the residences, I could sneak past Joshua's front door without him hearing me. I didn't want to talk to him. Being near him made me lose sight of what was right in front of me—just like it always had. This time around, I wasn't going to derail my whole life because of my inability to control my feelings for one Joshua Luca. Tomorrow was moving day; I could take my backpack and whatever else I'd accumulated these last three months in London and shift my postcode from W1 to WD6. Starting tomorrow morning, I'd be living nearly fourteen miles away from Joshua. He was more likely to go to Milan than make the trip from Zone 1 to Zone 6, so I'd be safe.

"Hartford, just the person I've been looking for."

I turned as Gerry came up beside me. It was nearly ten, and as much as I didn't want to see Joshua, I did hear my bed calling.

"I'm being interviewed by the BBC tomorrow and I'm thinking I might bring up this Merdon thing. There are rumors floating about Calmation being filed with the regulator tomorrow, so I can probably get away with commenting on what I've heard through the grapevine—no risk to my source. You mind taking a look at my notes?"

If anything was going to keep the adrenaline flowing, it was the fight against Merdon. "Absolutely, and actually I have something to tell you about that." I followed Gerry into his office.

"I've been researching how to file a complaint to the health regulator," I said.

Gerry sighed. "We need to do this in an organized way. We need lawyers to advise us and prepare a complaint."

"Sounds expensive."

"It will be," he replied. "But it's a generation of children who are going to become zombies if we don't do something about Calmation. Every two-year-old having a tantrum is going to be given this stuff."

It didn't bear thinking about. "Do you think they'll actually get it through?"

"Merdon has a lot of dollars."

"You think they'll bribe people?"

He shrugged. "They'll pay millions to make sure this application is successful. And they'll pay their lawyers to exploit every loophole they can find."

"And millions more to advertise it when it passes." Some of those millions would be going to Joshua. I'd tried to push our night together out of my brain. I'd tried to forget what I'd seen. The contract. The different Calmation logos. The shiny, kid-friendly packaging that would make a dangerous drug seem safe. I didn't want any of it to be true.

"Exactly. We're going to need some money from somewhere to fight this properly."

We couldn't compete. But we needed to try. The only wealthy people I knew were the ones Joshua had introduced me to, and they weren't about to take my side over his. Even though he was dead wrong.

"We could set up an online fundraiser. You could mention it in your interview tomorrow. It might help pay for a lawyer."

"Good idea. Here are my notes." He passed me two folded sheets of plain paper covered in what would, three months ago, have been indecipherable scrawl. Now I could read Gerry's handwriting perfectly.

I scanned down the page, making sure he'd taken the agreed approach, which was to say that the use of this type of drug was effective only in limited circumstances that had to be established by a doctor. "I think it's worth pointing out that Merdon is in the business of selling drugs, not solutions to medical conditions."

"I like that idea." Gerry started adding to his notes.

"Perhaps you can even mention that we're fundraising for legal costs in your interview. I'll set up a GoFundMe page people can contribute through."

Gerry sat back and steepled his fingers together. "I knew I was right to hire you the moment I met you. You're a clever, caring doctor. And a good colleague."

"Thank you, sir." Coming from Gerry, that was about the best compliment I could ever hope to get. "But I have a confession to make."

I took a breath and told Gerry about my conversation

with Joshua, where I didn't mention any names but told him we were getting ready to campaign against an ADHD drug for children.

"Well, he's a bright man. He will have known you were talking about Calmation." Which was why it was all the more hurtful that he'd not said anything to me. I'd trusted him, but he'd not done the same in return.

"I'm really sorry."

Gerry shook his head. "You didn't say anything that isn't already circulating as industry gossip anyway. You've not done any damage. Now, go home and try to get some sleep. Tomorrow's going to be a big day."

Sleep wouldn't come easily. I had too much to think about. Too much to do. The irony was that the person I wanted to go home and share all this with, the one person who might be able to help, was also the last man I wanted to see right now.

THIRTY-THREE

Hartford

I'd almost missed my tube stop because my eyes were so heavy with the need to sleep. It was five to midnight by the time I stepped off the lift to spend my last night in the hotel residences. Just over twenty-four hours ago, I'd ridden up this lift with Joshua, giddy from a romantic picnic, about to have the best night of my life.

How could so much change in such a short space of time?

Joshua would be in the bath or asleep by now. At least I wouldn't have to see him. I'd had a busy day and every valid excuse not to take the four missed calls I'd had from him.

Even if I hadn't been busy, I wouldn't have answered. There was nothing to say. Seeing that Merdon pitch on his dining table had unfogged my brain and brought me back to reality. These last few months, I'd slowly and unwittingly lowered my forcefield until it was barely more than a line in the sand. Now I was being reminded of the reasons it was there in the first place. I just wish my heart didn't feel quite so dense in my chest, knowing I had to walk away.

I stepped off the lift and tried to tread as lightly as I could to my front door. My heavy heart plunged to my feet when I heard the familiar sound of Joshua's door opening behind me.

"You snuck out this morning and haven't returned my calls," he said, his tone even—not super friendly. Not angry.

"I know," I said.

"I want to talk to you about your concerns with Calmation."

I didn't turn around, pretending instead to rummage for my keys in my bag. "There's nothing to say."

"So that's it? You've won me over and now you're dumping me?"

He was trying to be cute. Charming. But I wasn't into it. My forcefield was back up.

I turned to face him. "Why didn't you tell me yesterday that you were working for Calmation? You must have figured out it's the drug Gerry and I are working against?"

His chest rose and fell. "I had a suspicion, but I wasn't completely sure. I was supposed to be keeping it confidential, and then we reached the picnic and—"

"And you didn't say anything."

"No, I was too caught up in what was happening between us. But I would have told you—I think. And if you'd have woken me up, we could have discussed it this morning."

My jaw clenched. "You *think* you were going to tell me?"

"I'm signed up to a watertight NDA. But yes, I think I would have told you if we hadn't gotten sidetracked."

I sighed. Of course he made it sound entirely reasonable. "I guess it doesn't matter if you told me or not. We're fundamentally opposed on something incredibly important to me."

"It's important to me too," he said, taking a step toward me. "You have it wrong about Merdon. They're genuinely trying to help people get the drugs they need. It's different in the US—the drugs aren't available to people who don't have good insurance."

I took a step back. "You're being naïve. This is about profits and money for Merdon. That's it."

"Merdon can't sell this drug over the counter without regulatory approval. Calmation isn't going to be sold on the black market. If the regulator thinks it's okay, it's going to be okay."

That was going to be the argument parents used when they decided to self-diagnose their children and administer mood-altering medicine without the support of a doctor. Any drug, even something like paracetamol, could be dangerous if it wasn't used correctly. And Calmation was way more powerful and potentially dangerous than parac-etamol, which was why it had to be a prescription drug. "Just because something's legal doesn't make it okay. It's legal to eat a hundred cheeseburgers in a day. It doesn't make it a good thing to do."

"I've seen the evidence—their planning. I've seen docu-ments. The studies proving the benefits. It's all on my computer. My client sent me thousands of pages of stuff." He opened his door and gestured inside. "I can show you. Their entire strategy is about making drugs available and affordable to people who wouldn't otherwise have access to them."

It gave me some comfort that Joshua clearly believed he was doing good. He'd been duped. "I believe that's what they told you. Hell, some people who work for them might really believe it too. But I'm telling you, as a doctor, a pediatrician, and a friend, that trying to get Calmation authorized as an over-the-counter drug is immoral."

His shoulders drooped and his eyes hit the floor. "You really think so?"

"I think so. Gerry thinks so, and so will the entire pediatric community when this all hits the press."

Joshua pushed his hands through his hair. "I had a meeting with them today and . . . something was off. What should I do?" he asked, almost as if he was thinking aloud. "Fuck."

There were a thousand things I could suggest, not least of which was look over my very amateur PR plan and see what needed to be changed.

But these last few hours since I'd left his bed had made something very clear. Something that I'd known all along but had lost sight of. Whenever I was thinking about Joshua, I took my eye off the ball. I needed to focus on my career. On Calmation. On my future. It was so easy for me to get so wrapped up in the man in front of me that I lost sight of what was really important. I refused to regress to my seventeen-year-old self, especially for a man who had a track record of casual sex and little else when it came to women. I didn't want to lose myself again for the sake of an orgasm.

"I need to go to bed," I said, turning toward the door.

"Can I come in?" he asked. "I want to figure this out."

"I don't think so, Joshua. I'm not in the mood for casual."

"Hartford," he said, his tone questioning and confused. "I want to put this right. You're not going to help?"

"You don't need my help to do the right thing."

"I might not need it, but I'd like it."

I turned back to him. "You remember when I told you about the accident I had when I broke my leg the first time?"

He frowned. "Sure."

"That night, I was coming after you." The confession was like heaving off an enormous weight. "I wanted you to notice me, to see me as an adult woman." Ironically, it had been such a childish decision—reckless. Foolish. And one I was still living with. "I made a stupid call by driving that night and as a result, I ended up losing my dream of dancing professionally." I never talked about what I'd lost to anyone. Not even my parents. Saying the words out loud brought it back as if it had happened yesterday. My scar split open and it was bleeding. "I won't make the same mistake twice."

Joshua scratched the back of his head. "What mistake?" he asked.

"Losing all sense of judgment because I'm crazy about you. And here I am again, over a decade later, in almost exactly the same place. Take another step toward me, Joshua, and I'm gone—drowning in you, losing everything that's important to me because all I can see is you. I told you about Calmation yesterday when I'd been sworn to secrecy. Next time, it'll be a mistake I can't row back from."

"Hartford?" He reached for me and I stumbled backward, desperate to escape his touch because I knew how powerful it was. How powerful he was.

"And you know what?" I asked. "It might be worth letting myself surrender to the pull if it wasn't all so one-sided. But I can't lose myself in someone who might or might not remember to share the important stuff with me, who may or may not want something more than just sex. I can't fall in love with someone who's never going to give what I give." I would always feel more for Joshua than he did for me. I couldn't live like that.

He shook his head. "What do you mean, give what you give, fall in love? You're moving at warp speed, a thousand miles down the road. We had our first date *yesterday*."

I looked up at him, his floppy blond hair, hard chest, and charming smile. God, he was pretty. "You're probably right. For sure I can see farther down the road than you, and despite wanting to hold back, I'm racing to go further. I can't stop myself. In any relationship we have, I'm always going to be ahead of you, Joshua. And I can't do it."

My forcefield lay in pieces at his feet. It was all there for him to see. Was I hoping he would tell me I was wrong and he was right there on the road next to me, holding my hand? Probably. Was I hoping he'd tell me he loved me and we could figure this out because we were going to be together until the end of time? If I was, I wasn't holding my breath.

I waited, one beat, then two, giving him time to fill the silence.

At least he didn't lie. He was who he was and who he always had been. It was me who had changed.

Eventually I slipped inside and closed the door.

We were done.

THIRTY-FOUR

Joshua

I swept into the meeting room, my top team gathered around the glass table, the London skyline in the background. I'd spent the last week replaying my last conversation with Hartford, trying to come up with something I could have said that would have made her stay.

In the end, my Genius Time told me that it was action not words that counted. I was going to show her how much I cared about her. How much I listened to what she had to say and how much I'd changed from the man who only did casual.

"I have an announcement." I took a seat and scanned the faces in front of me.

"Today I called GCVB and told them that Luca Brands won't be working on any accounts for Merdon." Yes I'd hope Hartford would approve, but I'd withdrawn Luca Brands from the Merdon account because it was the right thing to do.

Gasps echoed around the room. They knew what that

meant: job losses. "I've not heard officially from Eric that Luca Brands no longer works for any of the GCVB brands, but I fully expect to." Eric would move fast and I expected him to fire Luca Brands before the end of the day. I wanted to get ahead of him.

A couple of hands shot up but I knew the questions everyone wanted answers to.

"I'll take questions at the end. Let me just finish."

I'd been up all night for a week brainstorming and strategizing. My Genius Time had paid off.

"I'm creating a new division of Luca Brands. And I'm looking for top quality internal candidates to head it up." Relief swept over their faces. "The division will do some of what we already do, but the clients of the division won't be luxury goods. We'll be working with charities and causes we believe in. We're also going to create a new lobbying arm to champion the priorities of these clients. The first project for the new division will be to roll out a campaign *against* Calmation being approved as an over-the-counter drug. We haven't got much time, so I'm going to need people willing to get started as soon as possible." Harford had been right—I didn't need her help to do the right thing.

Val, my right-hand woman on the original Calmation campaign, stuck up her hand. "I'd really like to head up this campaign. I know the drug, I know the issues, and I also have a kid with ADHD. The drug should be on prescription only."

I was stunned. I liked to think I knew my employees, but Val had never said anything about her son, Oliver, having ADHD. And she'd worked tirelessly on the Calmation campaign without any kind of hint that she might not agree with it.

"I would welcome your leadership on this, Val," I said.

"I actually have some ideas already. Because there are just pockets of opposition out there, rather than any organized anti-Calmation campaign, I think the first thing to do is create a group we can push forward as the face and voice of a unified opposition."

"Great idea. I know who you might want to contact to start that process." I'd put her in touch with Gerry. I'd seen his interviews; he would be a great advocate.

"Just a quick question." Val looked up from her notes. "If we don't have any kind of budget, where is the money coming from, and what can I spend?"

"I'm setting up a charitable arm of the company. And your budget for this anti-Calmation campaign is unlimited. Do whatever you need to do to make sure this drug isn't approved for over-the-counter use on either side of the Atlantic."

Murmurs through the room told me this was a welcome announcement. Maybe I wasn't the only one who'd had second thoughts about Merdon. Maybe this would be good for everyone at Luca Brands, even if they weren't directly involved.

"I'll make sure it doesn't happen." Val beamed at me.

"Whatever you need from me, you have. Don't hesitate to ask. Any questions?"

John at the back of the room raised his hand. "I think this is great and everything, but if we've pulled out of the Calmation campaign, then we've lost GCVB as a client. That's got to mean jobs are going to be lost."

"It's a good question and I'm going to make an announcement to the rest of the company when we leave this meeting. We'll have to adapt our approach when GCVB inevitably pulls their accounts. It starts with staffing the new division. Then, we're going to go out and get new business. It will mean looking at industries beyond luxury brands. I'm open to your suggestions, and I have a few ideas myself. I'm going to do my best for you all, to make sure that no one has to leave Luca Brands if they don't want to." It was going to be a struggle, and I was going to have to have Genius Time on a daily basis for the foreseeable future, but Hartford had inspired me.

Hopefully Luca Brands would stop Calmation being approved by the regulator—it was the best possible outcome for vulnerable parents and children. I also hoped it would be enough to show Hartford how I listened to her. How I respected her opinion. And how much I could change in all areas of my life.

THIRTY-FIVE

Hartford

Carrying my hospital-issued iPad, I crossed the corridor from Children's Accident and Emergency into the break room.

"Hartford," Jacob called out as I grabbed a coffee cup. I glanced up. "Wanna do me a favor? I hate to ask before you've even had a cup of coffee."

"No problem. Better busy than bored." Jacob was a nice guy and things had been easy between us since our date. We'd tacitly agreed there was nothing romantic between us, but both of us seemed happy to settle into collegial friendship.

"I've just been called into A&E to see a patient but Gerry wants to speak to me. Would you take it for me?"

"Sure. No problem. What's the case?"

"Not sure. All I know is that it's an eight-year-old with Down syndrome."

I was more than happy for the distraction. I retraced my

steps and headed to the desk to see which bay I was going to.

"Bay Two," the receptionist said. "This is her chart." She frowned at me. "No offense but I wish Dr. Cove had answered."

I laughed. "No doubt every female would prefer Dr. Cove over me." I flicked through the observations. Nothing out of the ordinary other than a high temperature.

I stepped around the curtain in Bay Two. "Millie?" I took a half step back when I took in the patient on the bed. She was an explosion of pink tulle and Lycra and wearing a grin as bright as sunshine.

"Hi," I said smiling. "I see I get to treat a ballerina today." Her leotard was a little too big and her hair a little too short for the bun it was fashioned into, but her happiness was infectious. I grinned at her.

I turned to the adult seated next to the bed. "I'm Hartford, one of the doctors. Are you mum?"

"Yes," the slender, graceful woman replied. "Our GP told us to come in. Millie's had a temperature since Thursday and it's just not going away."

I nodded and turned back to Millie. "How are you feeling?"

"Beautiful," she replied. "I'm a ballerina. Just like my mummy." I smiled. "Do you mind if I ask your mummy some questions about you?" She shook her head as she swept her arms up into first position.

I took a seat and went through some basic questions with Millie's mum. "So your GP suggested you come in for some blood tests to check for infection?" It was always good to know why someone had been encouraged into A&E.

"Yes. Just a precaution, she said."

"Makes sense. The temperature isn't too high and she seems in good spirits, so there's nothing in particular to worry about, but as I'm sure you're aware, Millie is a bit more prone to infections. It's good to be cautious." I stood to talk to Millie. "Can I take a feel of your tummy and listen to your chest?"

Millie nodded.

"Have you just had a ballet class?" I asked as I began to examine her.

"No," said Millie. "I'm always a ballerina."

I glanced at her mother, who was grinning. "She loves to dance. I used to dance professionally and she found all my old costumes when she was about three. She's been obsessed ever since. We've just come from seeing Romeo and Juliet at the Royal Opera House."

My heart swooped into the floor, my heart began to gallop, and I tried to keep my smile in place.

"You used to dance professionally?"

"When I was younger I went to the Royal Ballet School. But . . . life happens and . . ." She shrugged. "I had Millie and now we watch. And we dance for fun around the kitchen."

I wanted to ask her what had happened. No dancer went to the Royal Ballet School and just gave up. Had she gotten pregnant, had an injury, lost a scholarship?

"Dancing for fun is good," I said, not really thinking about what I was saying. It was the exact opposite of what I believed to be true for me.

Millie's mother sighed. "It really is. And we go to the ballet a lot, don't we Millie?"

Millie nodded. "Dancing is the best," Millie's mother beamed at her. I could almost believe them as I watched them.

"I'll order some blood tests. We'll keep an eye on things,

but I'm not concerned at the moment."

The idea of dancing just for fun or going to the ballet wasn't something I'd ever entertained. My parents had tried to convince me, told me over and over that my injuries didn't mean I couldn't dance. Or couldn't enjoy watching a performance. The problem was the accident had meant I couldn't dance as well as I once had, so I couldn't make it my future. I'd decided if I couldn't dance professionally, I wouldn't dance at all. I wanted to block every trace of dance out of my life. But looking at the joy on Millie's and her mother's faces as they talked about dancing made me remember how much I'd loved it. I'd loved hearing the music and being able to move my body in a way that honored it and watching others do the same. I loved the feeling of making the leap or spin or complex footwork. I loved seeing new choreography and how it interpreted the music differently. I'd left a lot behind.

As I walked back up to the break room, I headed for the lockers. I dove into my backpack to see if I could find the card Joshua had given me weeks ago.

Could I recreate some of the pleasure that dancing had brought me by just watching? I'd spent so many years avoiding anything to do with dance because of a stupid decision that had sent me into a ditch. Was I going to let myself continue to pay for that for the rest of my life?

Joshua had told me I could go to the ballet any time I'd wanted. Maybe it was time to remember the joy of dancing. Sure enough the card he'd given me was tucked into the internal pocket of my bag where I'd stashed it. I turned it over, in my hand, wondering whether or not I could recreate some of the pleasure that dancing had brought me by watching the best of the best.

I'd never know unless I tried.

THIRTY-SIX

Joshua

The bath was a perfect thirty-eight degrees and a glass full of chilled water with a twist of lime was in arm's reach. I wasn't exactly sure I got the frankincense, but I could definitely make out the lavender in my new bath oil. It was a special blend, supposed to de-stress and unleash creativity. Even so, I couldn't sit still and I wasn't coming up with any new ideas.

Instead, my mind was stuck on a loop of my last conversation with Hartford twenty-one days ago. I'd been trying to figure out why I hadn't tried harder to stop her from turning her back on me. It was the same thing that was stopping me from going after her now. There was a roadblock in my way I hadn't worked out how to dismantle.

She'd told me what she needed from me. I just had to figure out if I could give it to her. What did I want? I knew I liked her and wanted something more. What I didn't know was whether or not I was capable of more.

One thing was for sure—I knew I wasn't going after her

before I knew whether or not I could give her what she needed. She deserved better than that.

I sighed and sank into the bath so the water covered my head.

Eventually I surfaced and pulled in a deep breath.

"Joshua?" Someone was calling my name. "Joshua?"

Who was in my flat? What the actual fuck?

I leapt out of the bath, pulled a towel around my waist, and snatched open the door.

Andrew was standing on the other side of it.

"How the hell did you get in here?" I grabbed another towel off the pile and rubbed it over my head.

"I came to talk." He sounded calm, like it was perfectly natural to be accosting someone in their own bathroom. "Put some clothes on and meet me in the living room."

"How did you get in here?" He didn't answer, just pulled my bedroom door closed behind him.

Did he have bad news? Was he okay?

I pulled on a t-shirt and some jeans as quickly as possible and raced into the living room. "What's going on?"

He was sitting on my sofa, flicking through a copy of *Conde Nast Traveler*. It didn't look like he was the bearer of bad news. He closed the magazine and tossed it onto my coffee table, then nodded at the sofa opposite. "Take a seat."

"Andrew, this is my flat. I'll sit if I want to," I replied as I sat down.

"I'm here on behalf of the group," he said on a sigh.

"What group?"

He tilted his head and gave me an are-you-really-that-stupid look.

"Is this an intervention?" I asked.

"Call it what you like, but I don't have much time, so let's cut to the chase."

"Why change the habit of a lifetime?"

"It's about Hartford."

My stomach whooshed to my knees. What had happened?

"We heard from Autumn or Hollie—I can't remember which, but one of the Americans—that you two had a disagreement. What's happened?"

He'd come here to tell me about circulating gossip? I'd been enjoying my bath. Sort of. "What's it got to do with you?" I asked, bristling at the interrogation.

"So, let's summarize. Last time we talked about this, you'd realized you really liked this woman but didn't think she'd take you seriously because you've never been in a committed relationship. So with help from the group, you decided you were going to prove to her that you could offer her more than just sex."

Wow. No one could ever accuse Andrew of beating around the bush. "Thanks for the recap."

"Well, did you convince her?"

Good God, this man was matter-of-fact. "Negative." I sighed, my defensiveness deflating. He was here because he was my mate. Not my enemy. He was trying to help. I sat back in the chair. "We had sex. But not just sex. You know?"

"You connected," Andrew said. "So, why am I here?"

"Who the bloody hell knows? I was minding my own business in the bath. Which reminds me, how did you get in here?"

He rolled his eyes as if it was the inanest question he'd ever heard. "I need a drink. And so do you."

He went over to the bar, pulled some whiskey from the shelf, and came back holding two glasses.

"From what I hear from the Americans, you and Hartford still aren't together. I'm here to find out why. It's not like you to fail when you set your mind to something."

I groaned, threw back the whiskey then reached to retrieve the bottle. The tawny, smokey pour soured in my stomach. I hated the idea that what Hartford and I had over the last few months was just gone.

I didn't know how to answer the question. "She told me she didn't want to lose herself in me. From what I can piece together, she's concerned that her feelings are deeper than mine."

"Are they?"

I tipped my head back on the sofa and tried to swallow down the spikey uncertainty stuck in my throat. "She's scared of caring more. And I want to show her there's nothing to be frightened of . . . but can I make that guarantee? I want to be able to reassure her. I want to be able to tell her that I'll never leave. But I can't. And neither can she."

Andrew tapped his index finger on the arm of the chair. "You're scared."

"She's important," I said. "Like, really important. I want her to be happy before I want her to be with me. Especially when . . . I have no idea how to have a relationship. I was a kid when I was with Diana. This is real life now, and I'm bound to make a complete hash of it. Do I really want to put Hartford through that? Of course I'm scared of hurting her."

"Hurting her—yes, I'm sure you don't wish to do that. And of course, you're scared of *being* hurt."

"No. I wouldn't—I mean, I don't—It's Hartford. I don't want to hurt Hartford."

"You're a good guy, Joshua."

"I'm serious. I don't want to hurt Hartford. Not ever. I don't want to be the guy that ruins her. That gives her emotional scars she has to live with for the rest of her life." I hated what she'd been through with having to give up ballet and throwing herself into her work. She was a good person and deserved someone who had some kind of lifetime guarantee.

"Loving and being loved by someone is a big responsibility. It's not to be taken lightly."

Finally he was getting it. "Right. And I want to be with Hartford. Today. And tomorrow. I can't imagine a day that I won't want to be with her, but maybe there will be one. I just can't say for certain."

"No one can."

"Harford needs someone who can."

"There won't ever be someone who can make that guarantee honestly. Not for Hartford. Not for anyone."

That was probably true. But that's what I wanted for Hartford. That's what she deserved.

"Which is why you need to figure out if there's enough trust," Andrew continued. "No one can see into the future but you have to trust yourself to take care of her heart. And you need to trust her to take care of yours. And if you do, ask yourself, are you willing to take the risk? Is it worth the risk of hurting her and being hurt?"

Andrew always managed to reduce problems down to their most basic elements. And now he had, the answer was clear. Hartford deserved my faith, my trust. My vulnerability. She deserved me fighting for her.

I trusted that Hartford would never say she was going to marry me and then get cold feet and not turn up. I trusted her to tell me everything she was thinking, whether or not I wanted to hear it. I trusted her to love me. And I knew myself well enough that I would do whatever it took to make sure that her heart was kept safe in my hands. I trusted myself to love her.

I drained my glass and slid it across the table. "I take it you can let yourself out, seeing as you let yourself in." I stood and headed to my bedroom to get dressed. "Anyone tells you you're a cold-hearted bastard, tell them I said they're full of shit."

Andrew saluted me and I gave him a nod.

I had somewhere to be.

THIRTY-SEVEN

Hartford

I'd gotten to know the labyrinth of corridors at the hospital now. I knew which lifts were the quickest and which stairwells were the easiest to navigate. I shoved my scrubs into the laundry skip and pulled on my backpack, ready to take all the shortcuts to the exit and begin the journey back to Borehamwood. If I walked quickly, I'd catch the next overground to West Hampstead and be home and pajamaed in forty-five minutes.

"Hartford," Gerry called from behind me.

My heart corkscrewed into my knees as I turned. I liked Gerry, and normally I wouldn't mind him catching me on my way out, but tonight I just wanted to go home and miss Joshua. I was getting really good at it.

"Have you seen this?" He waved what looked like a stack of newspapers, then beckoned me into his storage-cupboard-slash-office.

On his desk lay the *Times*, the *British Medical Journal*, and the *Health Service Journal*. The BBC website was open on the news page, and the words *Merdon* and *Calmation* instantly grabbed my attention.

"What happened?"

"I have no idea but it's great news. I think."

I stepped closer, dropped my backpack, and looked more closely. "It's like . . . some kind of campaign against Calmation."

"That's exactly what it is."

"This is all paid advertising." I flicked through the various publications.

"Mostly," Gerry said. "And then the HSJ have done an article picking up on the campaign. You should read it."

He handed me the journal. I took a seat and read the headline. *Luca Brands launches campaign against Merdon's ADHD drug.*

"Joshua did this?" I asked.

"I thought you put him up to it? He doesn't seem to be doing it on behalf of a client. He's quoted as saying that his firm will be taking on campaigns for good causes and charities from time to time going forward. You didn't know anything about it?"

I shook my head as my heart inched higher in my chest. Why hadn't he said anything? I guess because he hadn't done it for me. He'd done it because he'd decided on his own it was the right thing to do.

I knew he would.

"He's a good man. I could tell the moment I met him," Gerry said.

Joshua had charmed Gerry's pants off that evening at his house. But what he was saying was true. Joshua *was* a good man. He always had been.

THIRTY-EIGHT

Joshua

Never in a thousand years did I think I'd make so many trips to Boreham-bloody-wood. Hopefully this would be my last.

As I got to the top of the second flight of stairs, nerves tumbled in my stomach. Stella had once described Hartford as a truth bomb, and she definitely had a lack of filter at times. And she deserved the same unfiltered truth in return. From me.

I pulled in a breath and knocked on her door.

I couldn't help but smile as she appeared before me in scrubs, her hair piled on her head in her usual bird's nest arrangement, her face bare of make-up. She was perfect.

"Joshua!" She didn't look angry, more . . . surprised. That was as good a start as I could have hoped for.

"Hartford." I wanted to snake my arms around her and drink in her familiar scent of cinnamon. "I'm sorry to just stop by. I had a few things to say and I didn't want to wait."

She glanced down at the suitcase I'd brought with me. "What's with the case?"

"I'll explain later. Things should be said in order."

"Come in. I was actually going to reach out. I saw your campaign against Calmation. It's . . . it's wonderful, Joshua. So smart and thoughtful and I think it's really going to work."

I couldn't ignore the warm buzz in my belly that came with her words. I was pleased she'd seen it and that she approved. She'd been the inspiration, after all. "I hope it works." I followed her into her tiny flat.

"I do too. But if it doesn't, you know you did what you could."

She offered me a glass of water and we awkwardly took seats across from each other at the small folding table under the window. I spotted what looked like a theatre program on the windowsill. I craned and made out ballet dancers on the front and the Royal Opera House logo on the top right corner. "You went to the ballet?" For some reason, hope bloomed in my chest that it was a sign that things might be salvageable between us.

"I did. I hope that's okay."

"More than okay. Did you enjoy it?"

She pulled in a breath and exhaled slowly. "More than enjoyed it. Thank you."

Perhaps next time, I could go with her. I was getting ahead of myself. Perhaps I should change tack and tell her that I should have realized my feelings for her were life-changing when I'd gotten the box at the ballet on the off chance she might use it.

"You see?" She glanced around. "I told you I could make Borehamwood look nice with a few bits from IKEA."

I hoped she wasn't too attached to the place, but I was skipping ahead again.

"It looks great. But anywhere looks great if you're there."

A small smile curled around her lips before she smothered it with a frown. "Joshua."

I glanced across the room at pink ribbons strewn across the sofa. "Are they ballet shoes?"

Hartford nodded. "Yes. I'm . . . laying to rest some old ghosts. And having some fun outside of work at the same time."

I grinned. "Sounds good." I was happy she was happy. Even if it was without me. I just hoped she'd be happier with me. I exhaled. I had to bite the bullet and tell her my whole truth. "Being with you over the last few months has brought a lot into focus for me. I've never had a real relationship other than Diana, and looking back, what we had wasn't that real."

She nodded as if I wasn't telling her anything she didn't know already. But I had more.

"You've told me about your forcefield . . . Subconsciously, I developed a forcefield of my own because of what happened with Diana. One borne out of fear of getting hurt again. Fear of being vulnerable with someone. Fear of being embarrassed again."

She shifted in her seat and reached to smooth her hand over mine. "I'm sorry."

"What I've realized since you landed at Heathrow three months ago is that I'd been living with a Hartford-shaped hole in my life for years."

Her freckles bunched as she screwed up her nose. "A Hartford-shaped hole? Sounds . . . painful, my arse is not small."

"Your arse is perfect. Anyway, my forcefield was wearing camouflage or something. Unlike you, I've never been particularly aware of it. And then the last time I saw you, when you asked me to step up, I became painfully aware of the walls I'd built around myself."

I turned my hand over and threaded my fingers through hers. She didn't pull away, and I said a silent thank-you.

"I couldn't tell you what I wanted in the hallway because my forcefield wouldn't let me. I'm here today to tell you, I've yanked the power supply from that thing and my walls are down." I took a breath and wondered how I'd kept away from Hartford for these past couple of weeks. I'd missed her so much.

"I love you."

Just three words but I hoped she felt their power.

She searched my eyes as if trying to satisfy herself that what I said was true.

"I know you think my feelings aren't as strong as yours," I said. "But I love you. I want you. I never want to let you go."

She sighed and closed her eyes. I knew she was scared.

"You're not going to repeat history and I won't let you lose yourself. In me. In work. In anything. I'm going to be the man pulling you back to the surface."

She opened her eyes and squeezed my hand. "The words are easy to say."

"It's not just words," I said, nodding to the door where I'd left my case. "I want us to live together. Be together. We can get married next month if you want. Or let's wait a while and plan something spectacular."

A small smile tugged at the corners of her mouth. "You brought your case so you can move in to my flat in Borehamwood?"

"Absolutely."

"Now I know you're kidding. There's no way—"

"Don't you see? I'll do anything it takes to be with you."
I paused—I was committed to complete honesty. "Although,
I can't lie. I'd much prefer you to come back with me to Park
Lane."

She laughed. "You really want us to move in together?"

"I told you, I want it all."

Her smile was all the more adorable because she was
trying to hide it. "Park Lane is nicer, there's no denying it.
But I don't want to live in a hotel."

I chuckled. "Then we'll find another flat. Or a house. I
don't care where I am as long as I'm with you."

She shook her head. "We're both going to turn off our
forcefields and really do this?"

"Mine's off. And I'm ready." I'd never been surer about
anything.

"And living together? You really want us to dive into the
deep end?"

"I wanna dive so deep, I'm going to need medical attention," I replied.

"Then I'm just the girl you've been looking for."

THIRTY-NINE

Joshua

I glanced out the tiny windows in Hartford's tiny flat to see if we were being watched. Of course we were—it was practically inevitable with buildings here so close together. I eased Hartford off my lap and crossed the room to close the thin curtains. "The neighbors shouldn't see what I'm about to do to you."

"I'm nervous," she said, transferring her weight from one leg to the other.

"Hey, we're in Borehamwood. Of course you're nervous."

She smiled and shook her head as I snaked an arm around her waist.

"I'm serious," she said. "Before it was . . . What happens if this time isn't . . . you know?"

"You're nervous that sex with me is going to be disappointing now we've discussed our feelings?" I said, dipping to place a kiss at the bottom of her neck.

She laughed. "Yeah. And I'm nervous that you'll be disappointed with me too."

I pulled back to make sure I heard her right. "Hartford, you could never disappoint me."

She exhaled another nervous laugh, but the worry in her eyes was far from funny.

"I'm serious." I cupped her face in my hands and pressed my lips to hers.

She sighed and inched closer to me. Thank God.

"Maybe it was so good because of the feelings that came with it?" she spluttered as I got to work undoing the buttons on her blouse. "Did we even have feelings at that point? I mean, my forcefield was seriously faulty. I don't know about you but perhaps that's what made it different. Or maybe it was—"

"Hartford."

She stopped and looked up at me.

"Shall we focus on actually *having* sex? And then if we're both desperately disappointed afterward, we can discuss it, do a full compare and contrast. Run a Monte Carlo simulation. Maybe even video it next time to see what we're doing wrong. But let's not doom it to over-analysis until there's a problem. Agreed?"

"You can run a Monte Carlo simulation on sexual performance?" Her forehead furrowed like she was working through what that would look like.

"I'm sure it's possible."

She sighed. "Maybe I need a drink. Like a tequila or something. I mean—"

"Hartford. Stop. Seriously. This is you and me. There's nothing to be nervous about. It's just you and me. I've never felt this way about *anyone*. When I came here today, I couldn't let myself think that you would reject me because I don't know what my life looks like without you in it anymore. And I don't want to know. I want to spend all my days with you. I love to talk with you. I love to eat cake with you. And making love with you is as good as life gets."

She tilted her head to one side. "I feel the same."

"I'm glad."

She hooked her finger into the front of my shirt and opened a button. "And it's just Joshua and Hartford, right?"

"Yes, just us."

She took a deep breath in and pressed her lips against my chest. "You smell good. But then, you always do."

I couldn't help but smile at her comment. I never knew she liked the way I smelled. I couldn't wait to find out more of what I didn't know. "Are you a beach person or a city break person?"

"Are you thinking we should go away?"

Now *that* was a good idea. "Absolutely. Where do you fancy?" I pressed my mouth to her forehead.

"Somewhere we don't have to wear many clothes." She began to pull off my shirt.

"Beach then." As she undressed me, I pictured white sands, over-the-water villas, never-ending sun. And Hartford.

I guided her over to one of the dining room chairs and took a seat, coaxing her to sit facing me, her scrubs still covering too much of her. I unpinned her hair, watching as it tumbled down around her shoulders. Sweeping it away, I pressed my mouth to her neck. I peeled off her top, revealing the smooth, pale curve of her shoulders and her perfect breasts.

I took a breath.

She was lovely.

I pressed my lips onto her skin, wanting to make this

moment—the moment before what came next—last as long as possible. She hummed in appreciation, the sound confirming for some deep-rooted part of me that I was with the woman I was made for. She trailed her fingers over my shoulder blades and up into my hair, pulling me close.

"I love you," she whispered.

Her words were like sunshine; the faded scar of my past dissolved into her warmth. I closed my eyes to take in this moment. I never wanted to forget it. God, how had I thought I might be able to give this woman up?

"I love you." I pulled her closer until we were chest against chest. I never wanted to let her go.

"I'm not going anywhere. Not ever," she said, reading my mind.

"I know." I was sure of it. Sure of her.

I pressed my lips up her neck as she traced her fingers over my collarbone. On a sigh she pulled away and shifted off my lap. She stood and pushed her scrub trousers off before sitting back on my knees.

"I like your penis," she said, devoted to the truth as ever, as she unzipped my trousers and pulled them down and off.

"I'm glad. I like it too."

"I've seen a lot of them in my time." She leaned toward me and circled her hand around my shaft, squeezing before pulling her fist upward. "Most of them on dead bodies. You know, in med school and—"

"Hartford, can we put a pin in the dead penis discussion for the moment? It's disrupting the mood a little."

She laughed, released my dick and kissed me straight on the lips. "I'm sorry."

I cupped her face and pulled her toward me for a proper kiss. At the moment, I could count the number of times I'd kissed her. I didn't want to be able to do that much longer. We knew each other far too well for us not to have kissed an infinite number of times.

She shifted and sat on my lap, opposite me. I closed my eyes at the feel of her slick warmth against my skin. I groaned and grabbed her perfect arse. "You feel so good."

I grabbed a condom and rolled it on. Our eyes locked and she lifted her weight off me, glancing down as I held my shaft firmly, ready for her. My jaw was tight just at the thought of her lowering herself onto me, and when her wetness enveloped the tip of my dick, I wanted to roar out at the fucking perfect glory of her. She lowered herself slowly onto me as if she were getting used to me.

"It's a lot, this way," she said, her breath huffy and her voice a little wild.

I nodded. "Keep going."

It felt like it took hours for her to sink down onto me, her hot, tight wetness yielding to me finally. I let my head tip back, trying to keep my focus so I didn't come right there and then.

"You okay?" she asked.

I smoothed my hands up her thighs. "Like you said, it's a lot."

She tilted her head and smiled at me. It was a gift she'd given me—the ability to illicit that smile. That I could possibly be part of what made her happy was the best thing I could imagine.

"You're so sexy," I said, cupping her arse. I started to encourage her to shift her hips slightly. Each movement fired off intense jolts of pleasure, and I needed to catch my breath.

"You feel so good," she replied. She was gaining confidence now, her movements growing bolder as she chased more and more sensation. Her breasts pressed against my chest and flickers of memories of picking her up from the airport crossed my mind. Had I known then that this was where we'd end up? That fizz of shock when I'd seen her, the way her smile had warmed something in me that I hadn't known was cold. Maybe part of me always knew it could be this good between us.

Her fingernails pushed into the skin of my shoulders and her cheeks flushed red. Christ, every time I though she couldn't get more beautiful, some new vision of her sent me reeling. Feeling her wrapped around my cock, her breasts against my skin, her fingertips tugging at my hair. Hearing her little moans as I began to take over the rhythm. I wanted to be relentless, wanted to fuck her until we were both spent and exhausted.

"More," she said, putting her hands over mine.

I grinned. She wanted that too.

I moved her off me and stood. "Hands on the table." I needed to able to move. To fuck. To plow into her with all the power she sent coursing through my veins.

I pressed a kiss to her spine and she pushed back, willing me to get on with it. I stood tall and anchored my hands on her hips, pushing in as she let out a groan. The tension built in my thighs as I tried my best to go slow—to hold back from fucking her so hard the table collapsed.

"Christ, you feel good. So warm. So soft."

She leaned back onto me, urging me on, deeper.

I picked up my pace, my chest tight and my muscles tense, entirely focused on filling her with pleasure and chasing my desire.

Her growing tightness, the distant shudder of my orgasm— "Fuck," I groaned into the air. It was so good and I didn't want it to be over so soon. I'd never be able to fuck her again for the first time after she told me she loved me, and I wanted to capture these moments, make them last forever.

She reached back and grabbed my hand. "Joshua. I'm so close."

I wanted to watch her come.

I pulled her down onto the floor and crawled over her, desperate to be inside her again. My instinct and need had taken over. She slid her thighs either side of my hips as I rocked in and out of her, over and over, bringing us both up together, higher and higher.

She opened her eyes and arched her back, her body tense, her orgasm bathed across her face as sensation channeled up my body and burst in my chest.

I collapsed on top of her as she skated her fingers over my back, humming into my ear.

"You're beautiful," I said.

"I'm yours," she replied. She couldn't have said anything that could make me feel any better, any more hopeful, any more grateful.

I managed to prop myself up so I could look straight into those beautiful blue eyes. "And I'm yours."

FORTY

Hartford

Standing right in front of the door to the penthouse, I hung up the phone from Gerry, just as Joshua walked through the door from work.

He met my eyes in a way that said *You okay?*

"I've never wanted to have sex with you as much as I do right now."

"Okay," he said slowly, as if there was a catch. "What do I have to do for you to think that every time I walk into a room?"

"Oh, I don't know—defeat big pharma. Save lives. Generally be the best guy I've ever laid eyes on."

His eyes sparkled and he held up a bottle of champagne in one hand and a cake box in the other. "You heard? I was going to surprise you."

"You knew? When?"

"I have a friend who has a friend."

"So does Gerry. That's how I know. When is it official? I want to shout it from the rooftops."

"Now. Merdon won't put out an announcement that Calmation is dead. The US regulator doesn't comment on drugs that don't pass their process. But we did it."

I couldn't believe it. Calmation was never coming to market as an over-the-counter medicine, and it was because my boyfriend was awesome. Luca Brands had been fearless when it came to opposing Merdon. They'd gotten Gerry on every TV show in both the US and the UK, and had gotten every TV doctor in existence to join in the campaign. He'd been amazing. "You want to do the sex first? Or the cake and champagne?" I asked.

"Let's toast and then take the champagne to bed."

I pulled two glasses from the cabinet and placed them on the marble countertop. "Did you hear anything about the hotel?" Luca Brands had been pitching for new work constantly since GCVB dropped them. He'd picked up a number of new clients, but I knew he was hoping that the owners of the place we called home would sign up with Luca Brands.

Joshua's dimple appeared out of nowhere. "Actually, yes. It's a day of good news. The chairman of the group called me today. Wants a meeting."

I slid my arm up his back as he poured out the fizz. "I keep telling you how irresistible you are."

The penthouse buzzer sounded and I glanced at Joshua. Was he expecting someone?

He shrugged. "I'll finish the champagne. You get the door."

"Andrew?" I said as I answered the door. "What are you —and Tristan! We weren't expecting you."

Andrew and Tristan filed in and then I noticed Tristan holding Gabriel's daughter's hand. "Bethany! Where's your daddy?"

"What are you two doing here?" Joshua asked as he saw Andrew and Tristan. "This one can stay," he said, bending to pick up Bethany. "But the rest of you—" At that moment, Gabriel, Beck, Hollie, Autumn, Stella, and Dexter filed in. Dexter seemed to be carrying a briefcase. Stella a cake box and everyone else seemed to have a bottle of wine or champagne in their hands.

"We've come to celebrate," Stella said.

Did they all know about Calmation? News spread fast in this city of nine million people.

"Yup, not every day Joshua makes a good decision," Beck said as he leaned in to kiss my cheek. "You're his best one to date." If there was going to be a man who made me swoon other that Joshua, it would be Beck. He always seemed to say the right thing. Stella was a lucky woman.

Everyone needed drinks. I turned to find Joshua muttering to himself and pulling champagne glasses out of the cabinet. "You okay?" I asked, sidling up beside him as everyone else spread out on the sofas. Tristan held Bethany by the ankles.

"She'll puke on you if you don't watch it," Autumn said to Tristan. "And I'll be the first one to say you deserve it."

"I won't sick on him, Autumn," Bethany said. "Just one more time."

"Don't say I didn't warn you," Autumn said.

"We were about to have sex," Joshua whispered in my ear, pulling my attention from Bethany's giggles. He sounded like he'd just been told to take his ball and go home.

"This is nice. Your family have come to visit."

"But why?" he asked.

"No idea. And we've got plenty of time for sex."

"Here," said Dexter, sliding his briefcase onto the counter.

Hollie slipped behind him. "I'm going to make everyone drinks while you play with your toys." Dexter grabbed Hollie by the waist, bent her down, and planted a kiss on her lips like they were in a Hollywood film. Then he released her and went back to business as usual.

"I'm thinking about some new designs and wanted to know what you thought, Hartford." I tried to check that Hollie had found the glasses but my attention was overtaken by Dexter as he opened the black suede case to reveal hundreds of dazzling rings. "What kind of shape do you like?"

I glanced at Joshua. "Subtle as a brick, mate," Joshua said. He turned to me. "Clearly business isn't going too well and Dexter's turned into a door-to-door salesman."

Dexter chuckled. "Come on, it's good to know this stuff. Just in case. You know?"

"Wait." It suddenly dawned on me what was happening. "Dexter, you're trying to find out what kind of ring I want if we get engaged?"

"*When*," Dexter and Joshua chorused.

"*When* we get engaged," Joshua repeated, snaking his hand around my waist. "I suppose it doesn't hurt to have a look." How could this man, who up until a month ago only did casual, talk so casually about marrying me?

"Brilliant is obviously the most classic cut. Like this one." Dexter pulled out a ring with a huge single diamond on it. And then he pulled out a second. "But you might want something more vintage-inspired, like an asscher cut— always been a favorite of mine. The cut is less expensive than a brilliant but there's no disguising the stone with an asscher cut. It has to be flawless."

"I love it when you talk stones," Hollie interjected from where she was pouring champagne into a never-ending row of glasses.

"I want something a lot smaller. I won't want to take my ring off for work, so it will need to be small enough not to rip my gloves constantly." If only my seventeen-year-old self could see me now, picking out a potential engagement ring with Joshua Luca. No one should ever tell anyone that dreams don't come true. "This is a lot to take in."

"Yes, well, I'm going to leave this case with you for a few days," Dexter said. "You can have some fun trying stuff on and then decide."

I had a feeling it might take more than a few days.

"Do we all have a drink?" Andrew asked from where he stood over by the fireplace. People raised their glasses. "Good. Let's toast."

"Wait a minute," Joshua said. "First I want to know how you got up here without the front desk buzzing you up. This is meant to be a secure building."

Andrew just shook his head.

"No such thing," Tristan said. "The Pentagon isn't a secure building with me around."

Andrew raised his glass. "To Joshua and Hartford. We wish you forever happiness."

"Very poetic for you," Dexter said, nudging Andrew.

"Thanks. I thought so."

"We have some news too, actually," Beck said. "We've finally set our wedding date. Christmas Eve, if you're free."

"Hold on, you're not married?" Autumn asked. "I thought you'd already gotten hitched?" Gabriel whispered into Autumn's ear and she nodded.

"About time," Tristan said. "As best man, I'll be there."

Joshua cleared his throat from next to me. "Tristan's not best man, is he, Beck?"

"Bloody hope not," Dexter said.

"You're all my best men. I hope." Beck raised his glass. "Cheers to the best men in London and the women who made them even better."

I glanced up at Joshua and he turned to give me a stupid grin. "You make me better," he whispered, and pressed a kiss into my neck.

EPILOGUE

A month later

Hartford

The residences of the Park Lane International were beginning to feel like home. But I wasn't about to admit that to Joshua or we'd never move out. I tucked my feet up on the bench as Joshua lay in his bubble bath. The man certainly knew how to relax and enjoy life. These moments with him when we shared some wine and discussed our days were some of my favorite times together.

I swiped the iPad, bringing up pictures from a house that had just come on the market. "I really like this one." I turned the tablet to face him.

"That bath is tiny. If you won't get in this one with me, there's no way you'll get in that one."

"You can't base every real estate decision on the size of the bath."

"Is that a rule I'm not aware of?"

I sighed. He was being so picky about where we were going to live. I wanted to get on with it. I couldn't bear the thought of all the money he was spending on this place.

"Actually, I have a surprise for you."

I narrowed my eyes. Surprises from Joshua were usually extravagant and unnecessary, but before I could ask him more, the buzzer on the door went. By the grin on Joshua's face, he'd been expecting the interruption.

"It better be nothing more than cupcakes."

"That as well."

He grabbed the sides of the bath and stood, the water cascading off him like he was Helios rising from the ocean. "You want me to tell Beck to get lost for half an hour?" he asked as he caught me ogling him.

I jumped up off the bench. "Beck is here? With Stella? This is my surprise?"

"Part of it, I suppose." He wrapped a towel around himself.

"I'll go and let them in." I grabbed my wine and the iPad and went to the door. When I had finished my hugs, Joshua wandered in. I set about making drinks for everyone.

"I'm going to put this into the TV," Beck said, holding something in the air.

I glanced at Joshua, who nodded his approval to Beck. At least one of us knew what was going on. I poured the wine and handed around glasses.

"Come sit down," Joshua said, reaching for me from where he was on the sofa.

Stella plonked herself down next to me and we all looked up at Beck, who looked like he was about to tell us if it was a film, a book, or a play.

Beck grabbed the remote control and pointed at the TV. "Welcome to Number Six Alford Street."

A film showed the exterior of a red and cream brick house. The camera swept up the stone steps and went through the large double doors.

I'd been ambushed.

I stood. "Hold it right there. Press pause." When the video stopped, I turned to face Joshua. "This is why you haven't liked any of the places I've shown you? You had this up your sleeve all along?"

He grimaced. "Not all along."

"Why didn't you say?"

"I want you to see what it's going to look like," he replied.

"It's not finished yet," Beck said. "But it will be by Christmas."

"And it's just around the corner from our place," Stella said, beaming at me. "It's going to be gorgeous. Trust me. And we can work together to get it exactly how you want it."

Joshua groaned. "No, that's not going to work. If we leave it to Harford, the place will be kitted out with IKEA furniture."

"There's nothing wrong with IKEA," I replied, sinking back down into the sofa.

"No, there isn't," replied Stella. "But this is going to be a sanctuary for you two. And Joshua likes the finer things in life so—"

"I'll do you a deal," I said.

"Name it," Joshua replied.

"I'll pick from options that Stella presents me with, no questions asked, if you agree to match whatever we spend on Alford Street and donate it to the Luca Foundation or

Medicine Sans Frontiers."

Joshua frowned, which I'd learned was a sign he was going to try to negotiate. But I was going to hang firm on this. "I'll donate an amount equal to what we spend on the fixtures and furniture to the Luca-Kent Foundation."

"The Luca-Kent Foundation?" I asked.

"I renamed it," he said, handing me his phone. He'd pulled up an email from his lawyer confirming the name change. He was the sweetest, most romantic man. Far better than any fantasy I might have had at seventeen.

"I don't need to have my name on the notepaper. I just want the foundation to get the money."

"Well, you're the person who inspired the foundation, so it's only fitting that it bears the Kent name. And anyway, I hope Luca-Kent will be *our* name before too long."

I tried to ignore the warm swirl in my belly. We talked about the future all the time, about having children and growing old together. But I knew the topic of marriage was a sensitive issue for Joshua. He'd been burned so very badly by Diana. "You know that a piece of paper saying we're together forever isn't something I need."

"Maybe not. But it's something I *want*. And I hope you do too."

I glanced over at Beck and Stella, who were both grinning at us like absolute loons.

I turned back to Joshua and pressed my hand on his chest. "I would love to be a Luca-Kent."

"And no, this isn't a proposal because I'm working on something"

"Maybe I'll save you the bother and take matters into my own hands."

"That would be so much fun," Stella said.

"I'm warning you, though," Joshua said. "I want a big,

lavish wedding. I'm the luckiest guy on the planet and I want the entire world to know about it. I want to watch you walk down the aisle toward me."

I wrapped my arms around him. There was so much unsaid beneath his words. He trusted me. He knew that I would never leave him, never humiliate him—and it felt good, because I loved him just as much as he loved me.

"I can live with that." If it was important to him, it was important to me.

Another three months later

Joshua

I'd been planning this moment for months. I couldn't wait to see Hartford's face when she saw what I'd done to our bathrooms.

·   "Have you put in a barbeque or something?" Hartford stopped walking and stood with her hands on her hips, blindfolded.

"Maybe I built one in *your* bathroom." I tugged on her hands, encouraging her into our bedroom. "Keep walking."

She started to move again. Just a few more steps and she'd be in our bedroom. "You know I think it's completely insane that we have our own bathrooms."

Tonight would be the first night we slept in our new house. Over the past week, we'd moved all our things in and were all finally set up to spend the night. "It's not insane. It's good for resale value and it's practical."

There was only one part of our new home that Hartford hadn't seen—the en suite bathrooms to our bedroom. She'd given me free reign and I'd made the most of it.

"The fact that I have to take so many steps just to get into our bedroom means this place is way too big." She sighed. "But I do love it. Okay, we hit carpet, can I take this blindfold off yet?"

"Nope. Not yet." I coaxed her forward until she crossed the threshold into her bathroom. The music I'd chosen was playing at the perfect volume and I pivoted her so the shutters wouldn't be the first thing she saw. I just had a couple more things to do. "Right. Stay right there."

Quickly I undressed and wrapped a towel around my waist.

"Is that Natasha Bedingfield playing?"

I grinned. I wasn't sure if she'd remember. "Yeah."

"It's the track that played all summer the year you left for university." She smiled and I could tell she was remembering those long summers of our childhood full of endless days of sunshine, tennis, and first crushes that became lifetime loves.

Nothing passed this woman by. Thank God I was lucky enough to be the man who got to try to keep up with her.

I liked the idea that when I got to the end of my life, I would have known my wife since the beginning. That we'd have lived so long in each other's lives. No one would ever know me better.

"I need to get you naked," I said.

"With the blindfold on?"

"Yeah, but it's not as kinky as it sounds." She was wearing a shirt and jeans, so I set about undressing her. When she was fully naked, reluctantly, I helped her on with a brand new fluffy white robe I'd ordered, *Luca-Kent* embroidered on the chest. I wondered how long it would take her to notice that.

I took a deep breath and slipped off the mask. "Your bathroom, m'lady."

She broke into a smile but she wasn't looking at the bathroom. Her gaze was fixed firmly on me. "I love it."

I chuckled. "You haven't even glanced at the room."

"I love it already," she said, looping her arms around my neck. "You did this for us, so I love it. But show me everything."

I pulled her toward me and gave her a whistle-stop tour.

"I still love it!" she said as she looked around. "And the bath is incredible. So deep. I guess I knew you weren't going to get that bit wrong. Is yours very different?"

"My bathroom is exactly the same but the marble is Portoro. I'll show you." I pulled back the shutters on the wall of her bathroom that was shared with mine, ready to reveal the cherry on the cake.

"Is this a pool?" she asked, her eyes wide with shock as she stared at the huge bath that sat between our two bathrooms. I'd made sure it was exactly thirty-eight degrees. A complement of the best bath oils money could buy had pride of place in a dedicated cabinet. During the last few months living together, I'd been able to encourage Hartford's Genius Time, and a mixture of lavender and frankincense were her favorites. We were perfectly suited in so many ways.

"No, it's just a very big bath." The bath was two meters by two meters—plenty of room for both of us. "And through there"—I pointed through to the other side of the shared bath—"is my bathroom. The bath sits between, so we can have joint Genius Time when the urge arises."

"Three baths between two bathrooms?"

"It's important."

She just chuckled. "Are we getting in?"

I dropped my towel. She grinned and shrugged off her robe. I held her hand as she stepped into the water.

She sighed as she sank in to her neck. "I think I could get used to life with you."

I chuckled and stepped in beside her. "Yeah? Well, I was hoping that would be the case."

Despite all the space in the tub, we wove our legs together and I handed her a drink. And a cupcake.

"A cookies and cream cupcake. In a bath opposite my favorite person in the world. In the most beautiful house I've ever laid eyes on. Does life get any better than this?"

"I hope so," I said.

"Joshua." She gave me a castigating glare. "We can't wish for more than this."

"Just one more thing." I took a breath. "Will you marry me?"

Her glare was replaced with a look of complete adoration. She put her uneaten cupcake down carefully on the side of the bath and kneeled over me, her slick thighs sliding either side of my hips. "A thousand times yes, Joshua Luca. My life is everything with you by my side."

And just like that, without another pound exchanged, I had everything I could ever want.

TO ORDER ANDREW'S BOOK, read **Mr. Bloomsbury**

HAVE you read

Beck and Stella - **Mr. Mayfair**

Dexter and Hollie - **Mr. Knightsbridge**
Gabriel and Autumn - **Mr. Smithfield**
Andrew **- Mr. Bloomsbury**

READ on for a sneak peek of Private Player

The Nights Series

Indigo Nights

Promised Nights

Parisian Nights

Faithful

Sign up to the Louise Bay mailing list at
www.louisebay/mailinglist

Read more at www.louisebay.com

Made in the USA
Coppell, TX
30 September 2021

63251783R00166